TIMELESS *Regency* COLLECTION

A Country Christmas

Josi S. Kilpack
Carla Kelly
Jennifer Moore

Other Timeless Regency Collections

Autumn Masquerade
A Midwinter Ball
Spring in Hyde Park
Summer House Party
A Season in London
A Holiday in Bath
Falling for a Duke
A Night in Grosvenor Square
Road to Gretna Green

TIMELESS *Regency* COLLECTION

A
Country
Christmas

Josi S. Kilpack
Carla Kelly
Jennifer Moore

Copyright © 2017 Mirror Press
Paperback edition
All rights reserved

No part of this book may be reproduced in any form whatsoever without prior written permission of the publisher, except in the case of brief passages embodied in critical reviews and articles. These novels are works of fiction. The characters, names, incidents, places, and dialog are products of the authors' imaginations and are not to be construed as real.

Interior Design by Heather Justesen
Edited by Jennie Stevens and Lisa Shepherd
Cover design by Rachael Anderson
Cover Photo Credit: Richard Jenkins Photography

Published by Mirror Press, LLC
ISBN-13: 978-1-947152-15-1

Table of Contents

Saints and Sinners
by Josi S. Kilpack
1

The Christmas Angle
by Carla Kelly
101

The Perfect Christmas
by Jennifer Moore
219

Saints and Sinners

By Josi S. Kilpack

Chapter One

Neville Franklin was inspecting the small village pub that smelled like yeast and grease—as it should—when his companion spoke from the other side of the small, rough-hewn table.

"Is Eloise promised to anyone?" Mr. Henry Burke asked unexpectedly.

The men had gone riding that afternoon until the cold had driven them indoors. First, they'd had hot cider, and now that they were fully warm, they enjoyed a hearty ale before journeying the remaining two miles to Franklin Farm, Neville's current home and future inheritance.

"Eloise?" Neville said, taken off guard by mention of his childhood friend. "I don't think so." He nearly added that Eloise wasn't old enough to be promised to anyone, but then he quickly calculated his age with hers and realized that she was nearly twenty years to his twenty-four—a perfectly eligible age. What an odd thought.

Burke wagged his eyebrows. "Really?"

Neville didn't like the roll in his friend's voice and narrowed his eyes. "Why do you ask?"

"Well, tonight's entertainment is a *ball*."

"And?"

"And it's been a while since we've had a kissing wager."

The connection Neville made in his mind was instantaneous.

"Not Eloise," he said firmly. He'd no sooner uttered the proclamation than he amended the rule. "And no other girl either. This is my village, Burke. We *will* be on our best behavior."

Burke slumped in his chair and let out a tortured breath. "All this prim and proper is driving me mad. A man has needs, Neville; you can't expect me to ignore them forever."

"My home, my rules. No kissing wagers. Your *needs* be hanged."

Burke rolled his eyes and took another drink.

The kissing wager was as simple as it was immature: a young woman was chosen, and the first man to steal a kiss received a drink purchased by the man who failed the task. It was a game Neville and Burke, along with a few other cronies from Oxford, had played when they'd first begun going to London—long before there was serious expectation of marriage.

"Besides, haven't we outgrown such childish antics?" It had been years since they had played the game. Why would Burke even bring it up?

"I'm simply trying to add a little excitement to our time here," Burke said.

"You think it's been dull?" Neville was genuinely surprised. "We have been to any number of dinner and card parties and hunted nearly every day. I thought you were rather pleased with the entertainment."

"Pleased enough, but a wager would spice things up, don't you think?"

"No, I don't think a wager would 'spice things up.' I think it would show us as silly schoolboys and I *live* here, Burke. No wager. We are too old for silly trifles."

Neville had come back from extended travel through America—with Burke as his companion—a few months ago, expecting to formalize a match with his cousin Lila, whose letters had sweetened during his absence. Between Lila's last letter and his surprise arrival, however, she had fallen in love with another. Aside from the blow to his ego, Neville had recovered from that setback easily enough to know that his feelings for Lila had never been all that strong. Lila was now married and on her way to India, while Neville was back in Shropshire and less opposed to country life than he had ever been before. In fact, he was excited to embark upon a gentleman's future of estate management with his father as his guide.

There was still the necessary business of finding a wife, but first, Christmas. And then January, during which time he would finish his formal proposals to Father about changes to the estate per his agricultural education in America, and then it would be on to the London season where the debutantes would be paraded about in search of potential husbands. He was not eager for such formal attempts at courting—could a young couple really get to know each other in such conditions? He thought of Eloise—good and saintly Eloise. And then he remembered the wager Burke had mentioned, and it stuck in his craw all over again.

"Why has Eloise drawn your attention?" Neville had

known Eloise all his life and had enjoyed spending time with her now that he was back in Hemberg, but she was not the type of young woman Burke usually took note of.

"There are three reasons Eloise has caught my eye," Burke said with a cock of his eyebrow. "First, I've gotten to know her better than any of the other girls in this forsaken place. Second, have you noticed the perfect shape of her lips? I have vast experience, you know, and I believe she has just the right fullness of mouth to give a most excellent kiss."

Neville's chest caught on fire—completely confusing him—but he took a drink to cover the unexpected reaction.

"And third, she fancies me."

Neville's hand tightened around the handle of his mug. "Eloise does not *fancy* you any more than she fancies any other man."

"Have you not noticed how raptly she listens to my stories and how often she compliments some aspect of my person?" Burke asked, quirking a brow. "She is very attentive to me every time we are together."

"I do not believe that's true." Neville shook his head. "She asks both of us questions and is well-mannered enough to give generous compliments to everyone. It's simply her nature."

"No, it's the dazzling effect I have on women—especially those with such kissable lips as hers."

Kissable lips? They were very nice lips, of course, but Neville had never considered kissing them.

Why not?

The thought startled him. This was *Eloise* he was thinking about—Eloise whose lips Burke was . . . maligning.

She wasn't some star-eyed deb in London wanting to feel the compliment of a man's attention, *and* she was among Neville's oldest friends. "If you try to steal a kiss, Eloise will slap you silly." *And then I will knock you flat.*

"Who said anything about *stealing* a kiss?" Burke asked, obviously enjoying the ire he was drawing. "One cannot steal what is gladly given. In fact"—a gleam lit Burke's eyes as he leaned forward across the table—"let's see which of us she prefers. Let's set that wager and make a night of it, for old times' sake and as an ushering in of this lovely Christmas season. I'll find us some mistletoe."

"No," Neville said, shaking his head, though his eyes were drawn for a moment to the rather bedraggled wreath mounted over the bar on the far side of the room—the only tribute to the season offered in the pub. "Eloise is my friend, Burke. I'd as soon kiss you as kiss her."

Burke raised one eyebrow and leaned back in his chair. "Truly?" he said, thoroughly surprised. "You have no attraction toward her?"

"I-I, well, to be honest I have never thought about it. She's just . . . Eloise."

"*Just* Eloise is a beautiful woman and an excellent conversationalist. I daresay she will make someone a very fine wife. If she was also a good kisser, why, I would be tempted to make her an offer myself."

The darkness that filled Neville's thoughts was as strange a sensation as he'd ever felt—likely how an older brother would feel about his sister, if it were she Burke was talking about so glibly. "Eloise would never accept an offer from you."

Burke raised both his eyebrows. "And why not?"

"Because . . . because she doesn't even know you."

"We've seen her dozens of times these last weeks at one event or another, and she gave me leave to call her by her Christian name as you do. I expect I know her as well as I know any other female, and my mother is eager to marry off her only son now that I've returned from my travels. She would be quite pleased with Eloise, I believe. She has preferred girls from the country for my brothers over a girl of the *ton*. Eloise would fit Mama's hopes for me very well, indeed."

Neville opened his mouth but didn't know what to say, didn't know what to think. This was such a bizarre conversation. Eloise a wife? Burke a husband? "No wager," Neville said to cover for the fact he could think of nothing else.

Burke finished his drink in one last swallow. "Fine, no wager." He put his mug heavily on the table. "But I will not promise there won't be a kiss."

Neville narrowed his eyes, but Burke spoke before he formulated a response. "And don't be surprised if one day I race away from this place and never look back. You expect too much restraint of me. Gads, you expect too much restraint of yourself." He pushed back from the table, grating the chair legs across the stone floor. "Well, we might as well get going. We've a country Christmas ball to prepare for." Burke stood, straightened his waistcoat, and headed for the door of the pub, leaving Neville to glower at his back and follow.

Chapter Two

Eloise looked at her reflection and swallowed nervously, putting a hand to the flat of her belly, just below the waist of the red dress she was wearing for the first time. Her golden hair had been arranged so that three thick ringlets draped over one shoulder. New stays had been necessary to accommodate the dress, and they accentuated her bosom in ways she was not used to. What would Neville think of her in this dress? Would he see her as a grown woman tonight?

"You will be the belle of the ball," Mama said from where she stood next to Eloise. She put one arm around Eloise's shoulders. "Do you feel as beautiful as you look?"

Eloise took a deep breath and tried to give herself a critical assessment, and yet she couldn't. "I do, Mama," she said, shaking her head in surprise. Normally she would never wear a red dress, but seeing as how they were in the country and it was a Christmas ball, Mama had agreed to the bold color when Eloise asked. Eloise would not be the only girl to wear a vibrant gown to the Websters' annual Christmas ball, but it was the first time she had presented herself so boldly. Mama's encouragement went a long way to enhancing Eloise's confidence of putting off her usual style choices. "Is it a sin for me to say as much?"

Mama laughed and leaned in to kiss Eloise on the right temple. "No, my dear," she said, giving one more squeeze and then dropping her arm. "We should order the same pattern in a color we can take to London. Perhaps after the New Year we can meet with the seamstress again and choose a sample fabric. You have a lovely figure, and I should have insisted on more flattering styles before now."

Eloise smiled, still anxious with this transition but ready, too. In the mirror, she watched her mother move toward the door. A different wriggling discomfort in Eloise's belly became too much to bear, however. "Mama," she said.

Mama turned from where she stood with a hand on the doorknob and raised her eyebrows expectantly. Eloise turned as well so that they faced one another across the room.

"Would you be very disappointed if I didn't go to London in the spring?"

Mama paused, then came back into the room.

"You don't want to go to London?" Mama asked. "Any number of your friends would love to have the chance."

There were parts of England where every girl of the gentry class was expected to have a London Season, but in Hemberg only those girls belonging to families with titles or parliamentary duties had such expectations. Eloise's father was a successful attorney in their village and had served as a clerk for Lord Terimid these last eight years during Parliament. The position afforded the family a reason to go to London, and, therefore, both of Eloise's sisters had London seasons where they'd made good matches. Everyone expected Eloise would do the same.

"I know I am fortunate to have the opportunity," Eloise said, looking down at the skirt of her dress, a sheer top layer the same red as the underskirt, with rosettes along the hem. It really was a remarkable dress. "And I don't mean to sound ungrateful, but, well, you know I don't care for large crowds or strangers."

"Yes, that's why we've waited this long—too long, according to some. You will be twenty years old in a few months' time."

She knows I am not saying everything I feel. Eloise took a breath, if she was truly ready to own her age and level of maturity, she needed to speak her mind more freely. "And I appreciate you and Papa being patient with me, but the more I consider the situation, the more I think I would prefer to make a match closer to home."

"Here? In Shropshire?"

Eloise nodded and looked up at her mother's puzzled expression.

"Have you someone particular in mind?"

Eloise hated that her cheeks heated up when she was attempting to take responsibility. Perhaps she should have waited to tell her mother, at least until after tonight, but every time her mother spoke of London, Eloise felt guilty for the hope she harbored that she would not go. The closer London became, the more preparations would be made.

"Eloise?" Mama said. "Have you formed an attachment to someone here in Shropshire?"

Eloise shook her head. "No. But, well, I hope that I might." It felt so presumptuous to say this out loud!

"Who?"

Eloise's cheeks burned even hotter. "I don't know if he shares my level of affection," she said, thinking over these last few weeks when she had sought out every opportunity to be in Neville's company. She turned away from her mother's intent gaze and fidgeted with the brush on her dressing table. "And I have ample reason to believe he has never seen me as anything more than a girl he once played with as a child, but I . . . well."

Mama gasped and crossed the distance to grip Eloise's arm. She opened her mouth to speak, but Eloise cut her off.

"Don't say his name!" Eloise said. "It will make it too real, and I will feel ridiculous." Eloise had been fourteen years old when she first realized how her heart rate increased when Neville Franklin entered a room. He was eighteen years old then, away at Oxford, but every time he came home, she hung on every word he said.

She had only just accepted that she was in love with him when her best friend—and Neville's cousin—Lila had confessed her own feelings. Eloise could not take anything from Lila, who had so many disadvantages, so she had kept her feelings to herself all these years. It wasn't until Lila's engagement to Mr. Lutherford that Eloise fully faced the fact that she could allow her own affection for Neville to play out.

Certainly her own feelings were no guarantee that Neville felt the same, but these last weeks she dared to hope he *might* feel something more than childish affection. He was always happy to see her and sought out her company at different events they attended. It took courage to present herself as something other than his friend, but she was ready to take that step.

Mama closed her mouth and then nodded. "Is *he* the reason you wanted this dress?"

Eloise looked at the ground and nodded, feeling foolish.

Mama put a finger beneath Eloise's chin and lifted it so that Eloise was looking into her mother's face again—her mother's *smiling* face.

"You are a woman, Eloise, and though you have been raised to be demure and proper, it is not a sin to feel beautiful, and it is not a sin for a man to see you that way. Marriage is a complex business, but you should be desired by the man who chooses you, and there is no sin in that either. We shall talk of him and London and whatever else we need to discuss when you are ready. For tonight, I want you to remember what I told you about feeling beautiful."

Eloise nodded and repeated her mother's words in her mind: *It is not a sin to feel beautiful.*

"I don't mean to appear . . . seductive," she said out loud. "I just want him to see me as a woman instead of a girl."

Mama leaned in, kissed Eloise on the forehead, and then pulled back. "You look beautiful, Eloise, without any reason to regret your presentation. Have a wonderful time tonight. We'll talk more when you're ready."

Chapter Three

Neville finished his third attempt at a decent knot in his cravat and eyed it critically before untying it, unwrapping it from around his neck, and throwing the rumpled fabric on the bed. He stalked toward his wardrobe for another starched article. He did not give into blue devil moods easily, but this disposition was growing darker by the minute as the Websters' Christmas ball loomed closer. His valet's mother had fallen ill last week, and he had taken the rest of the month to spend time with her in the next county over. Until now, Neville had not missed him too much, as he had become used to dressing himself during his American tour. He didn't think he'd need assistance tonight and therefore hadn't asked his father's valet or one of the footmen to help, but apparently he should have.

The door to Neville's bedchamber opened, and Burke came in, reminding Neville of why he was in such a black mood. Burke quickly ascertained Neville's difficulty with the tie and crossed the room in a few long strides. "Let me be 'ere ta 'elp ya wit dat cloth, gov'ner. Bit sticky fer ya?"

Normally Neville would find Burke adopting the cockney accent hilarious, but tonight it was yet one more thing to annoy him. He lifted his chin obediently and let Burke fix the cravat while attempting to calm his riled emotions. A minute later, Burke stepped back and put his fist beneath his chin, assessing his handiwork.

"That is as near perfect as any necktie I have ever seen." Burke beamed with pride, and despite Neville's sour mood, he had to agree. He looked in the glass and could find no argument with Burke's work.

"Thank you, Burke. I seem to be all thumbs tonight."

"Well, it is certainly due to the excitement of tonight's entertainment," Burke said sarcastically, then rolled his eyes. "I am certainly *tickled* to have the opportunity to attend the annual Websters' Christmas ball. I hope there is punch."

"The ball is a village tradition, and I have missed it the last four years for one reason or another." He paused and took a breath, knowing he was about out of time to speak his mind. "And I will remind you of the company I keep here and the reputation I uphold. We are to be on our best behavior." He said "we," but he meant Burke, and they both knew it.

Burke gave an exaggerated yawn, then sighed deeply. "So you have told me," he said with boredom. "But perhaps you should give such advice to your dear Eloise, not I."

He didn't stay to hear Neville's reply and instead stalked out of the room, saying he would wait for Neville in the foyer. Neville looked from the man's retreating form to the looking glass and quickly undid the knot, which was suddenly inferior.

Was Eloise interested in Burke? Neville began the twisting and tying all over again. Eloise was as much a fixture of Neville's hometown as his father's house or the village church. She had always been there, always drawn a smile, and he rarely thought about her when he was gone. He would be more settled here in Hemberg, now that his schooling and travel were finished, and he'd been glad at the assurance that the easy camaraderie he had always felt with Eloise continued. Eloise was always nice to look at, but with her round face and large blue eyes, she still looked very much like the girl he'd always known. Neville had never seen her as a young *woman*. Just Eloise.

Neville may have only just realized that she was a grown woman destined to make a match, but he had no qualms about saying she deserved a better man than Burke. Being raised in the country would give her no understanding of a man like him. He could flatter her into a kiss entirely too easily, but her heart would be broken when she realized it was all a game. The thought made Neville's chest burn as it had in the pub that morning. He hurried to finish the knot—not nearly as well done as Burke's had been—and then went to the foyer with his mind made up. He would keep an eye on Burke, but he would also be attentive to Eloise to see if, in fact, she had developed a *tendre* for Burke. If she had, he would do whatever it took to talk her out of it. A lifetime of friendship had earned her his protection in this, and he would not fail her.

Chapter Four

The Websters' ballroom had been transformed for the holiday. Small pine trees were placed throughout the room, swags of garland draped from one corner to the next, and all of the greenery was festooned with red and gold ribbons befitting the season. Hundreds of candles lit the room, and the air smelled of cinnamon. The Websters never failed expectations, and Eloise basked in the glorious ambiance.

"You look lovely," Mama said, putting a hand on Eloise's arm as she passed. "I am off to visit with Mrs. Partridge. Join us should you need me."

"Thank you, Mama."

Mama gave her a quick smile and then turned toward the larger portion of the crowd, already surrounding the refreshment table, which was filled with Christmas treats: mincemeat pies, plum tarts, ginger cookies, and shortbreads. Eloise was glad Mama would not be hovering around for confirmation of her suspicions of what man Eloise wanted to draw out, but there was little doubt she would be watching her daughter closely from any corner of the room. Eloise scanned the crowd once more; he wasn't here yet, it seemed.

"Eloise?"

Catherine Moore, Eloise's closest friend now that Lila was gone for India, stood a few feet away, looking Eloise up and down with wide eyes.

"What do you think?" Eloise asked, lifting the sides of the skirt and swishing them to and fro. They rustled like wind through tree branches.

"I think you are the belle of the ball, and every girl here will hate you for it."

Eloise dropped her hands to her sides. She hadn't meant to inspire envy. This wasn't a Season event, after all, and the debutants were not vying for gentlemen's attention like they would should they end up in London together—something Eloise hoped to avoid.

"You look breathtaking," Catherine said with a smile, reading Eloise's expression. Catherine quickly took Eloise's arm and began walking her toward a group of young women, some whom Eloise didn't know very well but always came to the Websters' annual Christmas ball, held two weeks before the holiday.

Eloise had come to this event all of her life—for years watching her older siblings dance and wishing she were one of them. The last few years she had danced as well—blushing, awkward affairs with boys as anxious as she was. Those nights had been great fun, despite no serious attraction between her and any of her partners, but tonight was different. Tonight, after years of school and world travel preventing his attendance, Neville would be here.

They reached the other girls and exchanged greetings all around. Janet Bothmeyer had an emerald green dress—with an uncomfortably low neckline—and Rachel Hoyt had a red and gold gown that flounced and flourished in every way imaginable. Eloise brushed a hand down the shiny skirt of her new dress with increased confidence that she was not the only one to make a bold presentation.

"Have you heard from Lila?" Rachel asked, drawing Eloise from her thoughts and into the conversation.

"Yes, just last week. She wrote before they left London."

"And is she enjoying her role as *Mrs.* Lutherford?" Catherine asked. The girls shared a common look of eager curiosity between them. They were all anticipating the upcoming Season—even those who would not go to London—and were rather preoccupied with the things that took place after the weddings that each of them saw as a matter of course come summer and fall. Eloise's blush betrayed how many details Lila had included in her letters these last weeks as she'd traveled rather leisurely through the countryside with her new husband. The girls read the expression on Eloise's face and quickly stepped forward, forming a closed circle.

"What did she say?"

"What did she tell you?"

"Can I read Lila's letters?"

Eloise shook her head. "The details are not fitting for discussion here, certainly." Eloise lifted one slim shoulder and gave a coy glance around the circle. "But should any of you want to come to tea, say, Tuesday next at three o'clock,

I could likely share a detail or two. Mama will be visiting my aunt that day, and Lila specifically said there are things she wished she'd known."

The girls erupted into giggles that betrayed their youth, then stepped apart again when the heads of other guests turned toward them. The girls tried to hide their smiles between sips of punch. Eloise was not used to holding a powerful position among her peers—she'd always been rather shy—but Lila's marriage had emboldened her somehow. In a matter of weeks, Lila had gone from young woman to wife. She held Mr. Lutherford's heart in her hand and had gladly given over her own. She was part of a whole now and would be forever connected to Mr. Lutherford and the children they would have. Judging from the content of her letters, the role of motherhood would not be far away.

Lila had found her destiny, and now it was time for Eloise to do the same—preferably without having to go to London. Would it not be perfect to find her destiny in the place she loved best? A mere ten-minute walk from the home she'd been raised in?

Neville could give her all of that, and himself besides. He'd always asked her to dance when attending such events in the village, but tonight could change everything if he looked at her the way she hoped he would. Anticipation hummed in her belly, and she took a deep breath in an attempt to calm herself.

As more guests arrived, and more young women joined their group, it broke into several smaller conversations, which left Catherine and Eloise standing beside one another as they surveyed the room that was filling bit by bit.

"Do you think Mr. Burke will be joining Mr. Franklin tonight?" Catherine asked. For a moment the question confused Eloise—why would Neville's friend come to the ball with Neville's father?—but then she remembered that Neville was Mr. Franklin to everyone else. Only *she* called him Neville, as she had since they were childhood playmates. The privilege set her apart from any other girl who might have her eye on him.

"I would be very surprised if Mr. Burke *didn't* attend. Neither man seems to go anywhere without the other." She hoped there was no bitterness in her tone. Mr. Burke was personable enough, but his continual presence these last weeks was Eloise's only complaint with Neville's return. She'd had to show as much interest in his stories as she did in Neville's so as not to seem rude. Not once in all these weeks had she had Neville's attention all to herself, and finally she'd had to accept that she likely never would as long as Mr. Burke stayed in Shropshire. She had made the best of it, then, and hoped that making a good impression on Mr. Burke would only help the good impression she made on Neville. She looked forward to time alone with Neville tonight. She could not dance with two men at once, after all.

"Mr. Burke is very handsome," Catherine said rather absently.

Is he? Eloise hadn't noticed.

Catherine continued, "More handsome than even Mr. Franklin, I'd wager."

"Certainly not," Eloise said with a huff of laughter. What a ridiculous thought. Anyone with two eyes and half a brain could see that Neville was the handsomest man in Shropshire. With his dark, thick hair and light blue eyes . . .

Catherine took hold of Eloise's arm. "I knew it! You're sweet on Mr. Franklin, aren't you?"

Eloise felt herself blush to the roots of her hair, realizing the trap Catherine had set for her. She turned toward her friend. "Please do not tell anyone."

"Of course not!" Catherine said, giving Eloise's arm a squeeze before she dropped her grip. "Only, I am so glad to know it. You are perfect for him."

The words washed over Eloise like warm rain. "Do you think so?"

"Absolutely," Catherine said with a confirming nod. "You love Shropshire, unlike the rest of us, who cannot wait to see somewhere new, and are the perfect complement to his wild ways."

Eloise didn't like the sound of that. "Wild ways?"

Catherine gave her a surprised look. "Surely you have heard the rumors."

Everything Eloise knew of Neville had come through Lila, and as Neville's cousin, Lila would not be the recipient of much gossip.

"I hear he was quite a man about town when he was in London," Catherine was not as hesitant to share this as Eloise would have liked her to be. "That's why his father sent him to America, hoping the travel would help him better find his place in the world and keep him from becoming an all-out rake." She looked at Eloise a bit closer. "Surely that does not upset you. Every girl dreams of a dashing hero capable of sweeping her off her feet. He certainly could not do so without a bit of practice." She bumped Eloise with her shoulder. "I would think Lila would have said as much in her letters. Surely her Mr. Lutherford had some experience that worked in her favor."

"Lila did not speak of that." Which was surprising, really, since Lila had spoken of so many other things. Catherine's words were troubling, and yet Eloise felt foolish to feel that way. Neville was twenty-four years old and had traveled the world. Of course he had met women, and every young man who spent time in London got in some trouble now and then.

"There they are."

Eloise looked up from the spot on the floor that had stolen her attention and felt excitement and trepidation and anxiety and bliss rush through her at the sight of Neville in formal dress. The blue superfine coat fit him perfectly, with tails that reached the tops of his polished boots, complete with silver buckles. His hair was combed forward in a Brutus, and the silver of his waistcoat complemented the darker gray of his breeches. She watched him scan the crowd, and time froze the moment he saw her. His eyes locked with hers and then traveled quickly down and back up, as though to confirm it was truly her. Her heart rate increased as his lips parted slightly in surprise and his eyebrows went up. When he met her eyes again, he quickly repaired his expression and smiled rather politely. He leaned in and said something to Mr. Burke, who was taking a much slower inspection that made Eloise's cheeks heat up. Why had she not considered anyone else's reaction to her presentation tonight? She had thought only of Neville, and yet something in *his* reaction seemed unexpectedly closed.

In tandem, the men began moving toward Eloise and Catherine. Catherine gasped and stood straighter.

The men came to stop in front of the two young women, and Eloise commanded herself to relax. *It is not a sin to be beautiful.*

"My, but don't the two of you look good enough to eat," Mr. Burke said, looking between them but lingering on Eloise. Eloise blushed again. A pox on her betraying cheeks!

Neville cleared his throat rather pointedly and narrowed his eyes at his friend. Mr. Burke ignored the look and turned his attention to Catherine. "Miss Moore, might I have the pleasure of the first dance tonight?"

"Oh, most certainly, Mr. Burke," Catherine said with a slight curtsey. "I would be honored."

Neville caught Eloise's eye and smiled. "Might I ask the same from you, Miss Hallstrom?"

It was always surprising to hear him address her formally when an event dictated such manners. Even still, there was something stiff in his expression—something keeping her out that made her anxious. He always seemed glad to see her; why not tonight? She felt her confidence tremble as though she'd stepped out of a cold bath on a winter day.

She inclined her head. "Certainly, Mr. Franklin."

Mr. Burke turned to her. "May I have the next, Miss Hallstrom?"

She swore she heard Neville's jaw clench, but when she glanced at him, he looked away. "Of course," Eloise said.

"We shall return in time to collect our partners for the first set," Neville said, bowing rather stiffly to them both and then leading Mr. Burke away.

"Gracious stars," Catherine said once the men were out of range. "I do so hope Mr. Burke is as experienced as Mr. Franklin. Might I please be so fortunate?"

Chapter Five

Neville stalked to the refreshment table and picked up a glass of punch before turning—almost against his will—to look at Eloise again. There was a reason debutantes were not supposed to wear such bold colors. *Gracious.*

The red set off her golden hair and drew the eye to the way the fabric fit her curves; since when was Eloise so . . . shapely? He was half tempted to tuck his handkerchief over her exposed bosom in order to hide the expanse of creamy skin from Burke's leering eyes. When had little Eloise, with whom he'd played tag and made mud pies, become such a woman? And where was her mother? Weren't mothers supposed to prevent their daughters from being so engaging?

"What did I tell you?" Burke said triumphantly as he stepped beside Neville, his own glass of Christmas punch in hand. "In a dress like that, she's fairly begging for a kiss."

"She is not," Neville said curtly. "And she does not understand the effect a dress like that can have on a man. She hasn't even had a Season. She's young and naïve and—"

"Stunning," Burke finished for him. He faced Neville. "You can't tell me that you aren't as affected as I am and wouldn't like a better view."

"There is view enough from here." And indeed there was. Neville's jaw was clenched so tightly he could feel the ache all the way to his shoulders.

Burke nodded to Horace Blaylock, with whom they had gone hunting last week, and made his way toward the other man, likely because Neville was turning out to be such stodgy company tonight. Imagining Eloise at the mercy of Burke's attention, however, was beyond what Neville could tolerate. Another acquaintance stepped forward, blessedly blocking Neville's view of Eloise on the other side of the room. Not that the distraction made him any less aware of her, but at least there was some kind of barrier.

After several minutes of small talk, Neville heard the orchestra warming up for the first set, which he would dance with Eloise. He swallowed nervously, not sure he was comfortable dancing with her when he still hadn't become accustomed to her presentation tonight, but at least Burke wouldn't be the first to lead her to the floor.

There had to be a way Neville could tell Eloise to be on her guard with Burke, who couldn't be trusted with women and most certainly not with someone as pure and naïve as Eloise. Especially if Eloise *did* fancy him. She might invite more than she was prepared to handle, and then she would be hurt and embarrassed. As a friend, Neville couldn't allow that to happen.

Burke had already collected Miss Moore by the time Neville reached Eloise. He bowed quickly, then took her hand and led her as far away from Burke as possible. They stood across from one another as the set lined up and his eyes moved up and down her person again before he realized what he was doing. He swallowed and forced himself to meet her eyes. She smiled nervously, and though he tried to smile back he feared it came off poorly.

How was he to know how to deal with awkwardness between them when they had never experienced it before? Even when Lila had confessed her feelings for Lutherford—with Eloise right there—Neville hadn't felt uncomfortable in Eloise's company. She'd somehow managed to be a friend to both of them, and they had moved forward accordingly. Yet now Neville was uncomfortable and fearful of the impressions she was giving without meaning to. And . . . that dress. He ran a hand inside his collar, feeling like an absolute wretch to realize he was ogling her as much as Burke had been. How could he look at her this way? This was Eloise!

"Is something wrong, Neville?"

He met her eyes and forced his smile a bit wider. "No. Nothing. Of course not. No. Certainly. Isn't. Wrong."

She pulled her eyebrows together, but then the leading notes were played. She put out her gloved hand, and he took it. When he looked at her again, she was looking at the ground rather than at him. A glance at the other couples showed them maintaining eye contact. The dance began, and Neville tried to get a hold of himself.

"I'm sorry," he said at a point when they came close enough to converse. "I'm a bit at odds with myself tonight."

They parted, then came together again. "Why?" she asked.

He considered how to answer, but then shook his head, hoping she would assume he didn't want to burden her with his worries—which was true. In greater truth, however, he simply did not know what to tell her. She would be so terribly embarrassed to know Burke's thoughts about her—kissable lips, indeed. What sweet, simple girl like Eloise should be exposed to the impressions of a rake like Burke? But Neville would feel like a poor friend if he didn't try to protect her.

They did not speak again—had dancing ever been so tedious? When the dance finally finished, Neville led Eloise from the floor. If it were not so cold, he could invite her to walk the garden so that they might have a private conversation, but there was snow on the ground and it was cold enough to rattle a man's teeth, to say nothing of what effect it would have on a woman with such bare . . . arms. He would not think about her . . . or her kissable lips. Or her golden hair. Or . . . blast, but it was hot in this room! Would no one open a window?

"Thank you for the dance, Mr. Franklin."

He hadn't realized they'd reached the edge of the floor. He met her eye and saw the concern in those wide blue depths. He was trying to think of how to provide a remedy when someone spoke from behind him.

"Are you ready, Miss Hallstrom?"

Neville turned to look at Burke with narrowed eyes. Burke ignored him.

"You are a vision on the floor." Burke put out his arm as though he were a gentleman.

"Thank you, Mr. Burke."

To Neville's absolute horror, Eloise's expression was repaired by the time Burke led her to the floor. Neville turned and watched them, forced to observe the other man with greater objectivity. Burke *was* handsome and relatively charming.

The couple took their position. Burke leaned in and said something in Eloise's ear. She laughed, her face lit up like it certainly had not been when Neville had danced with her. A pink flush tinged her cheeks. Neville had made her uncomfortable, but Burke was making her laugh.

I've gone about this all wrong, Neville thought when she laughed again and shook her head at whatever outrageous thing Burke must have said. Neville had arrived with the plan to warn her away from Burke, but all he'd done was drive her to him.

The dance began, and Neville watched her—really watched. She was so graceful in her steps, fluid almost. The skirt of her dress moved with her like water—and the bodice was tight enough to be a second skin—but the cut of the dress accentuated her narrow waist perfectly. Her sleeves were off her shoulders, showing her creamy neck and collarbone and . . . other assets. He forced himself to look away and swallow before looking back again with an attempt at decorum. She *was* beautiful, and yet he knew in a way that Burke did not that her beauty was more than the dress and the hair and the kissable lips. Eloise was kind, witty, smart, and optimistic—the perfect example of how inner beauty could be reflected on the outside. Neville had known and appreciated her inner grace and goodness all his life; how had he not noticed her blossoming into the external beauty he saw now?

Burke had noticed before Neville had even considered the possibility.

Chapter Six

By the end of Eloise's set with Mr. Burke—an energetic reel, which left her questioning the wisdom of such tight stays—she was nearly recovered from the uncomfortable dance with Neville. He'd been so severe that she had been fighting back tears by the end. Had she misinterpreted their ease in one another's company? Had she seen what wasn't there?

She'd felt foolish for wearing this dress in hopes it would help him see her as more than a childhood playmate. He was too out of sorts to notice. Beyond that, she worried about what had him so irritated. It was not like him to brood, and she wished she knew how to help. Was something amiss at the estate? Was his father feeling poorly? Had he received bad news of one kind or another?

"That was the loveliest dance, Eloise," Mr. Burke said when they reached the edge of the floor. Neville had been standing nearby when they'd taken the floor, and she'd seen him watching them a time or two, but he was gone now. She wondered where he went. "You are the very vision of

Christmas in that dress, and I thank you for gracing me with your company," Mr. Burke continued.

"Of course, Mr. Burke," she said, still glancing around the room in hopes of finding Neville. "Thank you for your compliments."

"Would it be frowned upon too severely if I took the waltz as well?"

Eloise hesitated to answer; she had hoped Neville would ask for the waltz. But he hadn't. And Mr. Burke had.

"Of course not," Eloise said.

Mr. Burke winked, bowed once more, and turned away.

"Is he not a fabulous dancer?"

Eloise had not heard Catherine approach, but smiled politely at her friend. "He is, indeed." She couldn't deny that he'd made her feel the way she'd hoped *Neville* would make her feel tonight—like the kind of woman a man enjoyed sharing company with.

"Did he request another dance?" Catherine asked with her eyebrows up.

"The waltz."

"Oh, you are a very fortunate girl."

Eloise smiled and nodded, but she had fantasized of twirling the floor in Neville's arms. Of course, she'd thought that before she'd known of his foul mood. But surely if they were in one another's arms, they could talk as they always had, and she could help him find a solution to whatever was bothering him. It seemed reasonable to assume that a good friendship would lead to a good match, yet there was a barrier between them tonight that she didn't understand. Somehow even their friendship seemed threatened.

Catherine was asked to dance the next set, and Eloise was considering some tea when Robert Hadley stepped before her. "M-might I h-h-have this d-dance, M-miss H-H-Hallstrom?" Robert was seventeen years of age and blushing to his ears. Asking her to dance had no doubt taken monumental confidence on his part, and she would do everything possible to put him at ease.

"I would be honored, Mr. Hadley."

He nodded furiously as she put her gloved hand in his sweaty one and smiled. "You look very handsome tonight, Mr. Hadley." She was determined to boost his confidence.

"A-as d-d-do you."

"Oh, thank you," she said, putting her other hand on his arm. "That is most kind of you."

She spent the dance complimenting how well Mr. Hadley knew his steps. By the time he returned her to her place on the edge of the floor, only his ears were red. She hoped he felt more comfortable now; she knew the difference a partner could make on one's confidence. She'd known such a thing before tonight, of course, but the lesson had certainly been brought to the forefront of her mind again. There was little time to think much about it before she was commandeered for yet another dance. She followed her newest partner to the floor and determined not to let her concerns for Neville's mood ruin the night.

After the set, Eloise found a chair away from the dance floor so that potential partners would know she was sitting out this set—she needed to catch her breath. The exertion and the crowd were contributing to a rather warm room. A few moments after she sat down, Neville slipped into the chair beside her. Despite her anxiety regarding his mood this evening, a thrill coursed through her to have him so close, and she sat up a bit straighter. He'd obviously sought her out. Perhaps he was feeling better, and they could now get on as they usually did, with comfort and equanimity.

"Oh, please do not ask me to dance, Neville," she said with a smile. "I am wrung out but will hate saying no to *you.*"

"You haven't turned anyone else down."

His tone was petulant, and she turned to look at him more closely. His jaw was tight, and he was not looking at her. She felt her irritation prickle for the first time. Why was he treating *her* poorly? Friends did not do such things to one another. Her response was clipped. "And, as I said, I am wrung out from it." She faced forward, almost relieved to be irritated with him since it saved her from feeling insecure. "Whatever the reason for your poor mood tonight, I would thank you not to act as if I am to blame."

Neville was silent a moment before he let out a breath and leaned against the chair back. "I am sorry, Eloise. I am out of sorts."

She instantly softened and turned toward him again. "What is bothering you? Might I help?"

He shook his head and made a point of watching the dancers. After a moment, she joined him. They sat in silence.

"Did you enjoy your dance with Burke?" Neville finally asked.

"Yes, I did."

"I hope you will not dance with him again tonight."

Eloise's irritation rose once more, but she looked ahead when she spoke. "He asked for the waltz."

Neville narrowed his eyes. "The waltz? *Two* dances. There will be speculation."

"It only means he asked me before anyone else did. It's not as though I shall give him a third, and it is the Christmas ball. Rules are always bent for such an occasion."

"As you have well proven." Neville faced forward and cursed.

"I beg your pardon," she said, raising her eyebrows at the double offense—his accusation and using such language in her presence.

"I am sorry," he said, shaking his head. "I am—"

"Out of sorts," she finished for him. "So you've said." She shifted in her chair, facing him more directly. "If you are unable to be sociable tonight, Neville, then perhaps you should leave so that the rest of us might not be drawn into your petulance."

The last thing she wanted was for him to leave, but she was losing hope of there being any way to redeem this evening. Each exchange she had with Neville seemed to only make things worse.

"You want me to leave?"

She pulled back slightly at the hurt in his voice. "N-no, I do not *want* you to leave, but . . . what is wrong? Why are you angry with me?"

"I am not angry with you." He ran a hand through his hair, leaving it adorably disheveled, and leaned forward to put his elbows on his knees. He turned his head to look at her. "I am just concerned, Eloise."

Eloise pulled her eyebrows together again. He sounded rather fatherly.

"You are very young, Eloise, and naïve to the ways that men . . . look upon a woman."

Her cheeks caught fire.

He waved in the general direction of her bodice. "When a woman presents herself . . . thusly, a man might get the wrong impression."

Eloise crossed her arms over her chest, horrified at what Neville was saying, while looking around to confirm that she was no less appropriate than any other woman here. Rachel Bastian, for example, was practically falling out of her dress and made a point to brush against each man who took her to the floor. Eloise's horror was amplified by the fact that she'd wanted Neville to feel attracted to her tonight, and yet now he spoke of such attraction as something untoward. Eloise could hear the blood pounding in her ears. "You are speaking beyond your realm, Neville," she whispered, shifting away from him in her chair.

He met her eye, and she could see that, despite how offensive his words were, his concern was sincere—confusing her once again. "I am speaking as a friend, Eloise. I don't want to see you hurt."

"Hurt?"

"By a man who might get the wrong impression when he looks upon your presentation tonight."

"And what *impression* is that, Neville?"

He grunted as though frustrated, not seeming to realize that she understood quite perfectly. She only wanted to make him say it out loud. Perhaps if he did, he would realize how horrid he was being.

"An impression that you want a man to . . . look at you,

to ogle you, in fact, and wonder at what charms you might be hiding." He gestured toward the bodice of her dress again and huffed. "Though I must say you are not hiding very much."

"How dare you say such a thing to me?" Eloise hissed, rising to her feet. Without saying another word, she moved toward the first doorway she could see on the nearest end of the ballroom, partially hidden by a screen painted in a festive Christmas scene. She could feel a dozen pairs of eyes follow her from the room. Unfamiliar with the Webster house, she looked both directions in an attempt to get her bearings.

"Miss?"

She looked to her left where a maid was standing with a tray of glasses, apparently en route to the ballroom, and felt her chin begin to tremble. "I need a place to be alone for a moment, t-to gather myself." She still had her arms crossed over her chest, feeling naked and exposed in more ways than one.

"The retiring room is just this—"

"Somewhere I can be alone," Eloise cut in, unable to face the other girls and women who would be adjusting their gowns or making idle gossip in the room set aside for such things. "Please."

The young maid nodded and waved down the hall, away from the ballroom. She began walking that direction—tray still in hand—and Eloise followed. "Certainly, miss. This way."

Chapter Seven

Neville barely noted Eloise's exit before he found himself alone. A few guests looked at him strangely, and he assumed they had seen Eloise's red face and hasty escape from his company. He opened his own mouth, as though to explain himself to the onlookers, but no words came out. Once again, he'd gone about things the wrong way. Perhaps Eloise was right; it would be better if he left. But now she was upset, and it was his fault. He couldn't leave without repairing things—never mind that he had no idea how to do that.

Explain. That was all he needed to do: explain himself. Eloise was a sensible girl, or, well, woman, apparently, and would certainly understand if he could explain in enough detail his reasons for saying what he'd said. If Eloise knew that his intent was her protection, she would certainly agree with him. She might even thank him for being such a good friend.

Neville stood, gave an awkward nod to the people watching him, and turned toward the door Eloise had used for her own escape. He soon found himself alone in a hallway with no idea which direction she'd gone. A sound from the left caught his attention, and he looked that direction in time to see a maid with a tray in one hand closing a door behind her. He stepped into a shadowed portion of the hall until she disappeared.

Several seconds later, Neville opened the door slowly, his eyes fixing on the vision of red facing away from him. Her shapely shoulders, narrowing rib cage, graceful hips—he looked away and gave the room a quick inspection instead. It was a study of sorts. It smelled of old pipe smoke and books, but it had a fire in the grate and, best of all, privacy. Eloise stood facing the window with her back toward him. A sniffle and swipe at her eyes betrayed how upset she was, and he felt his stomach drop. He left the door of the room open as he stepped inside.

"Eloise," he said softly, pulling his handkerchief from the pocket of his coat. She turned and winced when she saw him before turning her back again.

"Go away, Neville," she said in a voice that was both shaky and firm.

He paused a step but then moved toward her and handed the handkerchief over her shoulder. She shook her head and turned away from him, but he pressed the handkerchief forward again.

"At least let me do something to try to make this right."

She sniffled again, then finally took the cloth from him. He stepped back, but she didn't turn toward him and she said nothing.

"Eloise," he said softly. "I'm sorry."

"For calling me a harlot?" she said without looking at him, her voice ragged with emotion.

"I did not call you a harlot," Neville said in defense.

Eloise spun around. "You most certainly did! And in the same breath accused me of being too dim-witted to realize that I was behaving as such."

"I never used harlot or dim-witted in anything I said." Her eyes remained narrowed, and so he put up his hands, palms facing her in surrender. "It certainly wasn't my *intention* to suggest either of those implications." He shook his head in a desperate attempt to redeem himself. "I'm sorry that I upset you."

She sniffled but said nothing as she dabbed at her eyes.

Now was his chance to give her a full explanation. "I feel a duty to look after you, Eloise. We are friends, after all."

"And that makes it acceptable for you to talk to me that way?"

"I believe that friends help one another, and that is what I was trying to do."

"By telling me I look like a harlot?"

"That is not what I said!" he protested, his irritation growing. "But *this*"—he waved toward her dress—"this is not you, Eloise, and I am sure a girl as good as you are would not want to give the impression you give in that dress. You are not a harlot, nor do you look like one, but you do send . . . signals to a man when you look as you do tonight."

She lifted her chin and stood up straighter, necessitating Neville's sudden interest in the bookshelf to his left. She really had no idea the effect she could have. *He* had no idea the effect she could have until now, and the idea of other men being similarly affected was unthinkable. "How do you know that I don't know *exactly* what impression I am making?" she asked.

"Because if you knew, you would not wear a dress like this." That didn't sound right, and he let out a breath while running his fingers through his hair. "You do not want men to look at you with . . . desire, Eloise, and a dress like this, well, it strikes something in a man that can be intense, I suppose is the right word."

She put a hand on her hip, and he looked away again, swallowed, and reminded himself that this was *Eloise*. He was acting like a big brother. So why was he so uncomfortable? "Does seeing me in this dress make you desire me, Neville? When you look at me, do you feel some *intense* feeling that perhaps you do not know how to handle?"

Heat crept up his neck and face without any permission on his part, but he forced himself to hold her gaze. "I was speaking on the behalf of other men, Eloise."

Some pained expression crossed her face before she repaired it a moment later, shutting him out. "I see," she said. "You are above such base reactions, I suppose."

He nodded but looked at the toe of his boot.

"And are you giving this same advice to all the other young women similarly arrayed this evening?"

"No one is dressed like you are tonight, Eloise."

"Aren't they?"

"No," he said with confidence, reviewing the other women in his mind. It was not difficult to compare her against the twenty or so debutantes in the ballroom. None of them—not one—looked like she did. She shone like a candle on a dark night or the first evening star. Gracious, he hadn't taken a second look at any one of the other girls yet. He was unable to keep his eyes off of Eloise. "They are all dressed *appropriately,* Eloise. Their bodices are higher, their dresses not so tight, and their color choices are far less bold."

Her eyes narrowed, and he hurried to explain himself more clearly—why was this not working? He was only trying to help her, and she was tangling him up in his own words. "We have been friends for a long time, Eloise, and I am sorry that I've hurt your feelings, but I am simply looking out for your well-being. It is not that you don't look beautiful—you look absolutely radiant—but as your friend, I feel it important that you understand how dangerous that can be."

"Because men might desire me?" Eloise said. "And you do not want other men to desire me."

Finally, she was beginning to understand. "Exactly."

"But *you* do not desire me?"

"R-right," he said. Why did he sense he'd just walked into a trap?

She took a step toward him, and the heat that had begun to fade from his neck increased again. When she spoke, her voice was lower, and it did odd things to his appendages. "I am old enough to marry, Neville, and I fully expect that the man I marry *will* desire me. Since you are so very *unaffected,* I would ask that you give me the margin I need to make progress toward a match."

Good grief. His mouth went dry as she continued to

walk toward him. "I-I am only trying to help," he stammered, willing her to stop coming closer. "L-like a b-big brother would do for his little sister." Even as he said the words he knew that his confusing feelings of this night were not nearly as brotherly as he would like to pretend them to be.

She stopped, only a foot or two away from him. That fire in the grate was far too hot! "I have a big brother, Neville." Her eyes were still pink from the crying he'd interrupted, and yet she was entirely self-possessed at this moment. "And a ball to attend—including a waltz with Mr. Burke. If you'll excuse me."

She stepped around him, leaving him with a scent of her perfume—which was as equally inappropriate as her dress. Had she no shame at all? The door closed, and still he did not move. *What just happened?* he asked himself. He wanted to believe he'd helped Eloise understand that he was only trying to help, and yet he was pretty sure that wasn't the case at all.

Her words echoed in his mind: *"I fully expect that the man I marry will desire me."*

Neville hated this fictitious husband already.

Chapter Eight

Eloise made sure to enter a different door than she'd escaped through a few minutes earlier, and then she ignored sympathetic looks directed her way. She'd have liked a few more minutes of recovery before returning—gracious, she'd have liked to run for home—but if she did, Neville would think she was reacting to his words. She would not allow that to happen, despite all her hopes for this evening having come to naught. She would mourn that later, too. She made her way to Catherine, but was claimed for a reel almost immediately. She pasted a smile on her face and reviewed in her mind what had happened with Neville, while executing the steps of the dance. The movements seemed to settle her thoughts, sift and separate them until the hurt and embarrassment faded enough to give her a clearer view. Why was he so concerned? Though offensive and harsh, he was sincere in his pressings and felt strongly enough to confront her. Was it protectiveness, as he claimed, or something else?

Neville was standing at the side of the room with a glass

of wine in his hand as the dance came to a close, and she made sure to lift her chin a bit higher and smile a bit wider at her partner. She would not give Neville the satisfaction of thinking she was heeding his offensive warnings. An inspection of the other guests while she danced proved that she was indeed no more "revealed" than any other woman here—even more proper than some.

When her partner returned her to the edge of the dance floor, Mr. Burke was waiting to claim his waltz. She glanced at Neville only long enough to see that he was watching them, his expression dour. The glowering set of his eyebrows only strengthened her resolve to look unaffected.

Eloise thanked her former partner before turning to Mr. Burke and placing her hand in his so that he could lead her to the floor—how she wished she could look at him and see Neville's reaction at the same time. Once near the center of the floor, she turned to face Mr. Burke and put her hand on his shoulder while he put his hand on her waist. She startled a bit when he stepped closer, bringing the space between them to almost nothing. His hand at her waist tightened.

"You look positively breathtaking tonight, Eloise," he said as they took their first steps in tandem. Her skirts made a slight rushing sound as they swayed back and forth with the tempo of the music.

"Thank you, Mr. Burke."

"No, thank *you*," Mr. Burke said. "I have not had such a visual feast since I don't know when."

Eloise swallowed and looked away from what seemed almost a leering expression. It was all she could do to keep Neville's reprimanding voice out of her head. She told herself that she was simply unused to such direct attention, and, as she had already confirmed twice now, she was equal to every other woman here, other than those who *were* putting themselves on display. If both Neville and Mr. Burke felt she was being too bold, however, she would have a difficult time justifying herself otherwise.

"Have you enjoyed the evening so far?" she asked, forcing her tone to be bright. "I'm sure a country ball is rather simple entertainment for a man like yourself who is so well traveled."

"I will admit I thought it might be rather dull," Mr. Burke said, flawlessly executing a turn. "But perhaps I have underestimated the charms the country has to offer, after all. I was considering going back to London for Christmas, but perhaps I will stay a bit longer. Would you like that, Eloise?" The hand at her waist moved half an inch lower toward her hip.

She kept her smile pasted in place. "That certainly isn't my decision to make, Mr. Burke."

"If I did stay, would you go riding with me? Tomorrow, perhaps? Just the two of us."

"Oh, well . . ." She had no interest in being alone with Mr. Burke, but then they reached the side of the room where Neville was glowering at them. She snapped her eyes back to Mr. Burke. "I would love to go for a ride," she said—wishing Neville could overhear but not sure that he could. "I have a wool riding habit and a fur hat that would be perfect in this weather."

"Excellent," Mr. Burke said, allowing his eyes to move down to her chest and then back to her face where her cheeks were aflame. Suddenly, some portion of Neville's warning made sense.

"I would hate to catch a chill this close to the holidays," Eloise said, deciding to fill the rest of the dance with chatter. "There is ever so much to be done, you know. There are evergreen boughs to gather, to say nothing of the holly and the—"

"Mistletoe?" he said, raising one eyebrow. "Perhaps we might find some tomorrow on our ride."

"Oh, well . . ."

Chapter Nine

"Morning," Burke said when he joined Neville in the breakfast room the next day. Neville had not slept well, which did nothing to improve his mood from the night before.

"Good morning," Neville said as evenly as he could manage. He kept his eyes trained on the paper in front of him while Burke prepared himself a plate from the sideboard. Neville tried to think of something other than Eloise in Burke's arms as they waltzed across the floor, but seeing as how he'd been unsuccessful in the hours they'd spent apart, he was less successful than ever now that the man was in his presence again.

Overnight, Neville's world had shifted, and he had not yet made sense of the new world in front of him. What he wouldn't give for a few days of his own company where he might stand a chance of sorting things out. As long as Burke was here as Neville's guest and constant companion, Neville saw no hope of coming to terms with his feelings toward Eloise.

Around two o'clock that morning, Neville had realized he was *jealous* of Burke. Neville wasn't sure he'd ever felt such an emotion but acknowledged now that he felt something for Eloise he did not want another man to feel. He had justified himself as being protective last night, as a friend, but staring at the dark ceiling of his room, with the chill of night taking over the air around him bit by bit, he could not convince himself of such noble intent.

Just Eloise was not *just Eloise* anymore.

While the red dress may have shocked him into admitting it, he could look over the last weeks and see that her presence was a big portion of why he felt so content here in Hemberg. She made him feel welcome, encouraged his efforts toward estate improvement, and laughed at his stories. She was an excellent conversationalist and a trusted confidante. She built him up in every way a man wants to be built up. Yet it wasn't until last night that he realized the full potential of the way he felt in her company. Until last night, he had not realized how his affections had been growing all along, and now his physical attraction had come to match his feelings.

"You do have a fine cook, Franklin."

Neville looked up at Burke taking a seat at the other side of the table and felt frustration building in his chest again. Burke had already made these realizations about Eloise. Without knowing her anywhere near as well as Neville did, he'd seen her potential and gone after it last night, while Neville had offended and embarrassed her in his bumbling attempts to protect her from his dissolute friend.

There was no doubt in Neville's mind that his feelings

were more valid than whatever Burke's might be—but was that enough? His feelings were only a portion of this equation with him and Burke and Eloise, and he had made a mess of his position last night.

The solution in his mind was simple: take out one of the players of this puzzle. A lifetime of friendship with Eloise gave him confidence he could repair the damage he'd done, but not if Burke remained here and pressed his advantage.

Advantage? Was that what Neville believed, that Burke already had the upper hand? The realization sparked a new level of urgency. Had Eloise been more attentive to Burke than Neville had noticed? Was it fair for Neville to attempt to counter her interest in another man?

"How long do you think you might stay?" Neville asked, trying to keep his tone unassuming. "You'd mentioned yesterday that the country was wearing thin on you. Perhaps you'd like to move on, as you suggested."

Burke leveled a look at Neville. "Trying to get rid of me, are you?"

Neville looked at his paper and smoothed the crease. "Not at all. Just curious."

"Ah, yes, curious." Burke began cutting his ham. "I daresay the impression of your quaint village has improved upon me since last night. I think I will stay a bit longer."

Neville could think of nothing to say that would not betray his feelings, so he focused on an article about a naval ship returning to Bristol last week.

"In fact," Burke continued, "I've asked Eloise to ride with me today and she's accepted."

Neville lifted his face slowly. "It is too cold for a lady to go riding."

Burke grinned. "She did not think so when she accepted my invitation, though it's unfortunate she shall have to be so bundled up against the chill."

Neville took a deep breath and let it out slowly. "What are you about, Burke?" His voice was dark and ragged, finally showing the emotion he felt. "I have told you that Eloise is not a girl to be trifled with, and I will ask you to stand down from this course to preserve her feelings."

Burke continued to smile, but a hardness entered his expression all the same. "Why do you continue to assume I am trifling?"

"Because it is the only thing you know how to do."

"Well, then, it's about time I learned additional skills, is it not?" He forked a piece of ham and put it in his mouth, chewing slowly as he watched Neville process his words.

"So, your intentions are honorable."

Burke winked and turned back to his plate.

Neville was gathering a more direct question about Burke's expectations when his father came in, effectively putting an end to this line of inquiry.

"Ah, good morning, gentlemen," his father said as he moved to the sideboard, turning his back upon the younger men. "I wondered if you would be up so early. Jessop said it was quite late when you returned from the Websters' ball. I hope your ability to rise so early is not proof against the Websters' ball having been a successful evening."

"Oh, it was a *very* successful evening," Burke said, lifting his eyebrows at Neville, whose thoughts were swirling again. Burke speared another bite of ham. "Very successful, indeed."

Chapter Ten

Eloise was already saddled on her speckled gray mare, Frost—aptly named for today's outing—when Mr. Burke arrived on a chestnut-colored gelding. Eloise wore wool stockings, two wool petticoats, a coat, fur-lined gloves, a fur cap, and a scarf. Even still, her nose was frozen within a quarter mile of the house, and she wondered why she had agreed to this ride and why he had requested it. Why not tea in the parlor?

Eloise convinced herself that she was glad to have accepted the invitation as they moved farther from her house, but she didn't quite believe it. Thankfully, Mr. Burke was an easy man to converse with, and they spoke of his family and the trip to America he'd made with Neville. Eloise had heard a good many tales about their travels these last weeks but never tired of the topic. Such adventure in a wild and primitive land. Mr. Burke told a story Eloise hadn't heard before about Neville having his bags stolen from a posting house where they had stayed the night.

"What did he do?" Eloise asked, imagining how

frightening it would be to have no possessions at all. Poor Neville.

"We bought a suit off a banker that kept him presentable until we got back to New York," Mr. Burke said. "The pants were two inches too short and the shoulders too wide, which made Franklin look ridiculous, but he still outshone every other man there. You've never seen such a place, Eloise. I can't imagine why any of them left our fair land or why they fought so hard to be independent from us—they're a bunch of ruffians with a gun on each hip and hardly a tailor to be found."

A gun on each hip? How barbaric. "What was your favorite place you visited?" Eloise asked.

"Nantucket, Massachusetts," Mr. Burke said. "An island just off the coast—we spent a good deal of that first summer there. Franklin didn't care for it as much as I did, though. He preferred to see the villages and frontiers—talked to a great deal of farmers."

"Farmers?" Eloise said, preferring the conversation when it turned to Neville. She was still angry with him, but interested in everything about him now that the chasm between them felt too wide to cross. Mr. Burke's insight might be the best she could hope for.

"He found it fascinating that so much of the farmland had been recently converted from forest and wanted to better understand how they prepared the land. If I had a shilling for every fence line he walked . . ." He paused and shook his head dramatically.

"And did he learn some things that will assist the estate?"

Mr. Burke shrugged. "I suppose. I forbade him to talk of agriculture to me after the first month. Boring stuff, really. Rotation, wheat strains, manures." He gave her a look and raised an eyebrow. "I warn you never to bring up the subject with him—you'll rue the day if you do."

"I think I would find his talk of farming quite fascinating," Eloise said, looking over the miles of farmland stretching before them. "Mr. Franklin is an excellent manager of his acreage, which is why their estate is one of the most successful in the area. I think it's to Neville's credit to want to continue that legacy." She could imagine the way the energy would light Neville's eyes—and yet, after last night, the ease between them seemed extinguished. "How is Neville today?" she asked almost absently. She'd avoided him rather studiously after their discussion in the study last night, so she did not know if he had at some point shrugged off their exchange completely.

"Cross," Mr. Burke said. "Why are you asking after Franklin when you are riding with me?"

"Oh, I'm sorry," Eloise said, though she was taken aback by the harshness of his comment. "Only, he was out of sorts last night, and I wondered if he was improving. He has been a dear friend of mine for many years, and I worry about his mood, which was so unlike him."

Mr. Burke did not comment directly on that and looked forward again, returning to talk of his American travels. Eloise listened quietly but found her irritation growing. First at Mr. Burke's complaint against her, and then at Neville for drawing her attention when manners dictated that she should be focused on Mr. Burke.

She'd avoided Mama this morning as well because she regretted having told her mother that she had a fancy and feared Mama would ask after it. That Eloise hadn't confirmed Neville as the object of that affection made no difference; Mama knew, and it must be killing her to wait on Eloise before she could share her thoughts. Her parents' approval was certain. Neville was an eligible gentleman, and their families had always got on very well. At least until now.

"Why don't we tether the horses and walk for a bit?" Mr. Burke said, drawing Eloise from her thoughts. She looked around them to orient herself and saw that someone had cleared the path around Bramble Pond—a favorite walking place in spring and summer. Portions of the trail were built up with a railed boardwalk, but most of the path was dirt and stone, currently cleared of ice and snow, for the most part. By the state of the ice on the pond, some enterprising citizens had been exercising their skating abilities. Perhaps it was they who had also cleared the path. "You've got hearty boots on, do you not?" Mr. Burke asked.

"Indeed," Eloise said. She was not opposed to the walk, only not terribly invested in this outing. She wished she'd found a way to refuse it last night. She'd accepted Mr. Burke's invitation because it might make Neville jealous, but that reason seemed lacking in the cold light of day. What had Neville to be jealous of? He'd proclaimed his disinterest quite ardently, and though at times she was tempted to think his protests were evidence to the contrary, it was hopeful thinking that had put her in this predicament in the first place.

If she'd never attempted to draw Neville's notice, she would never have had such an offensive exchange with him that had now created more distance than his trip to America had. After only one day, she missed their easy friendship—missed thinking of him and only having warmth and joy surround her thoughts. Now there were questions and regrets and embarrassment and irritation. If she could go back in time, she would not have risked their friendship for the hope it might become more.

They made their way to the posting area, and Mr. Burke helped Eloise from her horse. She had to throw her long skirts over one arm so they would not drag on the ground, but it was not long before she was glad for the exercise. It helped warm her legs, and it was a lovely winter day. The sun turned the snow cover to crystals and lit the sky like summer. Eloise tried to keep her thoughts from Neville, but they returned again and again. Was he angry with her? Did he regret what he'd said? Every thought added to the weight in her belly. They would overcome this, right?

"Ah, it is a beautiful view," Mr. Burke said, reminding her whom she was with.

They'd reached one of the boardwalk sections of the pond, and Mr. Burke stepped forward and rested his elbows on the railing. They were nearly halfway around the pond, and could look out over its length and across the snow-covered moorland, where only clusters of shrubs and trees broke through the glittering white. Eloise took a position beside him, but did not rest her elbows as he did.

"It is," she said, sentimental of this place she loved best above any other part of England. "I know many people prefer the southern counties, where it is temperate the year round, and they can avoid the harsher effects of winter, but I cannot imagine living without each season of the year being distinct from the others."

"I don't mind the snow," Mr. Burke agreed. "But there is something to be said for sunshine all the year long. It is not so hard to visit the snow and get your fill, you know."

"Ah, but a visit does not connect you to the changes, and I like to feel connected. I like knowing which month I'll trade out my summer frocks for winter ones, and that there will be full days that I don't leave the house—I have an array of projects I can do indoors for days such as that. And we'll have more stews in the winter, and greens in the summer, and adapt our lives to the land we live on. I love it."

"Hmmm," Mr. Burke said.

His noncommittal response drew her eye, and she found him staring at her. She looked away, brushed at some nonexistent speck on her coat, and then turned toward the path. "Perhaps we should finish our way around."

She'd taken two steps when he took hold of her arm and somehow spun her around until the rail of the boardwalk was pressing into her lower back. He stood directly in front of her and leaned forward so that his arms were on either side, trapping her. He smiled at her warmly, suggestively. She had her skirts thrown over one arm, leaving only one hand free to put against his chest. "Mr. Burke," she said, trying to sound firm. The result of his taking her by surprise, however, added a breathless quality to her voice that made his smile grow wider.

"There is but one thing keeping me in this part of the

country right now," he said, looking from her eyes to her lips and back again. "Is it too bold to say it's you?"

"Me?" she asked, swallowing against the sudden dryness in her throat.

"You're a coy one, I'll give you that, and I have to admit that it took me some time before I understood your intent, but then last night sealed it in my mind."

"Sealed what?" she asked, looking to both her right and left, even though she knew they were very much alone. She kept her hand on his chest and felt the railing pressing into her back, despite the layers of clothing.

"Your attraction to me," he said, still smiling and oblivious to her discomfort. He leaned in, and she pushed against his chest—hard. He stumbled backward as she righted herself and swallowed her rising fear. She would not allow her fear to be misconstrued, however, especially since it seemed that Mr. Burke had already misconstrued a great deal. "I am very sorry if I gave you an impression of affection, Mr. Burke. You are personable and kind, but it is only your friendship I have interest in pursuing."

He stood still for a moment but then stepped forward, sweeping one arm behind her back and pulling her toward him so quick and hard that the air in her lungs was pushed out in a sound very much like a gasp which he, also, completely misinterpreted. "Ah, yes, your country manners are enchanting. I would have liked to have found some mistletoe, but all the same . . ."

Eloise opened her mouth to protest again, but his lips immediately pressed against hers, and his hand moved to the back of her head, trapping her in a kiss she did not want. She dropped her skirts and pushed against his chest with both hands, but he quickly captured both her hands in his free one and pressed his mouth even harder against hers.

Eloise knew nothing of kissing; she had seen very few in her life and experienced none. Mr. Burke was insistent and crushing, and despite her ignorance, she knew that a kiss was not meant to be stolen and hard and driven by something that was not beautiful.

Anger reminded her that she was not powerless. She raised her foot, pushed it out from under the folds of skirt now further encumbering her, and then raised the heel and drove down into the top of Mr. Burke's boot. The thick leather prevented any injury, but it did startle him enough that he pulled back and loosened the grip holding her hands. Eloise pulled back one hand and slapped him as hard as she could, the crack of it ringing through the trees as he stumbled backward with a grunt. She did not waste a moment gathering up her skirts in a messy bundle that exposed her petticoats. She held the skirts to her chest as she turned back the way they'd come and ran.

Without her arms for balance and limited view of the ground in front of her, she worried she would stumble on the uneven ground, but she pulled the cumbersome clothing closer to her chest and picked out the easiest portions of ground before her. She could hear Mr. Burke behind her, calling her name, but she did not stop. What a horrid man! Tears rose to her eyes. "Don't you dare cry," she told herself as she blinked away the moisture.

"Eloise!"

He was getting closer, and she increased her pace, even though she knew she couldn't outrun him—not with a dozen yards of heavy fabric working against her. And then the inevitable happened: she placed her foot wrong, tripped, stumbled, and fell forward. Only those yards of heavy fabric protected her from landing on her face, but when she tried to scramble to her feet, the skirts wrapped around her like tethers. She felt Mr. Burke's hands take hold of her shoulders and tried to pull away while throwing her elbow back to connect with his ribs.

"I am only helping you up," Mr. Burke snapped when she wrenched one shoulder out of his grip. "Don't fight me!"

She *would* fight him, if it made sense, but it suddenly didn't make sense. She gave in, letting him help her to her feet and straighten out the skirts of her habit so that she could once again hold them folded over her arm in a decent manner. They stood there, then, looking at each other. Her chest was heaving, and her face was hot. Someone had to say something, but she would not thank him for helping her to her feet!

"I have no interest in you, Mr. Burke," she said hotly. "And I am offended that you would take such a liberty with me. You are not a gentleman."

"I beg your pardon," he said tightly. That he was angry instead of embarrassed was no credit upon his character. "But perhaps you ought to guard your attention better than you have. I had every reason to believe you were interested in improving our connection to one another after the interest you've shown in me."

"In *you*?" she spat. "Only an arrogant man would assume he was the recipient of a woman's attention above all others."

Mr. Burke's eyes squinted in confusion, widened in

understanding, and then narrowed in offense. "All others," he repeated. "Or just one."

She said nothing, but her cheeks turned hot all over again. She looked away and fussed with her skirts, wishing she had guarded her tongue. She expected him to say something—tease her or laugh, at least—but instead he pushed past her on the path and continued toward the horses. Eloise rolled her eyes and then fell in step behind the *gentleman* who was anything but!

He arrived at the horses first and had one foot in the stirrup before he looked her way and let out a heavy breath of realization that she would need his help to mount—how she wished she didn't! He came forward without a word and helped her into her saddle. They journeyed back to the house in silence and only when they reached the lane to Eloise's house did either of them speak.

"It was a wager," he said suddenly, causing Eloise to look at him in surprise.

"What was a wager?"

"The kiss." He seemed to be trying to keep hold of some sort of bravado. "It's a game Franklin and I have played for years—the first to win a girl's favor is the victor—and so that was all I was doing, trying to win."

Eloise's mouth fell open, but no words came for several moments. "Neville put a wager on . . ." She couldn't say it—couldn't finish. It was a game they had played for *years*?

"Yes," Mr. Burke said with a crisp nod. He did not meet her eye. "I'm sorry for the distress it caused you. Apparently, country girls are different from those in the city. You have my apology and promise that I shan't seek your attention again." With that, he turned and kicked his horse into a run.

Chapter Eleven

Neville was watching out the window and pacing in front of the hearth, as brooding men are apt to do, when he saw Burke returning through the front gate. He paused only long enough to confirm it was him before hurrying to the armchair beside the fire and picking up a book so that it would not look as though he had been watching through the window while pacing in front of the hearth. He listened intently for the door to open, Bribson to take Burke's coat and hat, and Burke's footsteps coming toward the parlor. Only when Neville focused on the page did he realize the book was upside down. He righted the book at the same moment Burke crossed the threshold.

Burke walked straight to the fire, stretching out his hands to the flame and letting out a sigh of relief.

"Ah, there you are," Neville said as though he'd barely noticed the other man had been gone. "Did you have a nice ride?"

Burke shot a somewhat glowering look over his shoulder, then paused, repaired it, and turned back to the hearth. "Yes, it was quite good."

Neville tried not to clench his jaw too tightly. "Good?" he repeated.

"She really is a most exceptional girl, that Eloise. Handsome, wholesome, but with a passionate side she keeps well hidden."

Neville swallowed. "Passionate?" His tone was as dry as a crust of bread.

Burke smiled over his shoulder and then turned toward the door. Neville was out of his chair and blocking the way in a thrice. "You did not take advantage of her," he growled. It was a ride on a very cold day. Surely that would prevent anything improper—to say nothing of Eloise's own boundaries. She would not allow Burke liberties.

Burke was not smiling as he held Neville's eyes, but Neville sensed a debate taking place in the other man's mind and tried to brace himself for details he might not want to hear. Yet he felt he had to know it. He had already concluded that it was not impossible that Eloise had affection for Burke and that Neville's attempts to warn her had driven her to Burke. What he would not do to go back in time and play his part differently last night.

"I did not take advantage of her."

Neville swallowed in relief and began to step aside so that Burke might leave the room after all. He should have trusted that Eloise would never—

"But I did win the wager."

Neville spun back around and stared at Burke. *There was no wager*, he thought, but Burke's cocky grin was back in place and Neville's stomach was stone. He could not make his mouth form a single word.

"Only," Burke said with the shrug of his shoulder, "I daresay my expert opinion must deem those seemingly kissable lips as rather deceiving."

Neville's hands began to tighten into fists at the mental image of Burke and Eloise.

Burke continued, "Yes, most definitely deceiving and rather disappointing, if I'm to be quite honest. It seems that a country girl really is no match for a man of Town, and as I made my way back from our ride, I decided to pursue my recreation elsewhere—in Newport, I think. My uncle's family is wintering there this year. I'll leave tomorrow morning and arrive in time for tea. Would you care to join me and throw off the shackles of village life while you've still got the chance?"

Neville's thoughts were a jumble, but his hands began to relax at his sides. "You are leaving?"

"Yes," Burke said, raising his eyebrows. "Is that not what I've just explained?"

"But you kissed Eloise."

Burke let out a sigh and busied himself adjusting the cuff of his sleeve. "So I did. And I found the experience wanting, so I shall move on."

"You can't kiss Eloise and then leave town," Neville said, battling with his own desire for Burke to go. He wanted nothing more than to be free of his friend, who had become a barnacle during the last day and a half, but if Eloise had kissed him and he disappeared . . . "You must do right by her." The words nearly stuck in his throat. He felt sick.

"Do right by her?" Burke said with a laugh. "I don't *owe* Eloise anything. It was a kiss. Just one. And plenty enough to make up my mind."

"And what of her mind?" Neville said, putting his hands on his hips and pushing away his own confusing feelings for Eloise in order to focus on his devotion to her as a friend. "Eloise is not one to hand her kisses out like lemon buns; if she kissed you, then she has affection for you. You can't leave without a word to her. She'll be heartbroken."

"And how many women have you kissed and never seen again?" Burke said without the playfulness he'd adopted to this point.

"That is in Town," Neville explained. "And I had no prior connection to any of those girls. It was a game." A game Neville was increasingly humiliated to have played. How could he be so ignorant of those young women's feelings? Could not those girls have all been like Eloise—kind and good and believing his attention was more than it was? Watching Burke play with Eloise's heart this way put his own actions in contrast, and the shame cut him deeply.

Burke held his eye a moment, then shrugged. "A game I am still playing," he pronounced. "And I am ready to cut my losses and move to a new table. Come with me or stay here; it makes no matter to how I'll play my hand." He took another stride toward the door, then paused and turned to look at Neville. "I must say I'm surprised at your cry for noble intention. I was beginning to think that you had designs of your own upon Eloise, but if that were so, you would be glad for my departure, I think."

"I will never be glad of anything that hurts Eloise," Neville said, steering around Burke's determination of Neville's feelings. *Designs* was not the right word to explain his interest, but the veil of ignorance had been removed from his eyes since that conversation with Burke in the pub—was it only yesterday?

Burke strode from the room without responding, and Neville stayed where he was, growing roots into the carpet as he stared into the fire. How quickly things had become complicated.

Chapter Twelve

Mama cocked her head to the side and continued to stare at Eloise with concern. "Are you certain?"

"Yes," Eloise said, looking up from where she was sorting her yarns. She had separated and arranged them by type—silk, flax, cotton, or wool—and then arranged them by color in the lovely sectioned wooden box her father had given her for her birthday six years ago. Until this week, the box had sat in the back of her wardrobe waiting for her to run out of anything else to do. What luck she finally had. It would be nice to have the colors organized.

She had also finished the cushion she'd been working on for six months; made up Christmas gifts for the servants; sorted all her clothing and shoes so that she would have a nice collection ready for Boxing Day four days hence; caught up on her correspondence, poetry reading, drawing, and painting; and rearranged all the furniture in her bedchamber with the help of an accommodating kitchen maid.

Mama continued to watch her daughter, as though at any

moment Eloise would drop this front and confess what was on her mind. Five seconds passed in silence, then Eloise coughed into her hand, apparently convincing Mama that she *was* too ill to travel. Eloise moved the silk turquoise skein one space to the left to make room for the cerulean. This arranging of threads was very detailed work. Mama put down her traveling bag and sat. "I think I should stay. We can both go after the holiday."

"No, Mama." Eloise shook her head. "I am not up to so much commotion for a few more days, and there is always greater celebration at twelfth night that I would like to rest toward. Please let me stay here through Christmas. I will be fine. You act as though I have never been home alone."

"You have never been home alone following a week-long illness," Mama pointed out. "What if your fever returns?"

"The fever lasted all of one evening, and it has been five days since. If my coughing should get worse, I will send for you." Eloise held her mother's eyes. "Go to Charlotte. She wants and needs you, and I know you want to see your new granddaughter. I shall join you in a few days' time, rested and prepared to enjoy the holiday to its fullest."

She watched the war being waged in her mother's eyes. Charlotte lived some fifteen miles away and had had her first child four days ago. If not for Eloise having been ill, Mama would have flown to her daughter and newest grandchild in a matter of hours, not days. "Perhaps your father shall stay, then."

"And do what?" Eloise said. "Pace the windows? He is as eager as you are. I shall join you when I know I am recovered and will not bring anything down upon a newborn child."

It took a bit more convincing, but finally Mama was worn through. She planted a kiss on Eloise's forehead, repeated every warning, and then took her leave. Eloise remained in the drawing room, which was an improvement over her bedroom where she'd spent the first part of the week, but not much.

She had not gone to any of the Christmas dinner parties hosted by their friends and refused visitors based on somewhat exaggerated claims of lingering illness. Not that she *hadn't* been ill following the objectionable ride with Mr. Burke—she had—but it was convenient to use the illness as an excuse to take some time to herself. If all the time in her own company had been more enjoyable, she would not even question her choice, but it had been a miserable week—outside of how productive she'd been with her projects—and she was no closer to making a decision on how to move forward than she'd been when she'd first blessed the fever that beset her.

Oh, that she had never wanted for more than friendship with Neville. She was the greedy dog in the fable who thought she'd seen a bigger prize and therefore lost the one she already possessed. Gluttonous. Foolish. Regretful.

She knew Mr. Burke had left the village—Mama had learned that tidbit of gossip from Lady Harrison who called three days after their ride—and Eloise was grateful. But no one had shared any news of Neville, and she didn't dare ask. She had canceled the tea to discuss the contents of Lila's educational letters, so there was no vehicle for gossip outside of her mother, who did not know how to fish for information about Neville the way Eloise had become quite adept at doing. Perhaps that was for the best, however. After all, she was nothing but the object of a wager. A piece in a game.

He'd been oddly protective of her at the Christmas ball. But that could simply have been an attempt at winning. He had warned her off of Mr. Burke.

But he made no attempt of his own to win the wager.

What would it have been like if Neville had claimed the kiss? Would it have been as harsh and lacking as Mr. Burke's had been? Probably—it was only a game after all.

Eloise let out a sigh and raised her hands to her temples. "Enough!" she said to no one but the fire. It was not as though any of these thoughts were new ones. They had been cycling through her mind all week and led her to no new destinations of thought. She was as miserable as ever.

She finished organizing her threads, then read part of a Scott novel, then went to her room. She took down her hair in front of her mirror and put it up again—inspecting the arrangement from side to side—and then wondered how anyone did their own hair in any presentable way and took it down again. She was brushing out her hair when she looked out the window and saw a horse and rider coming up the lane. She leaned forward and then walked quickly backward from the window when she realized it was Neville on that horse. What was he doing here?

She ran for the bell and pulled. When a chambermaid peeked in, Eloise explained that she needed to dress and have her hair done as quickly as possible. Without Mama's maid, it was up to the downstairs staff to make her presentable. The chambermaid nodded and disappeared while Eloise began rifling through her dresses. When she saw the red dress, she scowled at it and continued through her wardrobe.

A few days after her ride with Mr. Burke, Neville had written her a card—as had a handful of her other friends—that wished her well and offered assistance should she need anything. Every other letter she received was just like it, and so Eloise had not allowed herself to read it over and over again in search of some hidden affection. Her conclusion was that he'd sent the note because he wanted their friendship to continue. She was glad of that, even if she had no idea how they might ever return to the comfortable place they'd once enjoyed.

A quarter of an hour after seeing him on the lane, Eloise took a breath and let herself into the drawing room. Neville rose to his feet while her heart flipped and turned in her chest. She must keep herself closed to his charm! *You were a pawn in his game,* she reminded herself, but seeing him made it difficult to keep hold of such reminders. She still ached to matter to him, despite knowing that she was just one more girl—the object of a wager. That he'd played such a game with *any* girl sat like a rock in her stomach; to know she was nothing more than any of them was a second stone.

"Good afternoon, Eloise," he said, bowing slightly. He did not put out his hand to take hers like he would have before. How she hated this strangeness, and yet she needed it to continue until she no longer thought of him with a tremble nor looked upon him with her pulse speeding up.

"Good afternoon, Neville," she said as she made her way to the settee opposite the chair he'd been sitting in. He returned to his seat. "I'm afraid my parents are gone for the holiday and therefore aren't here to receive."

"So I heard. I believe congratulations are in order—you are an aunt?"

He'd known she would be home alone and still came? As a family friend, he had visited her alone before, but it had never felt like this. She could not let him see a reaction; she could not afford to interpret the reaction herself. "As the youngest of five—all of them well engaged in the commandment of replenishing the earth—I have little originality of feeling over this role, but thank you. New life is always worthy of celebration, and as this is Charlotte's first child, it is an exciting event."

He smiled. She smiled back but found it difficult to hold his eyes and so turned her attention to smoothing the skirt of the lavender day dress she'd chosen for his visit. Lila had always said Eloise looked exceptional in lavender, but she felt ridiculous for thinking that would matter now.

Neville cleared his throat. "I brought a jar of molasses from America for your family—a Christmas gift." He picked up a jar she hadn't noticed from next to his chair and handed it to her.

"Molasses?" she said as she took the item and turned it in her hands. The substance inside looked like honey but was black as coal.

"Similar to what we call black treacle here in England, only thicker, sweeter, and stronger in flavor. They have it in great quantities in America, and I thought you might enjoy the newness of it. Tell your cook it's exceptional in ginger cookies or cakes. She has always done a remarkable job with such things, and I thought of her—and you—when I had molasses cookies for the first time."

He thought of me in America?
Keep your heart closed!

"Thank you for such a thoughtful gift," she said, genuinely touched. "I believe my mother had some spiced bread taken around from our family to yours before leaving town."

"Yes, it was delicious."

Eloise felt a tickle in her throat and coughed into her handkerchief as delicately as possible.

"How are you feeling? Did you receive my note?"

Eloise nodded. "I did, thank you. I am behind in my replies, for which I apologize." In truth, she had not planned to reply. She'd felt he'd sent the note as an olive branch that she had no choice but to accept. "I'm feeling much better; it is only a lingering cough that now besets me. That's why I did not go with my parents. I want to be full recovered before I meet my new niece."

"Have you no plans for Christmas, then?"

"No," Eloise said. "I will save my strength and celebrate twelfth night at Charlotte's." And she had no interest in being social right now. "Have you holiday plans?"

"Aunt Hannah and her family are coming tomorrow and staying for the fortnight. She's already informed Father and me that we shall be celebrating Christmas in all its splendor. Since Lila was always the one to head up such celebrations, we are indebted to her."

"Your Aunt Hannah is lovely," Eloise said, remembering the many times the family had visited Hemberg over the years. Eloise knew Aunt Hannah nearly as well as she knew her own aunts. "And it will be lovely for you and your father to have family around for the holiday."

"I suppose," Neville said with a smile. "With six children and the eldest not yet fourteen, it will be loud if nothing else."

Eloise smiled. They lapsed into silence until finally Neville cleared his throat rather pointedly. Eloise prepared herself for even more discomfort. "Eloise, I tried to find a way to say it in the letter but could not get the right words. I cannot stop thinking about the Websters' ball. I—"

"It is all right," she cut in, unprepared to face this topic. "Let us leave it there."

"I was inappropriate and unfair with what I said to you that night."

She continued to stare at the jar in her hand, turning it so that the substance rolled slowly back and forth. "It is all right, Neville." But emotion was rising up, and her anxiety was increasing. Next would be the remembered embarrassment. The wager. A prize he did not claim himself.

"I hate to know that I've damaged our friendship," Neville said. "That was not my intent, and as I have pondered on that night, I've realized—"

"It was a game," Eloise cut, gathering all her courage and looking up at him. "I understand. We are still friends, Neville. Let us leave it at that."

Neville pulled his eyebrows together. "A game?"

"The wager?" she said, unable to keep the edge from her voice. "I am only one of many players. I understand." Except she continued to hold it against him. "But it will be much harder to forget it ever happened if we are to discuss it."

Neville's mouth fell open. "Burke told you it was a wager," he said in a breath.

Until that moment, Eloise hadn't realized that some part of her held out hope that Burke had been lying, yet Neville now confirmed that he had not. She felt small and used all over again.

Neville moved forward in his chair, "Eloise, I never—"

"I understand Mr. Burke has left Hemberg," she said in an attempt to fill the air with something other than the topic of the wager. "I assume he's not coming back." She looked at the jar as an excuse *not* to look at him. Neville had carried this across the ocean for her. How could he be so thoughtful and thoughtless at the same time?

"You wish he were coming back?"

"No, of course not. It was all a game. I know that." *Why would you put me into such a game?* she screamed in her mind. *And why did you not claim the prize first? You had ample opportunity to do so!*

Saying such things out loud was ridiculous, however, especially since at least some measure of her preparation for the Websters' ball had been to present herself as that very prize she was embarrassed to have unwittingly become. At least to Mr. Burke. The confusing thoughts rattled in her mind until she quickly stood, prompting Neville to do the same. She gathered all her courage and met his eye with a polite smile and a closed heart, though her feelings pressed and clawed to be released.

"Thank you for the gift. Happy Christmas, Neville." She turned toward the door.

"Come to dinner tomorrow night," he said in a great hurry of words, causing her to stop and turn back to face him.

"We'll be having a Christmas dinner, of course, and I would like you to come."

There was a rashness in his offer that made it feel pitied. "I have not been well, Neville. I do not think it wise for me to go out or risk infecting others."

"We are a hearty lot," he said in that same quick-step manner. "And I shall send our carriage with bricks and robes to ensure you're warm. Please come, Eloise. I-I have a Christmas gift I would like to give you."

A Christmas gift implied some forethought that his tone did not suggest. She lifted the jar she held in her hand. "You have already given my family a very thoughtful gift."

"I have another one," he said quickly. "A better one. Please, Eloise." His voice was as rich and thick as the molasses. "Let me start toward making things right between us. Please."

Even as she held his eyes and told herself to refuse his hasty offer, she knew that she could not. She loved him—so help her, she did—and though she feared the deepness of those feelings were in vain, she wanted to return to the comfort they once shared, if it were possible. "All right," she said softly and watched the relief ease his tight expression.

Neville reached out and took her hand, his touch sparking warmth and confusion and sorrow all at once. That pressing clawing at her heart increased, and she stepped backward to break the connection that was too much to bear.

"I shall send the carriage at six," he said.

Eloise took another step back and nodded. "Yes."

He moved past her toward the door, but before he quit the room, he turned back and smiled. "I will make this right."

She wasn't sure he ever could, but she nodded.

Chapter Thirteen

It was a hard afternoon's ride toward Newport, and then Neville had no choice but to stop at a posting house still outside the city when the dark and snow set upon him.

Even the best room was flea-bitten and moldering, which made it easy to quit first thing the next morning and take the last few miles to Newport. He had the name of Burke's uncle—a Mr. Jonathan Burke—and it took under an hour to find the man's rented rooms not far from the square. Quick inquiry showed that the Mr. *Henry* Burke Neville was in search of had already left for the day, or rather not returned from the night before. They expected he was at the Cherry Stone Pub on High Street. The pub wasn't open for business this early in the day, but Burke had made a quick friend in the owner's son and enjoyed the delights of the resort town before hours. All of this was shared through the services of a far-from-loyal footman, who seemed already out of favor with the young master.

Neville found the pub soon enough and made his way to the back door where several sets of footprints in the snow and the pitch of both male and female laughter gave away the expedition. Neville took a breath and pushed open the heavy wooden door before picking his way past crates and counters forming the kitchen and storage area. He finally pushed through the pub and blinked to adjust his eyes to the dim light.

There were two men and at least four women laughing in the far corner of the room. One of the women was attempting to dance but looked a bit overindulged, as she could not keep balance on her high-heeled shoes. The scene was not much different than a dozen others Neville had encountered with Burke; he always seemed to make friends with a pub or saloon owner's son when he reached a new city. Predictability was Neville's friend today.

None of the high-spirited companions noticed Neville until he strode purposefully in their direction. It was easy enough to make out Burke's form in the group. Neville quickly took hold of his collar, pulled him to his feet, and pushed him toward the door while Burke sputtered and stumbled and bumbled along. Burke's companions found this terribly funny and therefore did not try to stop Neville's retreat, for which he was grateful.

Once outside, Burke raised his hands to his eyes and cried out that he was blind. Neville folded his arms over his chest, waiting for Burke to adjust to the light and the cold. When he finally did, he squinted. "Neville? What on earth are you doing here?"

"I am cleaning you up and bringing you back to Hemberg." Neville ran his eyes up and down Burke's person. What *did* Eloise see in him?

"Beg your pardon," Burke said, looking around until he found a crate. He pulled it underneath him as a seat. "But I'd rather not return to Hemberg. This place, however, is top of the trees. Let me introduce you to Daniel; he knows a lot of girls who, for a shot of whiskey, will—"

"I've no interest in the girls or meeting Daniel, thank you very much. I need you to come back to Hemberg."

"Need me, eh?" Burke said, folding his arms across his chest and squinting up at Neville, though the sky was overcast and it was not exceptionally bright. "And what do you need me for?"

"*I* don't need you," Neville said. "But you need to come back for Eloise. She is . . . sad."

Burke lifted his eyebrows, and the action nearly toppled him from his seat. "Sad?"

"You kissed her and left," Neville said, pointing in the direction of Hemberg. "She's kept to her house ever since, and when I went to look in on her, she asked about you."

Burke looked confused. "She asked after *me*?"

"Yes," Neville said. "And so I've come to fetch you. Come back to Hemberg and give her another chance. Get to know her without any games or devices to interfere. If we leave right now, we can get back in time for Christmas dinner. It would mean the world to her to have you there and a great deal to me as well."

Burke's eyebrows seemed fused together as he tucked his hands under his arms. "I've had a bit to drink today, so let me make sure I've understood this properly. Eloise asked after me, and you've come to fetch me for her, even though you're plumb in love with her yourself."

The pronouncement took Neville off guard, yet he could not deny it. Not honestly. "I want Eloise's happiness," he said evenly. "And your leaving has upset her. Please come back to Hemberg and see if the difficulty between you can be repaired."

"You want her happiness over your own, then?" Burke said.

Neville did not know how else to explain it, and so he simply nodded.

Burke scrubbed a hand over his face and took a deep breath. "I am not the man who will make her happy."

What a stubborn buffoon! "Just take some time to get to know her before you make such a decision, then it will be a choice based on something of substance rather than dismissed out of hand. She is not like other women you've met, I'll give you that. She has depth you can't possibly understand after such a short acquaintance. I believe if you spend more time with her, you will better appreciate all the matters of character that make her so wholly exceptional."

Burke lifted his head and peered at Neville. "But you hope the decision is ultimately that she and I do *not* continue forward."

Neville furrowed his brow. Was that what he hoped? A quick reflection showed that he'd said as much. "If you are well suited and will find happiness together, then I would want that for you both."

"But in your heart you don't wish for that, do you, Franklin? In your heart, you want her for yourself."

"You make her sound like a prized horse," Neville said, but he stared at his shoes and kicked at a clump of snow.

"And *you* have avoided this question in three different forms now—are you in love with Eloise?"

In love? Neville didn't know how to answer that. He had never been in love with anyone, so how could he know if he were in love with Eloise in a matter of days since first realizing she was more than the girl he'd made mud pies with? With Burke staring at him, he felt as though he were on trial. "I don't know," Neville said.

"You enjoy her company," Burke said.

"Yes, of course, but I enjoy the company of many women. Well, not to say *many* women, but, well . . ."

"Do you enjoy her company above all other women with whom you are acquainted?" Burke asked.

Neville only considered the question a moment. "Yes." There was a freedom to say it, a kind of release, as though something having bound him was loosened. He did enjoy Eloise's company above all other women he would consider friends. He was comfortable with her, engaged by what she had to say, and never eager to leave her company.

"And you are physically attracted to her," Burke continued.

Neville let out a breath. "To say as much makes me feel as though I am admitting to some kind of indiscretion. As though I am attracted to my own sister."

"Which would be a problem if she *were* your sister, but she is not. You had no qualms admitting that you were attracted to Lila, your cousin."

"No, I did not, but I was in America when things sweetened between Lila and me. Then they soured quickly, and I'm not sure I ever felt any sort of physical draw to her."

It was oddly simple to sum up his thoughts on that, though he'd not spent much time pondering them before now.

"Is Lila somehow interfering with your acceptance of seeing Eloise differently than you have until now? Are you still pining for Eloise's best friend?"

"I am not." It was the easiest question to answer, though he wondered at Burke's rather sober inquisition. "None of this matters, Burke. What *does* matter is that Eloise is pining for you, and I have promised her a Christmas gift tonight at dinner. If we are not on the road within the hour, we will not make it back in time."

Burke grinned. "And I am this Christmas gift?"

"Yes," Neville said, dropping his voice and his shoulders. "Please come, Burke. If ever we've been friends, please do this for me. Assure Eloise that she did not waste that kiss on a man unwilling to invest some time with her. Please."

Burke rose to his feet with a groan, steadying himself on the doorway once he was standing. "I daresay that if this inheritance of yours falls through, you could be a cracking good barrister, as you have presented me an argument against which I cannot defend." He nodded crisply. "I will go to Hemberg with you, see Eloise, and set her heart at peace once and for all."

It was an odd way of saying he would do as Neville asked, but he'd agreed to come to Hemberg, so Neville was in no mind to argue.

Chapter Fourteen

The carriage, complete with warm bricks and rugs as promised, arrived at ten till the hour. Eloise wore a light blue dress—purposely avoiding anything more festive that might remind her of the Websters' ball—and tried not to fret about the evening ahead. If not for wanting desperately to return to a place of friendship with Neville, she'd have never agreed to this. His family would be there to belay any awkwardness, which she was glad for—Eloise loved children and found they were priceless in the way they could set a mood. Besides, what was Christmas without children?

It will be fine, she assured herself, but still kept adjusting her wool cape around her shoulders and pleating and repleating the muslin of her skirt.

She was shown into the drawing room upon her arrival and greeted warmly by Aunt Hannah and her six children. Aunt Hannah's husband, Mr. Campbell, would be joining them on Christmas Day, once he concluded some last-minute business that had prevented him from traveling with the family. The adults chatted amiably while the children worked on a puzzle on the far side of the room for what seemed too long, until Aunt Hannah said they would go into dinner without Neville. "I'm sure he'll be here soon," Aunt Hannah said. "But I hate to have dry goose on Christmas Eve of all days."

They moved into the dining room, and though Eloise noted two empty chairs instead of only one for Neville, she did not comment—perhaps they hoped Mr. Campbell might arrive earlier than expected.

Dinner was delicious and certainly orchestrated by Aunt Hannah, as she related each course to some part of the Christmas story. The clear onion soup, for instance, was in similitude of the atonement of Christ, which cleared all of our sinful souls so that we might live again with God. The haddock in lemon sauce related to the many parables Jesus had told regarding fish and fishermen. They were on the main course—goose, to remind them of the bounteous blessings from the Lord—when the Franklins' butler announced that Master Neville had arrived and that he and Mr. Burke would join the party as soon as they had freshened up.

Eloise nearly choked on her bite of goose, then hurried to take a drink. "I'm sorry," she said, realizing that most of the table was watching her. "Did he say Mr. *Burke* is here?"

"I believe so," Mr. Franklin said, looking at her with concern. "You are acquainted with Mr. Burke, are you not?"

"Yes, I am," Eloise said, trying to gather her wits about her. *Mr. Burke? Here?* "I just understood that he'd left Hemberg, and I did not expect him to return so soon."

"Neither did I," Mr. Franklin said. "In all honesty, I thought Neville a bit relieved when Mr. Burke left last week, but then I make it a point not to interfere too much in my son's affairs. He asked to have a place for Mr. Burke at the table before he left to fetch him yesterday, and that was enough for me."

Eloise forced a polite smile as her mind turned new thoughts, round and round enough to make her dizzy. She had asked after Mr. Burke yesterday during Neville's visit and tried to remember what Neville had asked her—"*You are missing him?*" That's what Neville had said, and she had assured him that she was not missing Mr. Burke. Yet he must have left shortly afterward to bring Mr. Burke back. Why on earth would he do such a thing?

Making sense of the situation was interrupted by the butler introducing Neville and Mr. Burke to the room. Eloise nodded a welcome but could not meet either man's eye. Was there any way she could leave without being the rudest woman ever to dine at Franklin Farm?

Mr. Burke was seated at Eloise's left while Neville sat directly across from her. She busied herself with cutting her portion of goose into tiny pieces.

Aunt Hannah picked up her presentation of the Christmas story while Eloise kept her attention trained upon her plate. She was well aware of Mr. Burke beside her but would elbow him in the ribs before she would pretend she was glad to see him. She felt sure she could feel him smirking—what was he about? He knew she didn't want him here, so why had he come?

Dessert was Christmas pudding, and Aunt Hannah

talked of the sweetness of life and the great blessing of redemption ushered in through Christ's birth. Eloise barely tasted it and hoped God would forgive her for not giving ample attention to the symbolic meal.

Finally, it was time for the ladies to depart. Eloise was the first out of her chair. She would go into the drawing room and proclaim herself too fatigued to stay. What luck that Aunt Hannah had included the spiritual aspects of the day into dinner so that Eloise would not feel badly for missing the entertainment. Very little about this day, aside from Aunt Hannah's tribute, had felt like Christmas, and now even the bit of holiday spirit she'd felt had departed. She wished nothing more than to return to her own home and hide beneath the covers.

Eloise had only just stepped back from the table when she noticed the men also preparing to exit the room. Apparently, the men were foregoing the usual round of port before they would join the rest of the company.

Once in the drawing room, the older children helped the younger children hang their stockings for St. Nicholas. Eloise was considering when best to make her excuses when she glanced at Mr. Burke and he winked at her. No, she would not be staying. Very likely she would be forever known as that rude girl in Hemberg who left Christmas dinner early, but she could not abide Mr. Burke's company for anything.

"I am sorry to cut the evening," Eloise began, drawing her eyes downward to feign discomfort. "But I have not been well this last week, and I do believe it has caught up with me this evening. Thank you for—"

"You can't leave," Mr. Burke said, raising his eyebrows at her from where he lounged in one of the chairs flanking the fireplace. "What about your Christmas gift?"

At the mention of a gift, the children looked up from their stockings, some hung, some awaiting. Eloise felt her face flush. Had she been used in another one of their games? A quick look at Neville, however, showed that she wasn't the only one taken off guard by Mr. Burke's words.

Neville stood, drawing every eye toward him. "Um, Mr. Burke, might I talk to you in private a moment? In the foyer, perhaps."

Mr. Burke waved his hand through the air. "Certainly not," he said as though it were a proclamation. "What you *may* do is confess your love to this woman once and for all so that I might return to Newport."

Aunt Hannah gasped, one of the children giggled, and Eloise closed her eyes as though she could pretend she were not here. The room fell silent as everyone seemed to wait for someone else to speak. In the silence, however, Mr. Burke's words lingered—*confess your love? Neville?*

"Well, let's get on with it," Mr. Burke said.

Eloise opened her eyes, finally, and looked only at Mr. Burke, wishing she could burn holes through him. She'd had enough embarrassment at his hand and could think of nothing but preventing more. She stood and began toward the door, too humiliated to speak.

"Wait, Eloise."

It was Neville's voice, but it was not his grip on her arm. She knew that grip and she knew from the placement of the room which man would have reached her soonest. She spun and slapped Mr. Burke as hard as she had hit him that day at Bramble Pond. The impact spurred her rage upward another degree, and when his grip slipped from her arm, she lifted both hands to push hard against his chest, sending him backward into a chair where he flipped heels over head. "I have had enough of you, Mr. Burke, and I will ask you to never set a hand on me again!"

Belatedly, Eloise remembered she was in a room full of people—many of whom were children. Her face flushed as hot as the soup they'd had for dinner, and she tried to sputter an apology when the sound of laughter drew her attention to Mr. Burke pushing himself to his feet. If not for the embarrassment she felt at losing her temper in front of an audience, she'd have marched forward and kicked him in the side to send him down again.

"Oh, yes, Franklin, I think she will do just fine," Mr. Burke said as he got his feet beneath him.

"Shut your mouth, Burke," Neville said, stepping toward the other man with his hands in fists by his sides. "You have said quite enough already. You will apologize to Miss Hallstrom and then kindly remove yourself from this house. I should never have brought you back."

"Remove myself?" Mr. Burke made an exaggerated point of straightening his coat. "But you invited me to come. I am Eloise's Christmas gift, am I not?"

"You?" Eloise spat and turned to look at Neville, who looked ready to run Mr. Burke through. The children were now gathered together, watching events unfold as though they had never seen anything like this—which they likely had not. What did Mr. Burke mean about being a Christmas gift? And what of Neville confessing his love? She felt small and vulnerable and furious.

"Yes, me," Mr. Burke said, still grinning like an idiot. No one else in the room was grinning. "Franklin told me how you were *pining* for me and *begged* me to come back and give you another chance."

Eloise turned shocked eyes to Neville.

"That is not what I said, and this is not how I expected things to come about. I thought . . . I thought he'd broken your heart when he left."

"More like answered my prayers," Eloise countered, yet something was settling into her chest. "Wait, but you thought I cared for Mr. Burke and so you fetched him for me?"

Neville held her eyes a moment, until one of the children said to another, "She loves Mr. Burke?"

Another child answered, "No, she loves Cousin Neville."

Aunt Hannah suddenly came to her feet. "Children, let's go on to bed now. Come, come."

"But I want to see her hit Mr. Burke again, Mama," one of the children whined.

Aunt Hannah hurried them out of the room, despite their protests of wanting to stay.

"What about our stockings?" one of them said.

"Will St. Nicholas still come?" said another.

Once Aunt Hannah and her brood were gone, Mr. Franklin made up the fourth person in the room. After looking at the other three faces, he nodded slightly. "I think I might enjoy a bit of port, if you don't mind, and leave you young people to sort this out." He made eye contact with

Eloise, however, and smiled. "I shall be only a shout away if either of these men need to be taken to the ground. Are such terms acceptable to you?"

Mr. Franklin was leaving her here? The momentary shock quickly gave way to acceptance and even relief. She and Neville and Mr. Burke would settle things; she would convince them both that she had no interest in Mr. Burke and then she would go home and hope that one day she and Neville might forget any of this had ever happened. "Yes, Mr. Franklin. I shall call if I need you."

"Very good," Mr. Franklin said with a chuckle. "Have at it, you young bloods. Mind that you don't get any blood on the carpet."

He left the room, and Neville, Eloise, and Mr. Burke looked between one another.

Mr. Burke turned his attention to Neville. "Have you nothing to say?"

Eloise looked at Neville, too, and remembered the accusation Mr. Burke had made earlier—that Neville was in love with her. It couldn't be true. Mr. Burke was just acting on his broken sense of a joke. *Wasn't he?*

"I believe I asked you to leave," Neville said to Mr. Burke. "I have not rescinded that invitation. You have done quite enough."

Mr. Burke shook his head. "If I leave, then this"—he gestured between Eloise and Neville—"might never be resolved. You see, I *am* this Christmas gift of which Neville promised, but not in the way he expected." The amusement had disappeared from his tone, and he looked sincerely at the two of them. "I have some confessions to make, and it is best you both hear it so that nothing gets confused in some future retelling."

Eloise narrowed her eyes at him. Mr. Burke had shown himself not the least bit trustworthy or admirable, and she was not prepared to give him any benefit of the doubt.

"Franklin," Mr. Burke began, turning toward Neville, who still stood with his clenched fists at his side. "I did get a kiss from Miss Hallstrom that day of our ride."

Eloise protested, "Only because—"

"Shh," Mr. Burke said, turning toward her and giving her a sharp look. "You'll have your opportunity to speak your piece." He turned back to Neville. "I stole that kiss because I was determined to prove myself the better man in a competition I knew I was losing."

"There was no wager," Neville said, holding Mr. Burke's eyes.

Eloise stared at him. *No wager?*

"Perhaps not, but competition all the same. Miss Hallstrom was not a willing participant in that kiss, and she let me know, with a force quite unexpected, that she was not open to my attention in any way. Tonight was not the first time she has sent me heels over bottom, so I would warn you not to trifle with her in any way. Turns out, all those times I thought she was basking in my company, she did not want me at all. She wanted you."

After all the embarrassment Eloise had suffered these last two weeks, she would have believed she was incapable of feeling more, but hearing her long-hidden feelings proclaimed with such stark rawness was excruciating. She felt Neville look at her and dropped her eyes to the ground she wished would swallow her whole.

"Me?" Neville said. "But you were so hurt that Burke had left Hemberg."

She would not look at him, but neither would she go mute and not speak in her own defense. "I only remarked that he had gone during a conversation that had turned awkward."

"And the wager," Mr. Burke interrupted, drawing both sets of eyes to him. "That is my next confession." He looked squarely at Eloise. "As Franklin said already, there was no wager. I made it up to preserve my pride when I realized you cared for Franklin above me." He shrugged. "Character has never been my strength."

"You made it up?" Eloise said.

"Well, I made *that* particular wager up," Mr. Burke amended, putting his hands in his pockets and rocking back on his heels. "It *is* a game we played in London, and I *had* wanted to resurrect it at the Websters' ball with you as the prize, but Neville wouldn't have it. I believe his exact words were 'No, not here. Not Eloise.'"

"It was a childish game even when I participated," Neville said, his voice quiet. "And I am as ashamed to have been a part of such a thing as I am for you to know it."

"There was no wager set upon me?" Eloise said again. That meant Neville hadn't used her as a piece in a game.

"No," Neville said, shaking his head. "What you must have thought of me."

"Which leads us to the next topic of discussion," Mr. Burke said, though Eloise continued to hold Neville's gaze. "Eloise, do you agree that the majority of your memories of Neville until these last few months were from your childhood?"

Eloise nodded, though she didn't understand the importance of this question.

Mr. Burke nodded and turned his attention to Neville. "And Neville, do you agree that the majority of your memories of Eloise until these last few months were from your childhood?"

"Yes," Neville said, looking as confused as Eloise felt.

"And, generally, do you both agree that men can be thick, cotton-headed idiots, especially in regards to anything of an emotional breadth?"

Neither answered, but Mr. Burke nodded as though they had. "And so, what we have here is Miss Hallstrom, who has been rather besotted with our Mr. Franklin for some time, I believe, and Mr. Franklin, who missed *every* signal and misinterpreted *every* attempt she made to get his attention, only to bungle it completely when, in fact, he does find Miss Hallstrom a most entrancing woman—as good a woman as any sorry man could want, if said sorry man could make up for being a dunderhead and, in the process, make everything right."

Eloise was looking at the floor again, repeating in her mind what Mr. Burke said but not having the first clue how she might respond to it. Neville *did* have feelings for her? That is what Mr. Burke had said, but then Neville hadn't agreed it was true and—

"I think you have said enough, Burke," Neville said in a softened tone, causing Eloise to look up once again to find him watching her. "Might I now ask that you leave us to sort the rest of this out ourselves?"

Mr. Burke let out a dramatic breath. "Well, I suppose

you might." He began moving toward the door but then paused. Eloise looked at him. He gave her perhaps the first sincere smile she'd ever seen on that man's face. "I do hope, in time, that you might forgive me, as I should very much like your respect." He quit the room, and then there were just the two of them.

"Well," Neville said, attempting to put a laugh in his words, which did not translate well.

"Yes," Eloise said, trying to look anywhere but at him. Her gaze caught the fireplace, and she moved toward it, trying to figure out how they would sort out this mess. In the process, she turned her back on Neville and inhaled sharply when he came up behind her—apparently taking the awkwardness in hand directly. He touched her arm, sending a trembling wave of awareness throughout her body.

They stood there, silent but connected, for the space of two breaths, then Eloise took a step backward, bringing her back against his chest. Hesitantly, he put his arms around her waist, paused, and then rested his chin on her shoulder until she finally relaxed into the embrace and wrapped her arms around his. It felt both strange and perfectly right to hold each other this way, and as the silence stretched on, she felt her fear and frustration and embarrassment melt from her. It was her belief in this very rightness between them that had prompted the red dress she'd worn to the Websters' ball.

"I'm sorry, Eloise," he whispered, moving the soft tendrils of hair by her ear with his breath and causing her own breath to catch. "I'm sorry for being a stupid schoolboy and for bringing Burke back tonight and for not seeing what was right in front of me."

What could she say? And what if she chose the wrong words and broke this tenuous thread between them? She closed her eyes and relaxed into him even more.

"Can I ask you a question?" Neville asked after nearly a minute of silence passed.

Eloise nodded, intimately aware of the scent of his cologne, the heat of his chest pressing against her back, and the way being close to him filled her up with light.

"Did you really wear that red dress for my notice?"

She nodded again.

He grunted and shook his head just enough for her to feel the movement against her shoulder. "And then I said what I said. Even now, I can't fully explain what I felt when I saw you that night—so beautiful, so striking, so . . . different than I had ever seen you before. Can you understand that, Eloise? It was as though my mind had already made its decision about you as a playmate and a friend, and so I was blind to who you are now."

"I can understand that," she said, opening her eyes and staring into the fire.

"And can you forgive me for the things I said?"

Eloise turned in his arms then, but he kept them loose at her waist. "Of course I can forgive you, Neville."

"And can we start anew?" he asked.

"Isn't that what Christmas is all about?" she asked, cocking her head to the side. "A season where our hearts are softer and our thoughts are higher?"

"God and sinners reconciled?" he asked, using the words of the familiar carol.

Eloise laughed, but when she met his eyes again, his

face was serious. "I've kissed a lot of girls, Eloise, but it was always a game, a lark of young men who haven't a reasonable thought in their heads. I'm ashamed of ever having been a part of it and assure you that I am trying very hard to be a better man than the boy I've been. Can you believe me when I say that my next kiss will mean more than all of those combined and then some?"

"I don't know," Eloise said, finding no room for anything but love, adoration, and gratitude in her heart, which felt freer than it ever had before. "Sometimes seeing is believing."

She saw just the first quirk of a smile before he lowered his face and she went up on her toes in response. Their lips met with tenderness. Her arms went around his neck, and his arms around her waist pulled her closer. There was something about this moment that transcended a man and a woman in a parlor on Christmas Eve to include a boy and a girl with muddy feet and smiling faces. They shared history and community, and now they shared something more than the past, more than the present. Now they shared a future, as rich and as beautiful as either could imagine. Full of promise. Brimming with hope.

When Neville pulled back, he looked at her with pleased surprise. Though she had limited experience, Eloise sensed that he had never been kissed like that before. She reached a hand up to trace the arch of his eyebrows, the bridge of his nose, and the line of his jaw. He was here. Close enough for her to touch and feel and hold. Throughout her inspection, he watched her, and when she smiled, he smiled.

"Happy Christmas, Eloise."

She rose up and kissed him lightly, already imagining a lifetime of Christmas Eve kisses between them. "Happy Christmas, Neville. The happiest, in fact."

About Josi S. Kilpack

JOSI S. KILPACK is the author of more than twenty novels, which include women's fiction, romance, mystery, and suspense. *Wedding Cake*, the final book in her Sadie Hoffmiller culinary mystery series, was released in

December 2014. Other books include her Regency romance novels *A Heart Revealed* and *Lord Fenton's Folly*.

Josi and her husband, Lee, are the parents of four children and live in Northern Utah. In addition to writing, Josi loves to read, bake, and travel. She's completed six half marathons to date, but may never run another because right now she hates running and does hot yoga instead.

Josi's website: www.josiskilpack.com

Blog: www.josikilpack.blogspot.com

Twitter: @JosiSKilpack

The Christmas Angle

By Carla Kelly

To my daughter, Sarah, who understands.

Chapter One

Sailing Master Able Six never minded a little walk. His naturally long stride had suffered some constriction in a French prison after the capture of his ship, the *HMS Swiftsure*, but that had been a mere trial to endure until he escaped through a long-forgotten drain into the ocean.

The three fellow prisoners brave enough to squeeze after him through the claustrophobic confines of a drain were quick to sing his praises when they swam to the *HMS Carlisle* in the Brest blockade. Praise was never a bad thing, especially for a talented fellow with ambition to be Sailing Master without "Second" after his name and pay rate.

Able's exploits meant prompt advancement, with one yawning chasm to his ambition. Sadly, time, tide, and the Peace of Amiens wait for no man, so here he was, a master now, but cast ashore by the unwelcome, pernicious peace treaty engineered by First Consul Napoleon Bonaparte and Prime Minister Henry Addington—drat their hides.

The Christmas Angle

Which is why the end of November 1802 found Master Able Six, half-pay cheque in hand, walking up from the Clerk of Cheques office in the Plymouth dockyard to a boarding house with not many more comforts than the not-soon-enough-forgotten French prison.

He didn't mind discomfort, up to a point. However, eight months of discontent, chafing about peace, wanting to be at sea again, tiring of cheap lodgings and cheaper food had taken the bloom off the rose for many a seaman stuck in Plymouth, Able among them. The thought of facing one more bowl of porridge with cream verging on blinky was more than he could manage.

He solved his breakfast dilemma easily enough. It was time for a fast, or nearly so. A cup of hot coffee, as served at the Seaman's Welcome, did the job. A few pennies saved on breakfast bought an extra pasty for noon. Night meant potatoes and gravy at the grandiloquently named Captain Hawkins, with its poorly drawn but still interesting murals of the doughty seadog's exploits at San Juan de Ulúa against a Spanish fleet. Able could sit there for hours, warming himself with potatoes and stories of others' days of courage and desperation.

Night came early now. He would still be full by the time he crawled into bed in his solitary room. Able knew he could have saved a few more pennies by sharing a room with one or two other waifs of the Royal Navy cast ashore by peace, but he chose not to.

And that was the deal: he could choose. He knew he had the luxury of changing his mind, but right now the pleasure of a room of his own outweighed better food. After all, a man born somewhere in Dumfries, deposited naked and squalling on the steps of St. George's Church, then taken to the parish workhouse was well enough acquainted with slim rations from an early age. The familiar, empty spot in Able's stomach was just that: familiar.

A lesser man than Master Six would have wasted time kicking himself that he had taken a portion of his first prize money back to St. George's Church for a headstone for his mother, found dead in the alley behind the church, bearing all the signs of having recently given birth. Her only possession, now his, had been a Book of Prayer with the name Mary written in childish script.

Of course, Able had no way of knowing if the dead woman had swiped the prayer book from someone, in which case, who knew what his mother's real name was? He chose—ah, that word again—to believe his mother's name truly was Mary. He had used some of his still-meager prize money earned in a hard way at the Battle of Aboukir Bay to buy a simple headstone to replace the wooden marker for No. 143. Able Six knew what it was to be given a numbered name. Whether Mary was his mother or not, at least No. 143 was gone.

As the Peace of Amiens wore on, that lesser man would have wished he had not bothered with the expense of that headstone and used the money to live on. Master Able Six was not, and never had been, a lesser man.

He still had his boat cloak, that durable bit of Royal Navy garb doubling as an extra blanket when his room turned cold and frost rimmed the underside of the ceiling. Generous by nature, Able had taken pity on a bosun's apprentice mate who had traded away his own cloak for food, and redeemed from pawn such a garment for the shivering lad.

That bit of philanthropy had occurred a month ago, when unseasonably cold wind roared into Plymouth and he was walking toward The Drake with Elias Caldwell, third luff on the *Swiftsure,* a confident fellow who had no idea how little he knew. Caldwell owed his freedom to Able because he had the good sense to follow the sailing master down that unused drain and into the ocean.

"You're a kind fellow," Caldwell had remarked, after the visit to the pawn shop and gift of a cloak to a cold sailor.

Able shrugged. "Could've been me," was enough comment for the occasion.

Speak of the devil—here was Lieutenant Caldwell now, coming up behind Able from the docks with his own half-pay cheque, which he waved to Able.

"Master, I am off to the country," he said. "Mother will have dinner on the table precisely at six, because she keeps country hours. I'll just pop in on the whist game first."

Master Six smiled to himself. He had seen Caldwell's dedication to whist and his less-than-stellar ability at the table, because he was no mathematician. By the time Mama sat down to dinner, her son would likely still be deep in cards at The Drake. If his usual pattern persisted, Lieutenant Caldwell would leave the table with barely enough to get a conveyance into the country, where he would bide his time until the next half-pay cheque. Caldwell—drat his hide, as well—had a home to go to, a bed and food.

But Able Six was not a bitter man. He could wait for the

tide to turn, as it invariably did, if not every twelve hours, at least soon enough. An ambitious man himself, the sailing master understood ambition in others. He knew First Consul Napoleon would not long be able to resist the siren call of war.

Until that happened, it would be porridge for breakfast as late as possible, potatoes and gravy in the afternoon, and an early bedtime for Master Six.

Nodding to Lieutenant Caldwell, Able ducked into the labyrinth called the Barbican that constituted Plymouth's famous—or infamous, depending—warren of shops and cheap lodgings. As a sailing master and therefore a warrant officer now, he could have stayed at The Drake, but since he had spent more years fore with the crew than aft with the officers, Able found the Lady Luck more to his personal taste and certainly cheaper.

After a visit to the postal office to cash his cheque, he repaired to the Lady Luck, paying the landlady for his pathetic room, and then her skinny daughter with chapped hands for washing his linens. He took the stairs quickly and flopped on his bed, already relishing the constant pleasure of his best friend—his nearly worn-out copy of Euclid's *Elements*.

The book was on the slanted night table next to his virtuous bed, a cot too small for more than one person. He reached for it, first patting Mary's prayer book as he always did. He didn't bother to open *Elements*, because he knew it by heart, the same as he knew every book he read for the first time. When *Swiftsure*'s captain had learned of Master Six's peculiar ability to never forget anything he ever read, he had quizzed him at length, then just shook his head, declaring that one hundred years ago in Germany, Able Six would have been burned to death as a witch.

"I'd probably have lit the fire myself," Captain Hallowell had commented, but only in jest, because he liked Able Six.

But this was Plymouth, England, in 1802, and geniuses who had such abilities needn't fear the burning grounds or Bedlam. His captain had suggested he not spread word about this unheard-of prowess. "You're a nice enough lad, though young to be a sailing master," Captain Hallowell stated. "You might make people nervous."

Able recognized good advice when he heard it, and kept his odd gift to himself. With Captain Hallowell's kind complicity, though, he had promptly gone about reading every book on the *Swiftsure*, including all logs. He stored up a wealth of knowledge, which might perhaps come in handy someday.

Able Six gave a contented sigh, rested *Elements* on his chest, closed his eyes, and whispered, "'Number one, a point is that which has no part. Number two, a line is a breadthless length. Number three, the extremities of a line are points.'"

Another sigh and he slept, content—or nearly so.

Chapter Two

To Able's surprise, Lieutenant Caldwell, who must have finally made it to the country, came to his attention only two days later in the form of a badly spelled letter. Able didn't even begrudge the two-penny postage he had to pay, because the novelty of a letter outweighed the expense.

The only other letter he had ever received was the official notice of his warrant status from the Navy Board four years ago, proclaiming him fit to serve as a sailing master on any vessel of King George. Captain Hallowell told him later in the privacy of the empty officers' wardroom that the Board had questioned Able's age. Twenty-two was young to receive such a warrant for the most scientific member of any crew, next to the surgeon.

"I convinced the Navy Board you were a bit of a prodigy, and besides, I needed a sailing master," his captain had told him. "The looks of skepticism ran higher than a spring tide in that room, but by Neptune's trident, Able, you're already the best."

Able had tucked away that letter and gone about his business. Four years later, here was another letter. Rain thundered down, so he ducked into a tavern two doors from the postal office, ordered a cup of coffee, and wondered what Elias Caldwell had to say.

The route to what *Swiftsure*'s third lieutenant had to say was pitted with misspellings. During a lull in the Doldrums a year ago, a month with Captain Hallowell's two-volume copy of Dr. Johnson's dictionary had provided Able with total recall of all the words crammed within. Granted, he had long suspected that proper spelling was a bit like beauty—something in the eye of the beholder—so he cut Lieutenant Caldwell some slack. Who didn't relish the occasional letter?

He sipped coffee and read. One virtue Elias Caldwell possessed was the ability to cut through layers of offal and get right to a subject. "Able, considering that I oh you my freedom from that French prisson," the sailing master read, "I have found employment for you, pervided you do not minde teaching arithemetic to two little boys."

"Not at all," Able told the letter, thinking of his own school days in the workhouse, where the overworked teacher, a bit of a bully, had thrashed him for being smart and ignored him ever after.

He read on, learning of Elias's mother's best friend from childhood, who lived a cluttered life as wife of a Church of England cleric. "Four children in five years, Able. Imagin."

Apparently, the lady needed some help, which made Able chuckle. What the lady needed was her own bedchamber, more like, but who was he to question such matters—he who slept in a narrow bed in a rooming house?

After getting a refill for his cup, Able read on. "It's nothing fancy, but I thot of you. Basicly, it's room and board and ten shillings a month. It should tide you over, because I no youre not used too much."

Trust Caldwell to be helpful and condescending at the same time. Able chuckled at the notion of Lieutenant Caldwell's philanthropy and knew it probably extended no farther than this offer. Still, it was honest work and sorely needed. He continued his perusal of the document, all smudged and ink-stained because Caldwell was no dab hand at committing thoughts to paper.

At the end of the page, there was a long line with an arrow pointing in a starboard direction, so Able turned over the letter. "P.S. Don't be alarumed if Mama hangs about yur neck and weps tears of gratitude, my friend," Able read silently. "Besids all this, youll be spending Cristmas with a fambly."

Now there was a novelty that intrigued Able Six almost more than the promised ten shillings a month. He had never spent Christmas with anyone and had no real idea how to go about such a venture.

The letter concluded with precise directions to Pomfrey, described by Lieutenant Caldwell as a "smallish villag" not terribly distant from Dartmoor with its vile prison. "Just show up, friend," the letter concluded. "I think youre only neded through the Cristmas hollydays, because the vicar will be in fiting trim once the hollydays are behinde him and he can continew teaching them himselv."

Able drained his coffee cup, shook his head at another refill, and stared out the window. He had just paid another month's rent at the Lady Luck, and his landlady wouldn't refund a penny of it if he jumped ship. His own natural caution made him willing to maintain the room, just in case Lieutenant Caldwell's offer of employment proved less than desirable. If he kept the room, he wouldn't have to take along all of his admittedly few possessions.

What did he have to lose? The scuttlebutt down at the docks was of French buildup of ships in ports in Spain and France, obscure harbors where the French seemed to assume a British spy had never set foot. The rumors had come in a circuitous route from a distant cousin whose brother-in-law's grandfather heard such news in passing by Admiralty House. Although not inclined to skepticism, Able was a realist: the peace could end next Thursday or last for years.

I'll do it, he told himself as he rose and swung his boat cloak about his shoulders. Once outside, he turned up the collar against the rain, which had tapered off to sprinkles, even though a cold wind blew off Plymouth Sound. *What could possibly be difficult about teaching two boys some math?*

A few words with his landlady had left her cheerful and probably glad he hadn't demanded a refund. Keeping his quarters through December meant money to her, with no need to clean, dust, or change sheets in that room tucked under the eaves.

He possessed nothing in the way of clothing except his sailing master uniforms, or what passed as a uniform, as the Navy Board hadn't yet taken the time to authorize one. Able had adopted the plain black trousers and black coat of other masters, which showed neither dirt nor blood. His smallclothes were ragged, but nobody's business except his own. They went into the bottom of his duffel bag. Shaving gear took its usual amount of space. He was cursed with a heavy beard that required shaving each morning, and occasionally at night, if he was summoned to eat at the captain's table. Comb and brush followed, and the little bottle of olive oil that proved highly useful to untangle his black curls.

He debated whether to take his sextant, then decided he would feel uneasy leaving it behind. He didn't think his landlady would hurry it to the pawnbroker, but he had no such assurance about her daughter. He returned the sextant to its padded box and set it next to the duffel.

Books came next, not that he needed to refer to the information inside the pages. Books were a comfort. After the rout of the Dutch Navy that was Camperdown, he had gone below, once the bloody work was done, eased himself into his hammock, and just held Mary's prayer book for the peace it gave him. He knew all the prayers.

And that was it. There was no window in his attic room, but he listened to the raindrops diminish. When all was silent, he shouldered his duffel and his boxed sextant and left the Lady Luck.

He stood on Notte Street as he called to mind a map of Plymouth and the surrounding countryside. He had pored over it for ten minutes one evening in the *Swiftsure*'s wardroom and memorized it, as he had memorized everything he ever read.

Ten miles was nothing for a man in good shape who still relished a walk for a walk's sake. Eventually, he would be confined to a ship again, and the luxury of such appealing exercise would be a thing of the past. Besides, shank's mare was cheaper.

Truth be told, the road to Dartmoor gave him the megrims as he swung smartly along. He had been there once to facilitate the transfer of a prisoner from the *Swiftsure's* brig to the formidable prison from which no one escaped. The felon he escorted had been a stoic lad who had broken down in sobs as the big prison gate swung open to receive him.

I know the feeling, he thought, remembering that French prison, where the only thing good that ever happened was the opportunity to learn to speak French with a Provençal accent. He still mourned the loss of his old sextant, appropriated by his jailers—may they rot in hell.

He turned west before Dartmoor and continued his journey until he came to the bank of the Plym River. The rain began again, but he knew he was close to Pomfrey. He would have to ask directions in the village, but another hour should see him to what Elias Caldwell described as a large manor house, home of the lieutenant's parents.

There it was, seen through a screen of rain. His shoes crunched on the gravel underfoot, and he was soon up the low steps and knocking on the front door.

Able was admitted with some reluctance, after he explained to the footman that he wasn't a journeyman seeking work, but the invited guest of Lieutenant Caldwell. Luckily, Elias came into the foyer in time to spare any further embarrassment.

"Able, you're all wet," Elias told him, as though it were news.

"You underestimate the power of a good boat cloak, friend," Able replied, happy to hand off the dripping garment, which easily weighed an additional ten pounds in rainwater. And yes, he was wet, but that was another advantage of black clothing.

Soon, he was drinking tea in a pretty parlor off a larger one and being stared at by Lady Caldwell, Elias's mother. While she hadn't thrown her arms about his neck and wept tears of thanksgiving for the rescue of her son from a French prison, Lady Caldwell did dab at her eyes and look at him at some length. He sighed inwardly, knowing what was coming.

"You're certain you are from Dumfries, Scotland?" she asked as she handed him a cup of tea.

"As certain as a man can be," he replied, amused.

"I mean, you *sound* like a man from Scotland, but, sir, you don't look like one," she replied. She spoke with that same air of moral certainty that her son employed upon occasion, which told Able Six that particular apple hadn't fallen far from the tree.

"No, I don't, Lady Caldwell," he replied. "That's what I am, though, and I hear your friend is in need of a teacher. Please tell me more, if you would."

There. That should fix the old biddy. I dare you to change the subject, he thought and reached for a biscuit, the kind with sprinkles of sugar that he liked though they played merry hell with a black uniform.

Knowing she was defeated, Lady Caldwell let the ship of his parentage sail away and told him of her childhood chum, Amanda Bonfort, who had married the vicar holding the living on the next estate. Now Amanda Ripley, she was the mother of many and in need of educational assistance.

"She specifically mentioned help with arithmetic," Elias threw in, "but I assured Mama that you can teach practically anything."

"How can that be?" Lady Caldwell asked.

"I read a lot, ma'am," Able replied with a straight face, even as Elias's eyes grew merrier by the moment.

She nodded and said nothing, perhaps at a loss. Able knew he had a commanding air about him. She wouldn't be the first person who chose not to question it.

"Where is this vicar's house?" he asked when the silence stretched on.

"Not far," Lady Caldwell replied, looking relieved to find the muse of conversation again. "You can, er, walk if you prefer it, but I know Mrs. Ripley's youngest sister is coming by soon in a dogcart to bring me something."

Lady Caldwell looked at the timepiece pinned to her sparse bosom. "Oh, the time. Will you kindly excuse me?" she asked as she rose.

And there they stood for a moment. Able thought she would escape from the room because he was obviously not a man of quality like her son, but he underestimated Lady Caldwell. Instead, she came forward, took both his hands, and kissed his check, to his amazement.

"Thank you for freeing my son, Master Six," she said, and there was no mistaking the tears in her eyes.

"We were all getting pretty tired of incarceration," he said, touched by her emotion. "I just wish others had followed those of us who left."

She nodded. "Not everyone is brave," she said and left the room.

"I didn't expect that," Able told Elias.

"I warned you she would weep a bit and hang about your neck," the lieutenant joked. "Mothers are like that."

I wouldn't know, Able thought as he followed his friend into a breakfast room, where luncheon waited. As he ate—the food was excellent—he nodded and smiled and commented where required, while the other half of his active brain had a sudden epiphany about his own mother. The master of the workhouse had told him of his origins—how he was found naked and crying on the steps of St. George's Church in February, left there by a drab who somehow managed to get from the church to the back alley, where she died.

"A trrrail of blood," the beadle had told him, relishing the drama of the incident. "In both dirrrections, lad, as though she birthed you in the alley, but took you to the front steps. Odd, that."

Able had taken the news in stride, which was the only way to take anything in a workhouse. He was never angry at the woman he never knew, but as he ate and listened to Elias Caldwell, he had the most marvelous feeling that his dying mother had made certain he was found, by dragging herself to the church steps. She wanted him found; she wanted him to live.

He looked out the breakfast room window at the sound of a wheeled vehicle on the gravel outside. He looked, mainly so Elias would not see the sudden emotion on his face.

He looked again because the lass driving the dogcart had glanced in the window at him as she drove by and halted the cart. She raised her whip to wave.

"What a pretty girl," Able couldn't help blurting out to his luncheon partner. He heard the doorbell jangle and resisted a sudden urge to get up and answer it, galloping down the hall to beat out the footman.

"She surely is," Elias said with a sorrowful shake of his head. "Poor thing, youngest of six daughters. I believe her father—God rest his soul—ran out of dowry after the first three. All I know about her is that she helps her sister, the vicar's wife, with the younger children." He stood up and gestured that Able do the same. "And here she is."

Chapter Three

The door opened on a young lady with the brightest blue eyes Able had ever seen. The rich color dominated her face and left a man no choice but to admire them. Her hair was brown and she had a dimple in her left cheek and the hint of one in her right.

"Able, let me introduce you to Miss Bonfort, your ride to the vicarage, even though she had no idea this would happen when she drove up, eh, Meridee?" Elias was saying. Strange how his voice sounded far away. "Miss Bonfort, this is Master Able Six, here to help educate your . . . your—"

"My nephews," she supplied, turned to Able, and gave him—him!—a curtsy.

Able managed a decent bow. He felt awkward beyond belief, silently blaming his clumsiness with a woman on the fact that he had never found a book on manners and etiquette aboard any of His Majesty's ships.

"My sister greatly appreciates your willingness to help us on such short notice," Miss Bonfort said.

Bliss to his ears. Miss Bonfort had the wonderful West

Country sound to her voice, which reminded him faintly of English as he heard it spoken in the United States.

"Happy to help, Miss Bonfort." Not only was she lovely to look at, but she smelled of roses.

Her relieved smile at his words suggested that life in the Ripley household was lively, indeed, and possibly exhausting. "Master Six, my sister wanted to assure whoever answered Elias's letter that if you wish to go home for Christmas, she wouldn't hold you to staying at the vicarage through the holiday."

"I have nowhere to go," he said simply, which caused those pretty eyes to cloud over.

She quickly turned her frown into a smile. "Then you have come to the right place to keep Christmas."

She next directed that kindly gaze to Lieutenant Caldwell, who seemed to have no difficulty breathing or maintaining his composure in the presence of such loveliness. "Sir, I trust I may take your friend away now?"

Do with me what you will, Able thought, looking around for his homely duffel bag, which leaned in the corner of the room like an overweight dog of unknown origin.

"Take him, Meridee," Elias said with a casual wave of his hand. The man obviously had no idea how remarkable Miss Bonfort was. The fact that he used her first name suggested a friendship of long standing, which Able suddenly envied.

Elias performed a little bow of his own. "He can teach any possible subject your brother-in-law can devise."

"Such a gift," Miss Bonfort said with a laugh, obviously not believing the lieutenant. "Very well, sir, shall we go?"

Tongue-tied, he followed her from the breakfast room and down the hall, where the footman had his cloak ready. From the way the smaller man staggered under the weight of it, Able knew it was as heavy with water as ever. Perhaps he would fall ill from the effects of pneumonia and require tender nursing at the hands of Miss Bonfort. When he expired, she would shed a tear or two, then bravely go about her business, a changed woman.

The idea was so ludicrous that he smiled. He was reaching for his flat-crowned hat when Miss Bonfort put her hand lightly on his arm.

"Silly me, but I have forgotten the principal reason for my visit." She pulled a tissue-wrapped package from her reticule and held it out to the footman. "Barkley, please give this to Lady Caldwell. I promised her tatting for her pillow slips."

The footman took the package with an appreciative smile of his own, suggesting that he wasn't immune to Miss Bonfort, either. He held open the door for the two of them.

Miss Bonfort spoke as she pulled on her gloves. "I tat for Lady Caldwell, and she has her seamstress attach the tatting to pillow slips, which Lady Caldwell then claims she did herself."

"You get no credit for your exquisite handiwork?" he asked.

"I get *paid* for my exquisite handiwork," she corrected. "Are you given credit for keeping a ship in trim?"

Upon my word, the lady knows something of the sea, Able thought in admiration, as they stood beside the dogcart. He gave a rueful laugh. "Seldom. The captain gets the credit, Miss Bonfort."

"My situation entirely," she said. "Just stow your . . . your—"

"Duffel."

"Under the seat, Master Six. What is in that box?"

"My sextant. I didn't want to leave it in the rooming house."

"Don't you trust the other roomers?" she teased, but it was no joke to him.

"I don't trust anyone, Miss Bonfort," he replied, then winced at how dour he sounded. "That is, I . . ." *I what?* He thought in desperation now, wondering whence his self-possession had flown. "I'm a master on half pay, living in a cheap rooming house, Miss Bonfort, while waiting out the Peace of Amiens. I wouldn't want anything to happen to my sextant."

Why did he have to be so forthright? Why did he need to repel this lady who would never give a moment's thought to someone who lived a life such as his? Nothing was going to happen this Christmas except a month's work, then back to the rooming house. *She knows precisely where I stand now*, he reminded himself. *That's not a bad thing.*

"I wouldn't want you to lose your sextant, Master," she said. She stepped lightly on the dogcart pedal and seated herself in the vehicle before he could even offer a hand up.

He saw his dilemma. He could squeeze into the narrow seat beside her, but he blushed to even think of sitting hip-to-hip with a lady of such slight acquaintance, no matter how much he wanted to. He climbed into the rear-facing seat and set the wooden box beside him, the duffel under the seat.

Reins in hand, she turned around slightly. "Master Six,

if you would feel more confident handling the reins yourself, I'll certainly let you. Some men are inclined to prefer such a thing, and I don't mind."

Since he had already told her he lived in a rough neighborhood and was a man on half pay, there was no point to ending his plain speaking. "Miss Bonfort, I have never ridden a horse before in my life, much less held reins in my hand and expected a horse to follow my lead."

She laughed, but he heard nothing derisive in the sound—and he was listening. "Honestly spoken, sir! I suppose you have been at sea for years and years."

"Almost seventeen, Miss Bonfort, since I was nine."

"And who sees a horse and cart in the middle of the ocean?" she asked and clucked to the horse, who responded with a toss of his mane and moved at a speed slow enough to gratify a man enjoying the fragrance of rose and the sight of a pretty woman.

To his amazement, she seemed to find him interesting, because she asked him to sit on the other side of his seat so she could see him better. "See here, sir, I like to meet new people, and I think a dogcart hardly conducive to conversation."

He did as she asked, pleased now to see her in profile as she capably held the reins in her gloved hands, her back straight.

"Would you like to know something about your little charges?" she asked, when he said nothing.

"Aye, miss," he said, sounding like a workhouse boy. He winced again at his tone, aware as never before how little he knew about conversation with ladies. "Their father usually has the teaching of them?"

"He does, Master Six, except that my brother-in-law finds himself extra busy this time of year, what with caroling and taking baskets to the poor and commiserating with parishioners who find holidays overwhelming." She rested her elbow on the seat back and looked him in the eye. "Gerald is ten and in great need of the basics of numbers. James is eight and knows more than Gerald."

Able smiled at that, thinking of himself and remembering all the workhouse boys he taught after hours, so they might avoid beatings the next day. "It happens. Your . . . your sister would like me to bring along Gerald and keep James interested without embarrassing his older brother?"

"Precisely. I would help you, but I have my hands full with the two younger children, and there is another little one on the way," she said.

He watched her face, curious to know if such a forthright comment would make her blush. When it didn't, he knew he could talk about himself, because he was certain she had questions.

He didn't have to wait long. She glanced around at him again. "I see your name stenciled on that wooden box. I confess I have never seen Able spelled that way before."

"That's not my entire name, Miss Bonfort," he explained. "Would *you* rejoice in the name of Durable?"

She laughed out loud, then her face turned rosy as she realized he was serious and she had just made fun of him. "I beg your pardon. I shouldn't have laughed."

If she had said nothing more, he would not have added to the text. She turned around again to look at him. "Forgive my impertinence, but why would parents name a child

Durable? If this is a peculiarity of Scotland, do forgive me, because I don't know any people north of the border."

Able could tell his story with some economy, so he did. "My mother gave birth to me in an alley on February 5, 1776. She managed to get me to the steps of St. George's Church before she returned to the alley and died. The rector found me."

"Oh my," she said softly.

"He wrapped me in his overcoat, took me inside the church, and then to the parish workhouse there in Dumfries. When I didn't die from that exposure, I was declared Durable by the master of the workhouse and named Six because I was the sixth such foundling in 1776."

He knew there were any number of things she could have asked him then, or remained silent as other women had, turning away as quickly as they could. She surprised him.

"What happened to One through Five?" she asked as calmly as if they discussed sines, cosines, and tangents—not that they ever would—but Able knew his strengths; discussing One through Five wasn't among them.

"No one has ever asked me that before," he said, buying himself a moment.

"I trust you have had conversations like this when someone questioned your name," she said.

"It generally came up in fo'c'sles and later in wardrooms in one sea or other," he hedged. "My mates laughed it off. The wits called me Able Seven or Eight, and eventually no one thought about it. The teasing stopped, because what a man *does* at sea speaks louder."

"One through Five?" she asked again. This was not a woman with wool pulled easily over her eyes.

"All dead. They weren't durable," he said simply. "And now your next question will be . . . ?"

She turned around to face the front again, minding the reins as the horse trotted along slowly, and he thought she was done with him. Or not. He heard her sniff back tears, and he wondered if his story touched her heart as it did his. Through the years, he had wondered why *he* was Durable, and One through Five were not.

Might as well air all his dirty linen now so she could share it with her vicar brother-in-law and older sister. He accepted the reality that even this ten-shilling-a-month job with room and board might end before it began. "The next question is generally, 'Why, Master Six, do you look so unScottish?'"

"That wasn't *my* next question," she told him, speaking with a little more spirit now. "I have an uncle who works for the navy in Portsmouth. I stay with him upon occasion. His dinner guests often include sailing masters and surgeons. I've never heard of a sailing master as young as you."

"We can blame Napoleon for that, Miss Bonfort," he told her. "I was Sailing Master Second until the middle of Aboukir Bay in '99. You might know it as the Battle of the Nile. The master was killed on deck by a splinter of railing, and I took over."

It seemed simple to say, but the reality had been intense and painful, considering his high regard for the man just superior to him, now dead. Able had stepped forward on the bloody quarterdeck and watched the sails, the wind, and the course of the battle. After a nod from Captain Hallowell, he calmly told the helmsman precisely what the *Swiftsure* should do and when, coming into battle late as they had. There was time for the shakes hours later when victory was in their hands, and Admiral Horatio Nelson's audacity stunned and then warmed a nation's heart. His was only a small part of the bigger picture, but the glow of pride had never gone away.

"No fears?"

Had he been afraid? Why didn't this woman ask the usual questions? "No, actually," he said finally, hoping he didn't sound cocksure. "I wasn't afraid at Camperdown, either, or any number of smaller encounters with the French or Spaniards."

"I would be afraid," she said.

He didn't know her, except that her questions revealed a lively mind. "I doubt that greatly, Miss Bonfort," he said. "What a man is, in battle, is busy, and no one is busier than a sailing master. A wrong order to the helmsman can court disaster. The time to fear comes after, when the battle is over and you are wondering why in God's name you are still alive. Oh, and the odd nightmare or two." Or three or four, but she knew enough already about him that would do for a brief acquaintance.

She turned in the seat again, and his heart softened to pudding at her brimming eyes.

"You're too tenderhearted, Miss Bonfort," he teased gently. "I am in the business of war, and you are not. I put to sea because I relish the challenge."

"Not to protect the people at home?" she teased in turn.

Why did she come up with such probing questions? "You're no better at small talk and chatter than I am, Miss

Bonfort," he told her, buying another moment. "I share a ship and a fleet with many men who have wives and children at home, and parents and cousins. I have no one."

"I speak for myself, then, in saying thank you," she said, and turned back to her primary duty of getting a slow horse moving faster, now that the rain had started again. She turned to him for a fleeting moment, just long enough to say, even as her cheeks bloomed with color, "I wish *I* had curly hair, Master Six."

Who wouldn't laugh at that? The rain poured down, and Able Six, competent fellow, strangely but thoroughly educated, realized he had just discovered the pleasure of honest flattery. Was this *ad hoc* teaching assignment only going to get stranger?

Chapter Four

Able scoured his brain for something clever to say and decided silence might be best. No one had ever thanked him for what he did. No one had ever envied his stupid curls. No one had ever asked about One through Five. He could have told her more about Four and Five, who shared the room where all the boys slept, sometimes three to a bed. He remembered the coughing and then the blood, and wondered why he was immune from such suffering.

Even as a little boy, he knew that children with mothers and fathers died, too, not just orphans. In one of his more enterprising stratagems to mine income for the workhouse, Beadle McNair rented out the little ones as mourners for funeral processions.

"It's easy work, lads," he had said. "Just cry and wail a bit."

Able cried and wailed, but never enough to suit the beadle, who vowed he could "give him summat to cry about, think on." It was but one of many beatings, but Able Six still could not be convinced to cry copiously in funeral possessions. What happened instead was a fierce urgency to put the workhouse behind him before he went the way of Four and Five.

And now I am here in Devon with gentlefolk, he thought as the dogcart trundled along. *I have certainly been in stranger places. Or have I?*

"Four and Five died of consumption," he told Miss Bonfort at last. "One through Three must have died before I was old enough to be aware of them. I ran away to sea at nine because I didn't want to die."

"And into the arms of the most dangerous profession in England," Miss Bonfort said with a shake of her head. "Master Six, you are a wonder!"

They laughed together, and he felt immeasurably better, except she didn't seem to be taking his low status and unfortunate birth seriously enough. He noticed no disgust on her face. Might as well spill the entire budget.

"My hair is black and curly because my father was perhaps a Spaniard or maybe an Italian," he told her. "Who knows?"

"Maybe Greek," she commented, still unperturbed.

"Funny, but I hadn't thought of Greece," he told her, falling into the same casual tone, as though they talked about the king's horses at Newmarket and whether they would win, place, or show this year. *Lordy, but this isn't even the most interesting thing about m*e, he thought, completely diverted, even as he started to shiver from the driving rain.

As much as he enjoyed her company, Able felt only relief to see a small village—perhaps Pomfrey—then a venerable church and a stone house hard by. "Is that the vicarage?" he asked, wishing his teeth didn't chatter.

"At long last," she assured him. "You must be freezing. I know I am."

She gave the horse a halfhearted slap with the reins, and the beast only turned his head to give her a reproachful look that made the sailing master chuckle.

"If I do that again, I will lose a friend," she remarked. "Goldenrod is in no hurry."

Name him One through Five, and he won't last long, Able thought. "I bow to your superior knowledge of horseflesh," he said out loud. "One would think the incentive of oats in a dry barn would hasten the velocity."

She laughed at that, calling him a scientist, which he bore with good grace, considering that he never thought to hear such a title applied to himself. He had a strong suspicion that when he stepped from the dogcart, he would be at least four inches taller from all the praise piled upon him by a lass who didn't cringe at his lower-than-low birth, his regrettable situation of half-pay, or his curly hair.

It wasn't even praise, really, he decided, as his analytical mind examined two or three sides simultaneously, as it tended to do regularly. In his world of war and nautical hierarchy, he never thought to find a comrade in a dogcart in Devon. It was the farthest thing from his thoughts.

He did have the presence of mind and manners to leap from the dogcart in time to hand her down from the high seat, which earned him another of those dimpled grins and a hearty thank-you. He wanted to raise his cloak and shepherd her under it to stay dry, except the beastly thing was soaking wet and probably would have drowned her. They squished to the closest entrance of the tidy house included in the living of a parish vicar.

"I'm back," Miss Bonfort sang out as she closed the door behind them. "And I have brought a tutor!"

Able smiled to see little heads pop out of a doorway, then pop back in. "I am probably not their favorite sight right now," he whispered to Miss Bonfort, leaning closer to get another whiff of her rose talcum powder.

"Your task will be to assure them that numbers are not the enemy; ignorance is," she replied, turning toward him.

She was close enough to kiss, but Master Six was smarter than that. For a second, he admired the small freckles sprinkling her nose, then straightened up.

"I can't," he said out loud, not meaning to, but there she was and so pretty, even with rainwater on her face.

"I believe you have to," she replied.

"I mean . . . I mean, I can't wait to do battle with ignorance," he said, his face aflame. *She will think I am an idiot*, he told himself.

Miss Bonfort was far kinder than he deserved. She handed her wet cloak to a servant and peeked in the door where the heads had popped out. "Come out, you two," she said in a gruff voice he found charming. The woman knew children.

And there stood his pupils—little boys with wary eyes. With a nod of thanks, he handed his soaking boat cloak and hat to the same servant girl, who staggered under the weight of them as she retreated down the hall.

"Front and center, lads," he said in the voice of command he had developed through years of hard service.

He knew they would obey, and they did. "I am your tutor for the duration of this month," he told them, something they probably already knew. "I am Master Able Six." He gestured. "Beginning with the older, now. Step forward and report."

The slightly taller boy took a step forward. His chin went up. "Master Gerald Ripley, ten," he said, then stepped back.

The next lad stepped forward with more assurance. "Master James Ripley, eight." He started to step back, then gestured with both hands. "I know you are more than six, sir."

Able glanced at Miss Bonfort, who was laughing behind her hand, her marvelous eyes getting smaller the more she tried to suppress her mirth.

"I am twenty-six," he replied, trying not to smile himself. "Master James, how much more is that than six?"

"Twenty years more," he replied promptly, then added, "You are old."

"I am, indeed," Able replied, charmed by his students. "A master at sea is a different title than the one bestowed upon a lad. At sea, it means I am the master of the sails, their trim, the placement of ballast, and everything that keeps a ship afloat and moving in the right direction. I even keep the ship's official log."

"Not the captain?"

"No, James. He might take notes. Mine is the official log."

"But Six?" Gerald asked, speaking up for the first time.

"That is my surname, Gerald," he replied, pleased the

less-assured child had added his mite to the conversation. "My name is Able Six, and you will call me Master Six." He nodded to them. "You may return to your posts. Tomorrow, we will begin the amazing study of mathematics."

The brothers looked at each other then back at him, the wary looks gone. They turned to leave, executing a smart about-face that tried Miss Bonfort even more.

"One more item, men," Able said.

They stopped and turned around just as smartly.

"Do you ever play jackstraws?"

"We like to."

"Like to . . . ?"

"We like to, Master Six," Gerald said promptly. "Are we going to play jackstraws?"

"Perhaps at first. We will do something even better with them, I assure you," Master Six replied. "It will be life-changing. As you were, men."

Chapter Five

Able's introduction to his actual employers passed off smoothly enough, conducted as it was in the vicar's study, a book-lined room that held his immediate attention for the few seconds required to examine all the titles on the spines and memorize them.

He was fast, but not fast enough for the man seated behind the desk, who rose and held out his hand.

"You like to read, sir?" Mr. Ripley asked as they shook hands. He seated himself and gestured to a chair.

"Aye, sir," Able replied. "I'm a fairly quick study."

The vicar laughed and steepled his fingers together, appraising him. "You're welcome to borrow any book you choose during your tenure here."

Book? Able thought. He took another quick glance at the bookshelves. *It's only 216 books. I'll read them all in two weeks.*

Here it came. The vicar looked closer at Able. "Provided we choose to hire you to tutor our older children."

"Fair enough, sir," Able replied.

The door opened, and Miss Bonfort returned with a copy of herself, one looking older and frazzled and wearing her apron high. He rose and bowed.

"Master Six, this is my sister, Mrs. Ripley."

Mrs. Ripley bobbed a curtsy of her own and sat down in the chair directly beside the desk. A glance at her current tonnage made him suspect she was due for confinement in a month or so.

"Master Six, pleased to make your acquaintance." Mrs. Ripley said. "My boys are already telling me that you will play jackstraws with them tomorrow."

"Jackstraws?" the vicar asked as his eyebrows rose into his forehead.

"It is a wonderful way to introduce plane geometry to lads, provided you don't mind if I snap some in half and in thirds," Able explained. He laughed. "The jackstraws—not the lads."

Stony stares. "All we are asking for is addition, subtraction, multiplication, and division," the vicar said, his voice firm and in control.

"Certainly, sir," Able replied, knowing he needed to come about and handsomely to placate this slower mind. "They will know those within a fortnight, which is why I propose geometry as well. Tomorrow will just whet their appetite and give them something to hope for, after we survive the tedium of rote cards and memorization."

Oh damn, he had gone too far. Two sets of skeptical eyes bored into him. He looked at Miss Bonfort, hoping not to see the same expression. To his relief but not his surprise, he saw only lively interest on her face. *Bless your imaginative heart*, he thought.

"I think Master Six will work wonders with my nephews," Miss Bonfort said.

"Yes, yes, but geometry?" the vicar sputtered. "Who needs that?"

Able opened his mouth to reply, but another glance in Miss Bonfort's direction silenced him. The shake of her head was nearly imperceptible, but there it was. He kept his own counsel on geometry as surely as if she had jabbed him in the ribs.

Miss Bonfort continued to smile so serenely at her brother-in-law, who set about straightening the papers on his desk. He looked for all the world like a man who hated to make a decision—or one who had never seen the likes of Able Six before, which was more likely.

"Brother, he can use the work, and he comes well-recommended," Miss Bonfort said quietly.

Fidget and fiddle a little more. The vicar gave a great, noisy sigh and capitulated. "Very well, sir. Begin tumorrow," he said. "I will pay you ten shillings a month for December."

"Thank you," Able said. "You won't be disappointed."

The result of that comment was another sigh. "So much to do this month," muttered the vicar, "otherwise, I would do it myself."

"Shall I ask Mrs. Ledbetter to show Master Able to his room?" Miss Bonfort suggested when the vicar had returned to the business of tidying up a tidy desk.

"Yes, certainly. We dine at six of the clock, Master Able," Mr. Ripley said. "See that you are prompt."

With a shy smile of her own, Mrs. Ripley, hand on her

belly, turned Able Six over to a housekeeper who, if appearances were not deceiving, must be the household supreme manager and she who must be obeyed. His suspicions were borne out by Miss Bonfort, who insisted on accompanying them to the guest room, fulfilling what he was coming to realize was *her* role as buffer in the Ripley household.

What he thought was a two-story house gloried in a short stairway to a third floor, that attic floor he was familiar with from his rooming house in Plymouth. He braced himself for disappointment.

A glance at Miss Bonfort showed him a lady almost beside herself with glee. When she opened the door with a flourish, he knew *she* knew his thoughts.

"Why, this is quite charming," he said in surprise after a glance around at a narrow bed as virtuous as the one he had abandoned in Plymouth, but with a fluffy pillow and blankets in evidence. He saw a rumpsprung armchair with a reading lamp beside it and a three-drawer bureau for his modest possessions. A wool rug, shaving stand, and pitcher completed the tableau.

"I will send a maid up to light the fire," was all Mrs. Ledbetter said before she nodded to them and left the room. The door remained open, perhaps as a reminder for him to behave himself in a bedchamber with a single lady, should he think to practice some evil design.

"She doesn't approve of me," Able remarked.

"It took me considerable time to worm myself into her good graces, too, so don't be despondent," Miss Bonfort said. "Will this do? I hope you do not bump your head on the eaves."

"It will more than do," he assured her. "I've never had a room this handsome, and I'm used to tight spaces."

"Dinner at six," she repeated and turned to leave.

He didn't want her to go. He wracked his agile brain for some tidbit to keep her in his orbit a little longer and came up with something.

"Miss Bonfort, your last name is familiar to me, except that I can't quite place it," he said, hoping he didn't sound like a man with designs on a lady.

Yet again she surprised him. "You know perfectly well why you remember Bonfort," she said, her tone kindly but firm. "I am beginning to suspect that you never forget a thing, Master Six."

"You've found me out," he said simply, hoping she would think he was joking. "There are Bonforts and there are Bonforts, but I think your uncle—cousin?—is Aloysius Bonfort, who is more than a mere navy employee in Portsmouth."

"You have me," she replied, and made him suddenly wish that were so. "Uncle Bonfort is the chief victualling officer for the Royal Navy in Portsmouth."

"I've seen his name on a document or two," Able said, recovering from a momentary and unaccustomed lapse in attention. "One of my tasks aboard ship is the proper displacement of cargo in the hold. I see his name and stamp often."

He wanted to ask why she wasn't spending more time in Portsmouth to be seen of any number of naval officers, each of whom would probably duel with the other for the privilege of proposing. Yet here she was in a vicarage in the

Devon countryside, seen of children and one sailing master who already knew he was infatuated, at the very least.

"He's a fine uncle," she said, her cheeks rosy, as though she could read his thoughts. "I like to visit him, but the war keeps him more and more in his office."

She looked around his little room as if wondering what else she could do to make it better. "I'll see that you have a glass and carafe of water—or something stronger, if you prefer." She went to the open door. "I'm coming, Mrs. Ledbetter," she said and flashed him a conspiratorial smile. "She watches out for me," she whispered, then spoke normally. "See you at six for dinner."

Dinner was sheer delight. Able found himself seated between his two little pupils, with a fine view of Miss Bonfort seated directly across from him. The blessing on the food went on too long, as though the vicar wanted to prove a point. Able sat as still as the lads on either side of him. James began to fidget before the amen, but Gerald held fast.

He had never eaten so well, either. Dish after dish came his way—they served country style—and moved on after generous portions on his plate, which promptly disappeared. The soft rolls were made in heaven.

Sixteen years in a hard service caused him to commit what he hoped was his only breach of decorum. From habit, he tapped the roll on the table, which made Miss Bonfort put her hand to her mouth in merriment.

He realized what he had done and turned to James. "Lad, I am so accustomed to banging out weevils from bread that

I committed a serious offense against the best bread I have ever eaten."

"Weevils?" James asked, his eyes huge.

"They don't eat much," Able added. Even the vicar had to smile at that one.

Little boys being what they were, one thing led to another and he found himself describing the Battle of the Nile—a slimmed down, less gory version—to interested listeners long after the final course. The footman lingered to bring out more sliced apples, which occasioned a visit from the cook, until Mrs. Ripley asked her more agile sister to hurry belowstairs to invite everyone up to listen.

He told them of the *Swiftsure*'s late arrival on the scene in Aboukir Bay because they had been sent to reconnoiter Alexandria, Egypt. Rear Admiral Sir Horatio Nelson was still unsure where the French fleet was and sent *Swiftsure* out on a frigate's duty.

"The frigates are the eyes and ears of the fleet, but Sir Horatio had none," Able explained, taking another slice of apple. "When we got wind of the battle, we crowded on sail for Aboukir Bay."

"And fired on the whole lot of the Frogs?" James asked, which earned him a frown from his father and a reprimand from his mother to mind his mouth.

"We couldn't. It was dark, and Captain Hallowell didn't want to risk firing at a Royal Navy ship," Able said, remembering that moment, as well as the precise latitude and longitude, the number of crew on deck, and the other ships on the water. "As it was, he nearly fired on the *Billy Ruffian*."

"There never was a ship named that," Gerald scoffed,

ever a realist. This earned him another hard stare from Papa, but nothing more, because everyone was focused on the story.

"Master Gerald, you are correct. It was the HMS *Bellerephon*, but British tars being what we are, we call it *Billy Ruffian*," he explained.

"You did end up shooting something?" James asked, sounding so impatient that Able nearly smiled.

"Aye, we did, lad. We pounded the French *Orient* until it exploded," Able said. He never forgot anything, but he wished he could forget that moment on the deck of the *Swiftsure* when the sailing master was skewered through with a splinter from the ship's own railing, and the job of sailing master became his.

"I became the sailing master after the master died," he said, knowing that was enough information for little boys who probably thought splinters were mere irritations under a fingernail. "Next, we subdued the *Franklin* and, finally, the *Tonnant*. Not a bad evening's work."

James uttered a sigh of satisfaction. A glance assured him that Mr. Ripley had fallen under the spell of the battle, and so had Miss Bonfort, her chin in her palms, her elbows on the table. Mrs. Ripley looked too gravid to be comfortable until the next Ripley put in his or her appearance.

"I have to hear more," Gerald said solemnly. "I simply must."

"Not tonight," his father said, vetoing any further sea stories.

"But Master Six, why are you here and not on a ship?" James asked, determined the narrative continue.

"Solely because the First Consul of France, Napoleon Bonaparte himself, and our First Minister, Henry Addington, struck a peace accord," Able told his audience. "I am living ashore on half-pay, along with most of the Royal Navy, as long as the peace holds."

"Will it be long, sir?" James asked, even as his father pulled back his chair and took him gently by the arm.

"No. There is more war to wage." Able clapped his hands together, suddenly tired of all his thinking and rethinking. "I will tell you more tomorrow, when you report to . . . to . . ."

". . . the classroom at . . ." Mrs. Ripley supplied.

". . . at two bells in the forenoon watch," he finished. "That will be nine of the clock. Good night to you."

It was all too much, he decided, as he started down the hall to the stairs. He wondered what it would be like to not remember everything, to not know chapter and line of every book he had ever read. To think he had assumed when he was poor Number Six in the workhouse that everyone learned the way he did.

"Does your brain ever hurt, Master Six?"

He turned around, almost surprised but not quite. He waited for Miss Bonfort to reach him. He knew he could feign ignorance and joke about the matter, but she seemed to understand him. How, he knew not.

"At times," he admitted. "Then I go to sleep."

She nodded and held out a book. He took it. "*The Lives of the Martyrs*," he read. "In case I get bored before two bells in the forenoon watch?"

"In case. Good night, sir."

He smiled as he opened the door on a room that was warm and tidy. Tired, he kicked off his shoes, stripped, and crawled into a firm enough bed but with no lumps. The pillow smelled of lavender, so he thought of great fields of the aromatic herb he had seen in southern France in more peaceful times.

Stomach full, heart in tune, Master Six settled into as much somnolence as his mind ever allowed him. He closed his eyes and noticed something remarkable. For the first time he could ever remember, he felt his shoulders relax and slope downward. He thought a moment, wanting to end a good day in a perfect way.

"'Chapter One: Common Notions,'" he murmured as cares slid from those lowered shoulders. "'Number one: Things which are equal to the same thing are also equal to one another.'" He thought through two, three, and four, his mind on Miss Meridee Bonfort, who seemed to be figuring out his great secret. "'Number five: The whole is greater than the part.' Is that so, Miss Bonfort?" he asked out loud. "Euclid thinks so. Shall we find out?"

Chapter Six

By two bells in the forenoon watch, Able Six was ready for his pupils. He stood looking out the window upon a winter's scene of rolling land and trees still shedding their summer's ballast. He stood on tiptoe, but no, there was no ocean in sight, which caused him some disappointment.

The room rejoiced in the morning sun, so he had no fault with the lighting. The chairs looked hard, though. The table contained two neat stacks of thick paper he had requested, as well as single sheets, scissors, and pencils, plus a ruler.

He looked up at a timid knock on the door and opened it to find his pupils standing there, each with a cylinder tube of jackstraws in hand. He glanced at the mantelpiece clock.

"Excellent, men," he said. "Two bells in the forenoon watch. And you brought along your jackstraws."

He thought about the hard chairs, then sat down on the floor cross-legged, instead. Gerald and James looked at each other, grinned, and sat down, too. Able opened one cylinder and poured out the jackstraws, setting them up, and releasing them. They played quietly through three rounds.

Instead of setting them up again and letting the jackstraws fall a fourth time, Able counted out ten and arranged them in rows, which took up a good portion of the floor. By now, the boys were lying on their stomachs, watching with interest.

"Gerald, take five away from the ten, and let's see what we have," he directed.

Gerald promptly did as he was asked, going through an entire row of numbers that got larger and smaller, then larger again as he added, subtracted, and moved around the jackstraws with increasing ease, according to Able's instructions. James watched and took his turn, with none of Gerald's hesitation.

Since it was just as simple to make practice cards sitting on the floor, the boys spent the morning each making a set of addition cards and then subtraction. By the time Miss Bonfort, a baby on her hip, called them to luncheon, the cards were done. Able smiled inside to see their reluctance to leave the floor and troop down the hall.

"After luncheon, spend some time doing what you wish," he called after them and was rewarded with a snappy salute from James.

"You're a wonder, Master Six," Miss Bonfort said.

"Numbers are fun," he said with a shrug as he got up from the floor with a groan.

"Feeling our age, are we?" she teased.

"I am but twenty-six," he replied. "I blame a cutlass jab to my hip that nearly did me in at Camperdown."

"You could use a chair, as nature intended," she reminded him, her eyes lively.

And that was the precise moment when Able Six, a strange man with the lowest background imaginable, decided to pursue Miss Bonfort, even though he didn't yet have permission to use her first name, and he was scraping by on half pay. She was bright, and he thought she was on to him. Better to find out now. He couldn't say things were moving too fast, because his entire life and mind moved too fast. Why waste a minute more?

He indicated Fox's *Book of Martyrs* lying on the unused table. "I can give this back to Mr. Ripley now," he said. "Better return it while I can still walk unaided down the hall, despite war injuries that would elicit sympathy from a more tenderhearted female."

She laughed out loud at that bit of hyperbole and did as he thought she might. She picked up the book and turned to the table of contents. "How does Chapter Five begin?" she asked, innocently enough.

Able rubbed his hands together, because this was a game he relished. "You picked a good one, Miss Bonfort." He closed his eyes and saw the words on some cosmic sheet of paper. "'When the reformed religion began to diffuse the Gospel light throughout Europe, Pope Innocent III entertained great fear for the Romish Church.' Am I close?"

She laughed again, shut the book, and lightly tapped him on the head with it. "You are right on, and you know it, smart man!"

They laughed together, but she wasn't done with him. She opened the book again. "The heading on Chapter Twenty-Two," she prompted.

"Oh, give me a hard one, Miss Bonfort," he said. "'The Beginnings of American Foreign Missions.'"

She didn't laugh this time. She just observed his face quietly, as though wondering how a human could pack so much inside his brain.

"When did you figure me out?" he asked.

"I watched your eyes when you were looking at my brother-in-law's bookshelf," she told him, setting the book down. "I've never seen eyes move so fast." She indicated the book. "And you read this monstrously dry tome that I had to read for punishment years ago when I prevaricated."

"That's punishment, indeed," he teased. "I read it this morning when I woke up early."

"It took you . . ."

"About twenty minutes," he said. "It *was* dry, after all."

She shook her head in amazement, then transferred the baby she was carrying to her other hip. "I don't know what to say, Master Able."

"Start by calling me Able, without master in front of it," he asked, hopeful.

"If you will call me Meridee," she replied, then rolled her eyes. "What a name! I am the sixth of six daughters, and my parents must have run out of ideas."

"I rather like it. It's not as silly as Durable."

"You have me there."

He just looked at her then, imagining a life with this lovely woman beside him. The little girl who rested so quietly against her only fueled his imagination further. He strongly suspected that love and thoughts of marriage and children didn't come so fast to most men, but he already knew he wasn't like most men. "I have not one single thing to recommend me," he said quietly. "Nothing beyond a strange talent, which, frankly, is more of a curse than a blessing."

Meridee Bonfort merely shrugged and directed her attention to the baby in her arms. Deep inside him, he was touched at her sudden shyness. He knew he was moving too fast; she knew it, too, but she didn't run from the room or turn cold. He knew she was bright; he also knew she was breathtakingly, superbly normal.

"Captain Hallowell, my captain on the *Swiftsure*, told me once—I thought in jest—that I would need a keeper," he said, coming not one step closer to this charming woman. "We laughed about it, but I believe he was serious."

She set the baby on the floor between them, and the little one began to pat her knees and rock a bit. Able stooped a moment and wound a curl around his finger, watching it bounce.

"Captain Hallowell knew, too?" she asked.

"Couldn't be helped. I was a loblolly boy at that earlier time, dumping urinals and carrying food to patients for the ship surgeon, a man with no imagination whatsoever."

"That must have chafed you," she murmured, not taking her eyes from his while sitting down.

"No, actually," he said as he sat down across from her. "He never suspected, so I was free to observe to my heart's content and squirrel away his surgical textbooks for nightly reading."

Meridee sighed. "I think I know where this is going."

"I am certain you do," he replied. "At the Battle of Cape St. Vincent, I was serving on the HMS *Captain*, with Commodore Horatio Nelson commanding that arm of battle.

It was a bloody run, and the surgeon died." He paused, wondering if she would believe what followed.

She was quick. She turned pale, her eyes relentlessly on his. "You took over."

"Aye. The pharmacist mate seemed paralyzed when Surgeon Bowie died. I had watched any number of amputations. I knew what to do." He shrugged. "Should I have stood by, idle?"

To his gratification, Meridee leaned across the table and patted his cheek. She blushed and drew her hand away quickly, probably chagrined at her spontaneity, but he silently blessed her for it. She tried to cover her impulse by reaching down to pat the baby on the floor.

"Did they all live?" she asked.

"Most. Some, no one could have saved." He closed his eyes for a second.

"Open your eyes," Meridee said. "They're moving too fast."

He did as she said, relieved to be stopped before he saw the whole scene again on that cosmic sheet of cursed paper that was his mind.

"And so you met Captain Hallowell then?" she prompted.

She held his hand now, lightly in her grasp, as though knowing intuitively that a tighter grip would frighten him. Some sense told him it was up to him to tighten the grip, and he did.

"Aye. He commanded the *Captain,* Nelson's flagship, and came to the sick bay." That was close enough, if not entirely accurate.

"Beg pardon, Miss Bonfort, but there is luncheon getting cold in the breakfast room. Miss Bonfort!"

They both swiveled around and let go of each other's hands at the same instant. The housekeeper stood in the doorway, her eyes as wide as saucers.

"Luncheon can wait, Mrs. Ledbetter," Meridee said calmly. "Save something for us, please."

"Are we in trouble?" he said, after the housekeeper glared at him, turned on her heel, and stomped away.

"Most likely," Meridee told him, her voice steady. "Mrs. Ledbetter is an estimable woman, but she will tattle to my sister and . . ."

". . . and I'll be gone by nightfall."

"No!" Meridee exclaimed, and slapped the table. "I intend to win this round. My sister needs me right now, and your retention will be the condition of my remaining." She leaned forward, her lovely blue eyes so intense. "You do need a keeper, Able Six. Please continue your narrative." She laughed. "I need to hear it, but I am hungry and I believe Cook made profiteroles."

Meridee picked up the little girl from the floor and set her in her lap. She laughed when the baby slapped the table in perfect imitation. "I am setting a poor example," she teased.

Able told Meridee about the gift of Sir Isaac Newton's *Principia Mathematica* from Captain Hallowell a month after the battle. "It was in English, of course, but with the Latin text in the back."

"You read it in English in fifteen minutes?" Meridee teased.

"Took me an hour. It's a dense read. And then I—"

"You read it in Latin the next afternoon, before . . . before one of those dog or cat watches."

He threw back his head and laughed. "You are a sorry excuse for a seaman! It's a dog watch, and no, it took me three days."

"Slow top," she teased again.

"Captain Hallowell pulled a string or two and had me transferred to the *Swiftsure*, his next command, where I served as sailing master second without having any experience." He chuckled at the memory. "Captain Hallowell took a beating from the Admiralty for such an impulsive act, but they left him alone when matters proved successful."

"You observed the sailing master," she said, a statement of fact.

"I did. Reuben Maxwell was the best. I learned from him and regret to this day his death during the Battle of the Nile."

He had nothing more to say so he was silent, enjoying the view of a lovely woman with troubled eyes. He had laid himself bare for the first time in his life, even beyond what Captain Hallowell knew. A yea or nay from Meridee Bonfort would allow him to hope or send him packing.

He heard her stomach growl, which made him smile and broke the tension, if that's what it was. "Should we adjourn to the breakfast room before you start to gnaw on that small girl in your lap?" he asked.

"In a minute." She waved off the suggestion in a way that endeared her to him enormously. "I want to know more about you, but you are probably loathe to keep explaining yourself."

"*Au contraire.* I have never told this much to anyone before. My gift or curse—call it what you will—is something I try not to mention. Ask away."

"When did you discover this about yourself, or . . . or did someone discover it for you?"

He sighed and started to close his eyes, but kept them open. "Miss Meridee Bonfort, no one in a workhouse cares too much about children who are numbered."

"Then you figured it out by yourself," she persisted.

He looked up at a knock on the frame of the open door. His face like thunder, the vicar stood there, a napkin tucked under his chin. "Meridee, I will speak to you immediately."

Able stood up. "Sir, I . . ."

Mr. Ripley had a chicken leg in his hand, which he pointed at the sailing master. The result made the effervescent and obviously unrepentant Meridee Bonfort put her hand to her mouth. "You will leave this house at once."

"No, he will not."

Chapter Seven

I have a champion, Able thought, curious more than fearful how this would play out, mainly because he suspected Meridee was just beginning to plumb the depths of her own involvement. From the look of astonishment on the vicar's face, he had never heard his little sister-in-law defy him.

"Meridee, go to your room!"

She stood up, clutching her little niece. "Edmund Ripley, I am twenty-five and not three. I will *not* go to my room. Yes, I was holding the sailing master's hand. You would, too, if you heard his stories of life on the blockade and the terrors of a French bombardment."

Her chin trembled, and her eyes filled with tears, impressing Able beyond all belief by so much prevarication and emotion. No wonder her father had made her read *The Book of Martyrs* years earlier as punishment for fibs. She appeared not to have learned a thing.

"I doubt I would be holding his hand," the vicar said, but his anger seemed to dissipate. He stopped pointing the chicken leg and merely looked at it, as though wondering where it came from. Able glanced away, wondering if anyone had ever perished of suppressed mirth.

Brother-in-law and sister-in-law glared at each other. "I vow, if your sister did not need your help so much, I would send you packing, too, Meridee," the vicar threatened, but with diminishing fervor. He rounded on Able, who gazed back. "As for you . . ."

Praise God, but Gerald and James tumbled into the room, their practice cards in hand. "I got them all correct, Master Able," Gerald was shouting. He did a creditable imitation of a sailor's hornpipe, while James, ever the conspirator, beamed at his elder brother.

"He did, Papa," James said. "We quizzed each other, just as Master Able taught us. Let us show you. Sit down, please, dear Papa."

Dear Papa sat, his eyes on his sons now. With a flourish worthy of a magician, James held up the first card, which happened to be five plus two.

"Seven!" Gerald declared in round tones.

Another card, another correct response. Ever the observer, Able watched the vicar's face soften as his son, who was admittedly not as quick a thinker as his little brother, sailed in triumph through five more cards. When he hesitated on the first of the subtraction cards, Able spoke up quietly, so as not to disturb the boy's concentration.

"Think of the jackstraws in your mind, Gerald. Picture them on a piece of paper, and you'll have it," Able instructed.

"Eight," the boy replied, his voice confident.

Meridee applauded, and Gerald took a bow. "What are we going to learn this afternoon?" he asked Able.

"The world of triangles," Able told him. "Almost my favorite place. That is, provided I'm here to teach you."

"You'll be here," the vicar said.

Able had to give the man points for changing his tack and finding a new course. Mr. Ripley leveled an avuncular stare at his sister-in-law, even as he gently plucked his little daughter from Meridee's arms. "There will be no more hand-holding, no matter how heartrending a tale you hear, Miss Bonfort. Do I make myself amply clear?"

She curtsied, looking not one bit chastened. The vicar appeared inclined to overlook her unrepentant state.

"And you, sir," he said to Able. "Remember your station in life."

"Aye, sir. I am reminded of it often," Able said.

The chicken leg held at his side now, out of reach of his daughter's grasp, the vicar left the classroom. Gerald turned to Able. "May we start on triangles now?" he asked.

"I haven't eaten yet, and your aunt's stomach is growling," Able said. "Did you leave us any profiteroles?"

Both boys nodded, their eyes serious, because this subject was, after all, dessert. Able looked at their eagerness, their youth, their well-fed faces, their clean and brushed clothing and wisely did not contrast it with his own childhood. Perhaps some things were meant to be put away and not remembered. He would have to ask Meridee about that, once he told her of his own education in the workhouse. Perhaps he could even tuck away all those bad memories, once she knew.

"Here is what I think you should do," Meridee told her nephews. "Go outside and walk around in the cold air. See what you can find that might interest Master Able. I'll send him out to join you as soon as he finishes luncheon."

"Well done, Miss B," he said as they walked down the hall to the breakfast room. He leaned toward her, but not too close this time. "How much trouble are you in?"

"None, I think," she said after a moment's consideration. For the smallest second, he envied her a quiet brain that required reflection before response. "Truth be told—"

"So you *do* tell the truth now and then?"

She had the good grace and sufficient conscience to flash him a look that held a measure of repentance in it. "I only tell lies to get myself out of trouble, and maybe you, too, as I'm the one who took your hand." She cleared her throat for dramatic effect. "As I started to say before I was so *rudely* interrupted, truth be told, my brother-in-law and sister have worried about Gerald's mental acuity."

"No need for them to worry," he said. "He simply needs a different approach to whatever has been tried before. I have noticed that some people need to see and touch what they are learning. Jackstraws are one thing, and I will find other methods for Gerald."

She turned to face him. "You realize you should be teaching children full time, and not just temporarily."

He couldn't help it that his hands went to her shoulders. By the mark, she was soft to touch. "You also realize I am in the Royal Navy," he said. "We are not at war at this moment, but I wouldn't wager peace to last too far into 1803. I have a job to do."

"I know," she said, sounding oddly deflated. She

seemed to perk up almost too fast to suit her mood. "Right now, I need a profiterole."

"It's dessert," he teased, relieved to be on what felt like solid ground.

Even though it was only lukewarm now, luncheon with Meridee was an unalloyed pleasure. She ate with relish, which he enjoyed. Eyeing her sturdy frame, he reckoned she never missed a meal. She was by no means plump, merely healthy and well-fed, as a woman ought to be. And shapely.

Not for the first time, he wondered what his mother had looked like toward the end of her likely short, bleak life. He had no idea how old she was when she died, but he had seen drabs and street woman in other ports and countries and knew she was probably not beyond her teen years. Life on the street was a great and harsh leveler. Come to think of it, so was his life in the fleet.

For the first time, he wondered what it would be like to teach children, just children. A man of logical if overcrowded mind, Able extended that thought to include his own children, well aware they would likely never be born, considering his dangerous profession and the realization that once war resumed, it would probably last a long time.

"What in the world are you thinking, Able?" Meridee asked as she passed him another sandwich, the kind with the edges trimmed and the bread soft and free of weevils.

"Do you truly want to know?" he asked as he took the proffered sandwich. "I am not a small-talking man. Think carefully before you answer me, Meridee."

It could have gone in any direction. *I have not known*

you for twenty-four hours, he thought in humility, as he watched her expressive face. He wanted to lean closer to see those minuscule freckles again, but he refrained because he was already balancing on thin ice in the Ripley household.

"I need to know what you are thinking, Able Six," she said finally. "If war comes today or tomorrow or in six months, something tells me I will regret the remainder of my entire life if I do not know."

He sat back, almost at a loss, except that he was never at a loss. Might as well confess. "I am thinking how much I would like to teach children; more specifically, my children, who will likely never be born, because I have not a thing to recommend me and I serve a dangerous profession."

He didn't know what she would do. This woman was a variable in the complicated scheme of his life that he had never encountered before. He smiled suddenly, thinking of Newton's Third Law of Motion. He turned slightly to face her and held up his hand. To his eternal relief and delight, she pressed her hand against his. He pressed back, and she pressed again. He twined his fingers in hers.

"According to Newton's Third Law of Motion—I'll simplify it—for every action there is an equal and opposite reaction. We just proved it," he whispered, not even wanting the delicate watercolor pictures on the walls to hear him speak his odd heart to this lady. "That's how arches stand up. I also think it's how a . . . a vessel could fly to the moon, if such a thing were possible, and it is."

He looked for skepticism and saw none, which made his shoulders relax as they had last night in bed. He knew he could tell her anything.

"You are always going to be thinking faster and farther

than anyone," she whispered back. She tucked their twined hands in her lap, which gave him a pleasant jolt even Newton couldn't explain.

"But you won't yield an inch. It's an equal reaction," he said. "We would remain in equilibrium."

"People? Us?"

"Why not?" He took a deep breath, in too far to back out, not that he wanted to. "I can't even imagine more wildly divergent spheres of society than you and I inhabit, but by the eternal, I don't care."

"What would Sir Isaac Newton say to that?" she asked, her eyes bright with the merriment he was already finding himself unable to function without.

He touched her forehead lightly with his, just a light touch. "By the eternal, I don't care."

Chapter Eight

By unspoken, mutual consent, Able and Meridee declared a strange sort of truce. Able knew truce was the wrong word, but he couldn't actually think of a better one, even as he scoured those cosmic pages in his ordinarily tidy brain. They were not at war with each other—quite the contrary.

It was the first time in his life that his brain could not think of the right word to describe what sort of person Meridee Bonfort was to him. He tried something new; he decided not to worry about it.

He realized what it was a few days later, when Gerald and James were busy forming and reforming triangles with their jackstraws. He watched the boys and recalled the Peace of Amiens, which was printed and given to every ship in the Fleet. He had imagined the Peace as a pulling away—a chance to regroup and rebuild their forces, but also to breathe, to think about what lay ahead.

This personal Peace he had discovered with Meridee Bonfort was no different. He knew he must slow down, and maybe that was the point of this peace of theirs. He wanted nothing more than to kiss and cuddle her, and he suspected she wanted the same—Newton's third law and all that it implied—but this was neither the time nor the place. For the time being, he must remain a man working for his ten shillings a month, room and board, who would disappear from everyone's life when Christmas came. It chafed him, but he was discovering hitherto unknown wells of patience.

Able decided Meridee was a bit of a tyrant, which made him remember Captain Hallowell's remark about his needing a keeper. One morning, when she was certain no one was watching, she pressed her hand against his chest, backed him up against the wall in the breakfast room, and ordered him to walk outside every afternoon with his pupils.

He obeyed her dutifully, although he did admit to her that the country was not entirely to his liking. "I was raised in a city," he protested, "breathing great lungfuls of sooty air. It didn't stunt my growth. Are you aware how loud winter birds scream early in the morning? I didn't think so. I rest my case."

"You are hopeless," she replied with some spirit. "I suppose you prefer the ocean. I've seen you standing on tiptoe at the schoolroom window facing south, as if thinking water will magically appear."

"Guilty as charged. You can keep your countryside," he said generously.

"Well and good, Master Six, but I want you to walk outside, breathe the country air, and *not* think," she insisted, which made him smile.

"I don't have any choice in that," he replied, because he didn't.

"Try, Able, try," she urged and melted his heart with the compassion in her voice.

He tried and discovered it was possible to enjoy crunching through leaves as the season advanced, and then even piling them up into mounds, turning around, and throwing himself onto the noisy pile to his students' delight, his mind blissfully free. That worked until James found a worn-out rubber ball that looked as if a dog had gnawed it. James tossed it to Gerald, who tossed it to Able.

Able bounced it against a tree, then bounced it harder, stepping back as the increased force meant increased resistance. He moved farther and farther back, then sat his charges down and explained Newton's Third Law of Motion and how someday man could use such principles to take a vehicle to the moon.

When he told Meridee what he had done, she shook her head. "You are incorrigible," she scolded.

"Aye, incorrigible," he replied, which meant he had to say the word over and over because she liked the Scottish way he twirled his r's around. Then they were both laughing as quietly as they could, sitting there on the top of the stairs that led to his attic room.

They had learned to wait until everyone slept before adjourning to the stairs for conversation and the simple pleasure of sitting shoulder to shoulder. She laughed when he told her about Gerald's confusing angles with angels, which meant the boys got silly and talked about the properties of scalene angels and isosceles angels.

"You turned it into a lesson, of course," she said, and he heard the pride in her voice. Whether it was for her nephews or for him, he wasn't certain.

"Aye, miss," he said and nudged her, which meant she could nudge him back. "Stay here." He got up and went to his room. When he sat down again, he had a handful of drawings, which he put in her lap.

"Once we got back to the classroom, after that *improving* walk in the country, we made Christmas angles. The jackstraw cylinders were on the table, so that was our model for angel bodies. Gerald favored scalene triangles for wings, and James preferred isosceles."

She held the drawings close to her face because the light was poor on the stairs. She pointed to the third drawing. "Yours?"

"Aye. I like a double pair of equilateral triangles, then a single one as a halo," he said.

"Are they having as much fun as you are?" she asked, placing his drawing on top.

"I hope so. Gerald pulls a long face when the afternoons are over." He leaned back and rested his elbows on the tread above them. "I work on their memorizations in the morning—we're up to multiplication now—and the afternoon is for fun."

"Geometry is fun?" she asked.

"For me," he said with a shrug, and then a smile. "And for the boys."

Meridee sat silent for a long moment. Able had come to recognize those quiet moments as preludes before personal questions. *Ask me anything*, he thought. The pleasure of lowering his guard was fast becoming an addiction, as long as the person asking had striking blue eyes and those tantalizing tiny freckles. He started to nudge her again, but instead of a nudge, it turned into a gentle lean, which he found he preferred anyway, especially when that third law of Newton's meant she leaned gently, too, and held him up.

"What?"

"When did you realize that not everyone learns the way you do?" she asked.

"That's a good way to put it," he said, temporizing because it wasn't a pleasant experience.

"Now you're stalling," she said, which made him wonder how well she knew him. It was a novel experience. "I was going to ask when you discovered you were a prodigy, but I don't want to swell your head."

"It's a curse, not a blessing," he assured her.

"What can I say to that?" she asked, then folded her hands in her lap and waited.

"I was six," he began finally, his voice subdued. "There were thirty of us foundlings in one small classroom, every age jumbled together. I suppose the only concession to our age was that we young ones were set up front so we could see better. You really want to know?"

"I do," she said firmly. "Master Six, I have never met anyone like you before, and I doubt I will ever meet anyone like you again, no matter how long I live."

He felt precisely the same way. She deserved an answer. "The instructor wrote on a big board—at least, it looked big to a six-year-old—words and more words. After a few days of observing what he said when he pointed to certain words, it started to make perfect sense."

"You just *watched*?"

"Aye. It's what I do best," he assured her.

"I saw how fast your eyes moved over the books in my brother-in-law's study," she said. "Up and down one bookcase and then the other two, all in about three seconds."

It was his turn for a question. "Why in the world were you even looking at my eyes?"

She blushed then. "Master Six, you are a remarkably handsome man. What was I supposed to do?"

He threw back his head and laughed, which meant she had to put her hand over his mouth and say, "Shh!", which meant he couldn't help kissing that hand, which meant her hand came away quickly and she blushed even more furiously.

"Well, you are," she said again, with a charming dignity that went to his heart. "Answer my questions, please."

The laughing ended as he remembered what his brain would never let him forget. "A big boy, maybe ten or so, was sitting behind me. The master called on him to read the sentence, 'In my father's house are many mansions.' I didn't know at the time it was from St. John, but I knew what it said." When he stirred restlessly, Meridee took his hand in hers.

"He couldn't read it—I mean, how can an ordinary person learn if he fears the switch? The master struck him with a switch and kept striking him. Like a fool, I leaped up and read it, so the master would stop hitting the boy behind me. Oh merciful heaven, the master stared at me, then started beating *me*. I never was sure why. I . . . I had assumed all children my age learned the way I did, but I was the only one foolish enough to leap up. What did I know then about how others learned? I was six!"

"You never did that again?" she asked.

He couldn't look at her, because her voice betrayed more emotions than he wanted to add to his own at the moment. "I did a few more times. Then the other children started avoiding me, and I got tired of being beaten."

"But why would he beat you?"

"You've never been in a workhouse?" he said. "Count your blessings."

Chapter Nine

He asked it so calmly. Meridee dabbed at her eyes and looked him square in his. "I begin to understand what you mean by a curse," she said.

She thought he might deflect her comment, but he nodded. "It's a curse not to be like everyone else. I learned to keep my mouth closed. The teacher ignored me after that and put me in the back of the room, where I couldn't see over the taller pupils."

"In your case, it didn't make any difference where you sat," she said.

"Not at all. Since I could read, all I had to do was find books somewhere, anywhere."

"No, I've never been in a workhouse," she said. "You're saying they didn't want the challenge of a child out of the ordinary."

"I am. The workhouses take what the cities and towns disgorge and turn little ones who are not at fault for their birth into dumb animals. I sat in the back of that classroom for three years," he said, still holding her hand as if he sought reassurance like the child he was then. "There was a row of old books behind me. I took one at the beginning of each classroom purgatory and read it five or six times. The teacher couldn't see me. I got sly and clever and started stealing books to read overnight."

"Bravo, Master Six," she whispered.

He startled her by taking her hand to his lips and kissing it. "When do I become just Able again, Miss Bonfort?"

"Right now, Able," she assured him, wondering how the top of the stairs in December could suddenly feel so warm.

She was grateful down to her still-cold toes that Able chose not to question her. She was having a difficult enough time trying to figure out this tumult of emotions that had showered over her ever since the man's recent arrival. Meridee had learned after her mother died that some hopeful doors of escape from the spinster life had been quietly closed to her.

The most glaring failure was a lack of dowry. A respectable man had the prospect of some compensation upon marriage into a genteel family. Genteel though her parents may have been, Papa was not a man prudent with finances. Three modest dowries for the oldest daughters had seen them married well enough, but that was all. The short end of that financial stick had seen her two undowered sisters marrying down a bit. Mama's passing had closed even that door for Meridee, the youngest, who suddenly had no home.

She couldn't fault Amanda for gently insisting that she come to live in the little country rectory, and her oldest sister did need her services. At the time, incarceration in the country after life in Exeter seemed ample payment for a roof over her head, and she knew she was biddable. She had been happy to furnish childcare for her fertile sister until this strange man arrived to teach her nephews for ten shillings a month. But Able needn't know all that. He was even poorer than she was.

Her toes were not getting warmer, even though her face and neck still felt on fire. "Able, I'm going to bed before my feet freeze," she said frankly, then couldn't help another question because she didn't want to leave his side. "Why in the world couldn't your teacher just have taught, instead of bullying children into additional fear they didn't deserve?"

"We were beaten and starved for questioning anything. Apparently, some people, when given a little power, use it most unwisely to wound others," he said promptly, which suggested to Meridee that he had given the matter considerable thought. *Of course he had*, she chided herself. *What does this kind genius do but think?*

Cold toes aside, Meridee couldn't leave. "I've seen how good you are with my nephews. Even Gerald seems to be learning. Did you know you had this teaching skill?"

"Not really," he said with a deprecating laugh. She felt his shoulders shake in more silent laughter. "Imagine what I am capable of."

"Able, you astound me," she said as she stood up. "You need to be a teacher of young children."

He rose, too. "Tell that to the Royal Navy. A man can't quit the service in times of war."

"But we're at peace," she protested.

"And the Admiralty grudges me half-pay as a reminder that I am still a sailing master."

"Maybe some things need to change," she told him, even as she knew this amazing, intelligent man would be gone at the end of December, when her brother-in-law had no more need of his services.

"Let me know if you see a solution to my current dilemma," he said, and then he kissed her.

It wasn't her first kiss. Pretty women do find occasional opportunity, and hers had been the brother of the man who married her just-older sister: one quick peck on the cheek, and then another on the lips before he laughed and darted away.

This was different. She was being kissed by a man who probably had some experience, and there they were, balanced on the staircase. His hand went to her throat to steady her. He leaned her against the banister for balance and kissed her several times—each kiss more successful, because Meridee, though not a prodigy, was a quick learner.

This can go nowhere, she reminded herself when he released her neck and stepped up to the next tread.

"I think that was more fun than is legally allowed in the country," he whispered, then kissed her forehead. "Good night, good woman."

She didn't sleep at all, but spent the night wrapped in a blanket in her window seat, staring out at the undulation of the Devonshire moors. Able was right about mornings in the country: the winter birds did scream rather too loud. About the time she heard the maid of all work tapping on the door to start a modest fire in her grate, she knew her comfortable, quiet, unchallenging life in the country was never going to feel anything but stultifying ever again. When Master Able Six returned to Plymouth and war inevitably began again—she did not doubt his comments on that eventuality—she would spend her increasingly void life wondering whatever became of the man who went back to sea.

Tears came finally when she knew she was doomed to scour every account of battles at sea from now on and wonder if he even still lived. She would wither and die with each piece of vague news until she truly became a dried out woman with no hope. Such a personally disastrous course had come about because she had fallen in love with the most unacceptable human being on the planet, a man so low in birth and fortune that her sister and brother-in-law would never for one second entertain him as a suitable match.

If there was a more discouraged and saddened woman anywhere in the world, Meridee Bonfort had no idea who it could be. And if a woman ever needed to hide such knowledge, she knew precisely who that was, too. The idea of pasting a smiling face on her countenance until the end of December seemed impossible; she could not consider that same face for a lifetime. Not yet, anyway—misery needed to be added upon gently, a stroke at a time, to become bearable.

She pasted on that pleasant face and started another day. She nodded to Able in the breakfast room and teased her nephews about making more Christmas angles, which meant she had to explain that to her brother-in-law. She found pleasure in the way his face lit up when Gerald raced away and returned with his Christmas angel with scalene wings.

"You, sir, are a remarkable teacher," Mr. Ripley said to Able over a cup of tea.

"I enjoy it," was the master's simple reply. "Didn't know I would, but I do."

Soon enough, he led his little charges down the hall to the classroom, and another day began. Meridee knew better than to look in the mirror, because that pasted on face had started to slip the moment Able left the room with her nephews. She wiped jam off her littlest niece's hands and lifted her from her chair, holding her close to enjoy the pleasure of a little one. The knowledge she was unlikely to have little ones of her own had never troubled her overmuch before, but it did now.

Still, to everyone except her, this was just another day. She took her other little niece by the hand and started down the hall to the nursery, where they would play and she could stew in peace and quiet.

She had been agitated before by small aggravations, the kind that came with daily living. This was different. She set her little charges down on the floor and sat with them. She emptied a box of blocks and starting stacking them for the girls to knock down.

Ordinarily, the fun of watching her nieces could jolly her out of any black mood. Not today—not when she knew that her life would only go downhill to the eventual sterile grave if she did not exert herself to at least try. But where to begin? She had no idea.

Grateful for any diversion, she looked up with relief when someone tapped on the open nursery door, then sighed inwardly to see her sister. She felt a shiver of fear dart down her back, because Amanda looked grim. *We were too loud on the stairs last night*, she thought in misery, as her phony expression slipped away entirely.

"May I join you?" Amanda Ripley said as she sat down on a stool beside Meridee. "I don't think I can manage the floor, but you understand."

Miserable, Meridee folded her hands in her lap and waited for the ax to fall. She hadn't long to wait.

"I don't sleep well because I am so uncomfortable, sister," Amanda said, choosing her words carefully.

Meridee said nothing, which made Amanda sigh.

"I heard you and Master Six talking and laughing at the top of the stairs," she said, handing back a block that her daughter handed to her. "Meridee, I don't know what to think. What is going on?"

Why should such a simple question be so hard to answer? Better to tell Amanda Ripley about the amazing man who was teaching her children. She started slowly, picking her own way through words, then warmed to her subject, because that was her generous nature. While the little ones played, oblivious, Meridee described Able's early life in the workhouse.

When Meridee dared to look into her sister's eyes, she saw only kindness there, accompanied by wistfulness.

"He should be teaching disadvantaged children," Meridee said and wiped tears off her cheek. "He deserves so much more." She took a deep breath. "How is it fair for life to be so hard for one so clever?"

Amanda looked down at her lap, then she looked into

Meridee's eyes. "It is unfair for you to be exiled to the country with no chance, really, to meet eligible men."

"What good will it do me when I have no marriage portion?" Meridee asked, genuinely dismayed to hear her sister's regret. "I am talking of Master Six here."

"And you love him," Amanda said calmly. "I am not a fool, either."

Chapter Ten

Meridee closed her eyes and rested her head against Amanda's knee. Her sister's hand went to her head and rested there as gently as a benediction.

"I didn't think I was wrong. Are you prepared to do something about Master Six?" Amanda asked.

"If I knew what to do," Meridee said, happy to turn some portion of her despair over to someone else. "I . . . I've thought about writing to our Uncle Bonfort in Portsmouth. Perhaps he has some influence. And there is Captain Hallowell, Able's former captain on the *Swiftsure*. I don't know of anyone else. I don't know what to do, sister, but don't tell me not to try."

"I won't," Amanda said, her serenity taking some of the pain from Meridee's heart. "What I will do is this: you are going to Portsmouth to visit Uncle Bonfort."

"I can't. You need me," Meridee said, which earned her a flick of a finger to her head, the same punishment Amanda meted out to her boys.

"You will lay this out before our uncle and ask for help," Amanda continued, as if Meridee had not spoken. "You will find out where this Captain Hallowell lives and visit him, too. Surely the navy can do without one sailing master."

"I don't think it's that easy," Meridee said.

"You will never know if you do not try," her eldest sister told her firmly. "Pack. Edmund will drive you to Plymouth to catch the mail coach. I wish we could afford a post chaise, but we cannot. I will let you have ten pounds for mail coaches, and such incidentals as you need for travel. I wrote a letter to Uncle Bonfort yesterday, so he will be expecting you."

"You did *what*? *Yesterday?*"

"You heard me."

"But, but, you cannot spare ten pounds," Meridee said.

"Before she died, our mother gave me twenty pounds to give to you, should you ever find someone suitable to marry and need a wardrobe and some money to set up housekeeping," Amanda said, calmly and quietly as she said everything, but with a relentless tone to her voice that told Meridee she didn't really know this older sister as well as she thought. "Master Able is eminently unsuitable, except that you love him and he appears to be smitten, as well."

"Are we that obvious?" Meridee asked.

"Completely. Even Edmund is wondering when you two will elope or do something equally improper."

"Good heavens."

"My thoughts precisely, Meridee," Amanda said. "When you send Master Six outside this afternoon to walk with your nephews, go along and tell him I am sending you to Portsmouth to visit your uncle."

"I have never traveled alone, sister." *Who is this person whining?* Meridee thought, wondering if she had any courage at all. "Besides, Able will think I am meddling in his affairs."

"You are! He needs a meddler!" Amanda retorted. "You're twenty-five, a spinster, and perfectly respectable," Amanda reminded her. "Tell Uncle Bonfort you need his advice."

"Sister, am I up to this?"

Amanda kissed her cheek. "Not for you the ordinary fellow, apparently. I should tell you: as we speak, my estimable husband is talking to Master Six. I think you will have a proposal soon."

"Speak of meddlers!" Meridee hugged her sister. She sniffed back tears because she hadn't time for them. She sat up, alert, when she heard firm footsteps coming down the hall.

Amanda's hearing was equally acute. She held out her hands to her daughters and informed them they were to come with her now. Meridee watched in wide-eyed amazement as these headstrong little females who occasionally butted heads with her did exactly as their mother said. She stood up, wanting to be on her feet when Master Six came into the nursery.

"Beg pardon, ma'am," Able said as he stood aside for Amanda and her little ones to pass.

"Close the door behind you, Master Six," her thoughtful sister said.

He did as instructed, then crossed the small room in two strides and grabbed Meridee around the waist. "I have been informed by the vicar who holds the living in this parish that I had better propose, as he is calling banns on Sunday."

Meridee put her hands to his chest, but she didn't push hard. "Don't do anything you don't want to do."

"You're quizzing me," he said, his eyes so intense.

She looked right into those amazing eyes of his, those windows to a brain so astonishing she would never be able to keep up with it—no one could. She thought about taking herself bravely to Portsmouth to plead his case for what, she wasn't even certain.

"I would never quiz you about loving me," she said, "but I cannot even fathom a more unlikely couple than we will make. I cannot begin to match you for brains, Able."

He laughed at that and pulled her closer. "No one can, Meridee Bonfort, but what is that to me? You have enough heart for both of us. My captain was right, however: I need a keeper."

"Do you? Propose to me."

He took her face so gently between his hands. "Here it comes. Miss Bonfort, I was found as a baby, naked and an orphan, on a church step and have not a single thing to recommend me. I have no money, no employment, and no prospects if war doesn't resume. If it does, I'll be at sea continuously and only show up now and then, provided I stay alive. Hush now." He held up his hand. "Or you'll find a way to keep me inshore and teaching children."

She touched his upraised hand and pulled it back to her cheek. "All you have done is list reasons why you are supremely unsuited. Here are my reasons: *I* have no dowry or money, either. Socially, we could not be farther away from each other." She stopped. "I can't think of any other reasons."

"Your list is shorter than mine, by far." He released her, then pulled her closer. "Here is what I do have: great love for you, plus respect and admiration."

Meridee found it distressingly easy to press against his back and haul him closer. Mama would have been scandalized, but she doubted Amanda Ripley would be. "That's precisely what I have, too."

"Meridee Bonfort, will you marry me?"

"I thought you would never ask. After all, it's been all of two weeks."

He laughed, started to kiss her, but broke it off when they were nearly lip to lip. "But is that a yea or nay?"

"You exasperate me. It's yea."

It all sounded so simple in the nursery. At noon, Meridee stammered her way through luncheon like an idiot, then just closed her mouth and listened to her nephews tell their father and mother about their adventures with fractions. Able Six looked on, beaming at his pupils, then gave her a slow wink.

"I'm going walking, too," she announced and had not the courage to look at her sister.

"We're taking Master Six to our favorite view of the moors," Gerald announced.

She walked beside the sailing master, pleased when he twined his fingers through hers. When she told him she was leaving for Portsmouth in the morning to speak to her Uncle Bonfort, he tightened his grip.

"Do this: ask your uncle if he knows anything about Trinity House."

"I don't even know what that is," she said, then had the good sense to smile at herself. "Master Six, there is far too much you will tell me that I will not have a clue about."

"Less than you think, Miss Bonfort," he said. "Trinity House manages all lighthouses in our realm and teaches navigation to seamen, among other things." He held up their twined hands while the boys skipped ahead. "My background will never open that particular door for me, although I wish it could. Maybe in another age." He kissed her fingers. "I have heard rumors that Trinity House also runs a school somewhere for the children of dead seamen. These are children with nothing in their favor—my kind of children."

Suddenly, the day didn't seem so gloomy. "I can ask my uncle about that. Tell me, where does your Captain Hallowell live?"

"In Portsmouth. I have his direction."

"Send him a letter this afternoon and tell him I am coming to see him, too. Can he help us?"

"Flash your beautiful smile at him, Meridee. Bat your eyes, tell him you've elected yourself my keeper."

She stopped and put her hands on his shoulders. "This is the world's strangest courtship, you realize."

"It's going to get stranger. If you are really lucky and if the sun is shining when you return, I'll show you and your nephews how to use a sextant."

Chapter Eleven

In this and so many other ways, Amanda Ripley was right. Meridee had no difficulty negotiating the mail coach from Plymouth to Portsmouth.

Able insisted on coming along with her brother-in-law to Plymouth as they took the modest family carriage to the inn where the mail coach waited. Since her nephews refused to be left behind, too, she watched Able go over fractions during the ten-mile drive. She saw Gerald's eyes light up when he got a correct answer and delighted in the way Gerald's father beamed at this slightly slower son of his, who was being brought along so patiently by a master teacher.

Holding tight to Able's hand, she decided on the drive that although his full name might be Durable, it could just as easily have been Capable or Reliable or Estimable. At times, if their lives were allowed to intertwine, she imagined Able Six also being Unfathomable but not Inflexible.

The sailing master touched her heart by his determination to see her well-seated on the mail coach.

"When you get to Portsmouth, speak for one of the jarveys about the inn to drive you to your uncle's house." He leaned closer, reluctant to be overheard. "If nothing happens, then nothing happens, and I will go to sea again when war returns. We may have to wait a while."

She knew he was right. She tried not to cry, but she felt the heaviness of tears in back of her eyelids. She willed the pesky things to remain in place and not slide down her cheeks. She was nearly successful. He patted her hand, unable to speak himself, then closed the door.

Meridee leaned back and found herself looking into other kindly eyes belonging to a woman long in years.

"Dearie, he's a handsome one," the woman said.

Meridee smiled through her tears. "Yes, he is."

"Where did you find him?"

"He came to teach my nephews," she replied, wondering about conversations on the mail coach. She could be silent and say nothing more because she was a lady of quality. She could also chat and find out about the ordinary folk who were probably going to be more a part of her life than people of quality, if she was lucky enough to marry Able Six.

She decided to chat, and the time passed quickly, with brief stops in Exeter, Dorcester, Bournemouth, and Southampton to change horses. The woman bid her good evening in Southampton and wished her luck with her handsome sailing master.

Night came early. Meridee was content to sit in the gathering dusk and think about what lay ahead as the coach made the final distance to Portsmouth. Able had tucked a letter for Captain Hallowell into her hand. She took it out of her reticule and nearly read it because he said she could. She didn't; she felt too shy to read a missive between two men, neither a relative.

There was so much she did not know about men or the sea, or any part of Able's hard world. Living as she did in the country, and certainly not permitted to read a newspaper because she was a woman, war had always been something vexatious but remote. As the coach bowled into Portsmouth, that Royal Navy base far larger than Plymouth, she stared at ship after ship at the numerous docks, each warship capable of carrying husbands and fathers and sons to death and destruction, all because a Corsican upstart thought he should rule the world.

"We are hinged, wooden creatures in the hands of a puppeteer who makes us dance to his tune," she whispered softly into the glass, fogging it over. "We must do as he dictates."

So it was that Meridee Bonfort, a woman now most serious, left behind her youth and childhood in the mail coach and knocked on her Uncle Bonfort's door, determined to do her best to help one hinged, wooden creature. Two, actually.

After the usual pleasantries over dinner—answers to queries about Amanda's family and the news of her other sisters—Meridee spent another hour in her uncle's book room, where the talk turned serious. She told Uncle Bonfort about Sailing Master Able Six, his peculiar genius, and his unmatched ability to teach. He chuckled over the Christmas angles Gerald and James had drawn especially for him. The angels' wings now included the proper degrees for each angle drawn small, which made Uncle Bonfort nod and comment, "Scrupulous about his angles is your lad, Meri."

Finally, he folded his hands on his desk and asked, "What is it that I can do for this interesting young man of yours?"

"Use your influence within the Royal Navy to find him a place to teach," she said promptly. "He mentioned Trinity House."

"Alas, that august group of Elder Brothers is not directly affiliated with the Royal Navy, where I do own some influence," her uncle said with considerable regret in his eyes and his tone of voice. He leaned back in his chair and folded his hands across a well-fed paunch. "I do know one or two of the Brothers. I'll send a note 'round first thing. Will that do?"

"It will help," Meridee said. "Master Six is a good man with no patronage or influence whatsoever."

She knew the interview was over when her uncle began to speak with fondness about her late father. He then expressed some regret that he could not have done more for her and her sisters. "War times are hard times," he said, as he ushered her from his book room and handed her off to his housekeeper, then closed the door.

She tried not to cry once she was alone, but she couldn't help herself. Uncle Bonfort was polite and kind, but that was all. She suspected he thought Able Six unsuitable as a husband and probably would not write any such letters.

Sad beyond belief, she dutifully knelt beside her bed, offering her whole heart to the Lord, even if He might not approve of Master Six, either. Finally, there weren't any words, only a silent plea to the Almighty that if some path could be smoothed for an extraordinary man, she would be a willing, loving, and efficient keeper.

She breakfasted with Uncle Bonfort, delighted when he showed her the letters he had written to two men known as Elder Brothers, who lived in London and worked for Trinity House, doing what, she did not know. She thanked him prettily.

He was kind enough to let her take his coach around to 63 Water Street, the address of Captain Hallowell, he of the White Fleet who was also cast ashore on half pay, hardly an onerous situation, in his case.

"Hang it, I'll accompany you myself," Uncle Bonfort told her as he was about to close the door and send her on her solitary way. "Move over, Meridee. Let's go see a captain of the Royal Navy."

The drive was a short one, to her dismay, because Meridee Bonfort did not know what to say to Able's captain of the *Swiftsure*, who had lost his ship and also served some time in that French prison before he was repatriated. She looked out the window at the bustle of Portsmouth, noisy even with the Peace of Amiens in force. She was far removed from her small world in the countryside and felt it acutely.

She and Uncle Bonfort arrived at the grand home at 63 Water Street of Captain Benjamin Hallowell, Massachusetts born and bred, but a victim of the American Revolution. Able had told her that much and more of his captain's audacious courage at the Battle of the Nile, which had earned him a place in Rear Admiral Sir Horatio Nelson's aptly named Band of Brothers.

"Does this man have any influence?" she asked her Uncle Bonfort as they stood together on the front steps.

"Possibly a great deal of influence," he replied, then nodded to the footman who opened the door. "I am Aloysius Bonfort, quartermaster of victualling in Portsmouth Harbor," he said. "We would speak with Captain Hallowell. My card."

Chapter Twelve

The footman, a supercilious tadpole, made them stand there a moment longer than necessary, which was sufficient time for Meridee's heart to plunge into her stomach, teeter there, and descend to her toes. *Dear me, we cannot even command the respect of a footman*, she thought.

Now or never. "And I am Miss Meridee Bonfort, lately from the country," she said, then felt like an idiot.

The footman's lips twitched at that, but he let them in and left them standing in the foyer, to the amusement of Meridee's uncle.

"He didn't even show us to the drawing room. What a pup," he whispered. "He is toying with the man who victuals ships of the fleet and a young lady who probably has more influence than I do."

"I doubt that supremely," she whispered back, then gulped as a much-chastened footman returned, followed immediately by Captain Hallowell himself.

She found herself looking at a balding man with a long,

sharp nose, intense eyes, and an expression announcing that the man had never suffered a fool gladly in his entire life. She swallowed and looked again, noticing that his eyes were on her now, and that expression softened. *Oh, please*, she thought. *Please help us.*

The captain bowed to her, and she curtsied as prettily as she could. He bowed next to Uncle Bonfort, then extended his hand.

"Kindly excuse the poor manners of my footman," Captain Hallowell said. "He's new and doesn't know what distinguished guests are, apparently." A frosty look at the footman made the man wilt before Meridee's eyes. "He will improve, or by the mark, I will impress him. Come with me."

Terrified and determined not to show it, Meridee grabbed her uncle's hand and hung on as they walked past a drawing room and into a room with a desk and comfortable chairs. Ignoring the desk, Captain Hallowell seated them in the chairs and joined them in front of the desk.

He was not a man for small talk. He reached behind him and picked up a letter. "Miss Bonfort, I received a letter early this morning from my sailing master, Able Six. For Master Six, it is a remarkably jumbled letter. If I didn't know better, I would suspect he has taken leave of his senses." He leaned forward and smiled. "But I know better, my dear."

Meridee felt herself relaxing. She willed her hands to stop shaking and pulled the note from her reticule that Able had handed to her only yesterday. "He wanted me to give this to you, sir."

He took it, opened it, laughed quietly, and handed it to her. "Read it, my dear. Read it aloud."

She took it, read it, blushed, and shook her head.

"No, no, I insist," the captain said, his expression suggesting huge enjoyment.

Meridee glanced at her uncle, who nodded. "Do what the good captain says, niece."

She cleared her throat. "'Dear Captain Hallowell,'" she began, in a voice not sounding remotely like the one ordinarily possessing her body. "'Here is my keeper. She is lovely and kind and intelligent. Please help us. I know of no one else who can. Yours sincerely, Able Six.' Sir, I . . .'"

"In a moment, my dear." He held up his hand and spoke to Uncle Bonfort. "I am delighted to make *your* acquaintance, sir, and can only echo the praise of other captains who appreciate the orderly way you run the victualling department. Between the two of us, what say you that we help this couple?"

Uncle Bonfort nodded. "Whatever I can do, sir. I must ask: why? Why would you help a good sailing master *out* of his position?"

"He is the single most brilliant man I have ever met in my life, but that counts for nothing, really," Hallowell replied. "He did me a singular service for which I can never totally repay him." He tapped Able's letter. "He has never asked me for a favor before."

Singular service? "I don't quite understand," she said.

"He's a sly one, is Master Six," Captain Hallowell said. "Did he mention my presence in the sick bay of the *HMS Captain* during the Battle of Cape St. Vincent?"

"He did," Meridee replied, on unsure ground.

"Well, we weren't even in the sick bay. That spot took

a direct hit and the surgeon died. We were in the stairwell of the orlop deck, dead and dying men all around."

Meridee nodded. "He said you were there."

"That's all? I am hardly surprised," the captain said. "For all his astounding intelligence, I think part of Durable Six is still that little boy in the Dumfries workhouse, unsure of himself and unable to comprehend what was happening to him." He leaned forward and gave Meridee a direct, searching look. "Which is why he needs a keeper."

She blushed some more. "What happened in the stairwell?" she asked.

Captain Hallowell directed his attention to Uncle Bonfort, who looked puzzled. "Able Six was a loblolly boy then, hardly an exalted position. After the surgeon died and the pharmacist mate seemed too paralyzed to act, Able rolled up his sleeves and calmly took over."

"Impossible!" Uncle Bonfort sputtered.

"In an ordinary man, I would agree. Able Six is not an ordinary man," Hallowell said. He turned his attention to Meridee again. "What he did was save my son's life."

"He would do that," she said softly. "He never told me."

"Cape St. Vincent was my son Charles's first voyage as a Young Gentleman. His leg was mangled by a chain shot fired from the *San Nicolás*. Able removed that portion of his leg below the knee as calmly as if he had done thousands of such amputations. My son is alive today and still active in the fleet, thanks to your man. What is it I can do for him? Just name it."

"Wait a minute!" Uncle Bonfort demanded. "He amputated a leg?"

"Several, in fact," Captain Hallowell said calmly. "The man is a prodigy. He sees something once or reads it once, and he never forgets. Never."

Uncle Bonfort gave Meridee his own chastened look. "You told me all this last night, and I did not believe you, my dear."

"It is hard to believe," she agreed.

"Come, come! Time is wasting! How can I help my sailing master?"

"He has an amazing facility to teach young children," Meridee said quickly. "He has been tutoring my nephews, one of whom is slow, where his younger brother is quick. Gerald loves arithmetic now, and James is still enthusiastic, because Able—I mean, Master Six—brings him along quicker without injuring Gerald's feelings."

"He would appreciate the worth of a little boy, I imagine," Captain Hallowell said, more to himself than to her, or so it seemed. "How can I help?"

"Captain, can you possibly find him a place to teach math and geometry and navigational reckoning to young students?" she asked.

Captain Hallowell rose and went to the window, where he stood a moment, hands behind his back, rocking on his heels. Meridee's heart, which had been slowly climbing back up to its rightful position, took another dive.

"Please, Captain," she whispered. "Please."

"I need him more than you do," Captain Hallowell said, still not facing her.

"No, you don't," Meridee declared, tossing away a lifetime of quietly doing the bidding of others. It was her turn. She went to the window, too, taking the august man's arm and tugging him around to face her. She gathered all her courage together and shook him. "You couldn't possibly need him more."

"My dear, we will soon be at war again," Captain Hallowell said gently as he took her hand from his sleeve. "Why would I willingly relinquish the services of the finest sailing master the Royal Navy will probably ever see?"

"Because you owe your son's life to him, and he has begged a favor," she said, her voice controlled and quiet. Shouting at this man would never do.

"My dear, what you ask is impossible," the captain replied. "I should never have said I would do anything for him, because I cannot. Duty forbids it."

What could she do but admit failure? The room was silent except for a ticking clock. She looked at Uncle Bonfort and saw sympathy on his face. She looked at Captain Hallowell and saw the same. All she wanted to do was go back to the country where she could continue hiding from the world. She would wither and die there because there was a man in the world who needed her and she could not help him.

"I believe I will leave now," she said. "I have squandered everyone's valuable time."

She left the room with no fanfare, resisting the urge to run. The front door looked miles away, but she minded her steps and retained her dignity. Just a few more steps, and she would be out on the street again. She had relinquished her coat to the footman, but he could keep the thing.

She stopped and felt an enormous anger building inside

her—so massive it frightened her. Was she going to be brave or not?

"Master Six has never asked me for anything before."

She stood there in the foyer, unwilling to turn around. "You have already said no, Captain," she reminded the dratted man. "I will . . . I will think of something else because I intend to succeed. Good day."

"There will soon be war again."

That was it. She rounded on the captain, her fists up, took two steps, and hit him in the face as hard as she could. It was no open slap, but her closed fist.

The pain to her knuckles was immediate, but she pulled back to hit him again.

"That's enough!" Captain Hallowell exclaimed as he grabbed her hand. "Look now, you've bloodied your knuckles. Calm down, my dear, calm down! I think I am about to change my mind."

Meridee gasped and burst into tears. She stood there, her knuckles bloody and Captain Hallowell holding her hand so gently now. In fact, his arm went around her shoulder, and before she knew it, she was sobbing into his shirt. "I love him, and he needs a keeper."

"If ever a man had a champion . . ." he said and smoothed down her hair. "Miss Bonfort, I will do everything in my power to help. I know just the place for your man, and it hasn't anything to do with Trinity House."

"Something better?" she asked, too shy to look at him.

"Aye, Miss Bonfort, although a bit of a secret." He chuckled. "Can I trust you?"

"I can keep a secret," she said as she crossed her heart.

He pulled out his handkerchief, handed it to her, and commanded her to blow her nose. She did as he said, then pressed the cloth to her knuckles. She made the mistake of looking at Captain Hallowell then and gasped to see his eye swelling shut.

"I didn't mean it!" she exclaimed.

"I believe you did, my dear," he contradicted. "I deserved it, too, after the enormity of what your man did for me. Come now. Let's find my wife, who will shed her own tears when I tell her what happened and probably scold me later. We can find some salve for your knuckles." He chuckled. "And maybe a beefsteak for my eye. Mr. Bonfort, had you any idea what a ferocious terror you have for a niece?"

"Not at all," her uncle said to her dismay. Meridee also thought she heard a little pride in his voice. "She was always the most biddable girl, perhaps biddable to a fault. This is a new Meridee, and I like her even more."

"Obviously, she has never been in love before," Captain Hallowell said, as he steered her toward the back of the house and told the dumbfounded footman who had witnessed the whole thing to find Mrs. Hallowell, and quickly.

"There is one more way I can assist you and that sailing master of mine, who has no business wasting his prodigious talents on a mere quarterdeck," the captain said.

Meridee blew her nose again. "Oh, anything, sir. I owe you such an apology, too."

"You owe me nothing," he said. "I had a massive debt to discharge, and you . . . er, reminded me." He stopped walking and put his hands on her shoulders. "My dear, we have an ace up our sleeve by the name of Vice Admiral Sir Horatio Nelson. I intend to call in a favor of *mine*."

"You can do that?" she asked, astounded. Everyone in England was familiar with Sir Horatio.

"I happen to be a member of an august informal little group called Nelson's Band of Brothers," he said. "I earned that title at Aboukir Bay, by damn! A letter from me would be well and good, but when the masters of St. Brendan's hear from Nelson himself . . ." Hallowell chortled and rubbed his hands together. "Tell me, my dear, do you have any objection to setting up housekeeping right here in crowded, noisy, infamous Portsmouth?"

Wide-eyed, she shook her head. "Anywhere Master Six is, is home to me."

He chucked her under her chin. "That is the right answer. Go home now, once we bandage your fingers, or better still, come with me to St. Brendan's."

Chapter Thirteen

I am too old for the fidgets, Able Six told himself as he walked outdoors with his star pupils.

Meridee Bonfort had been gone too long—never mind that it was only four days. The first day of her absence, he had dutifully walked with his pupils after luncheon, breathing great lungfuls of healthy air, before they returned to the schoolroom for more geometry, followed by more Christmas angles, which the vicar himself requested.

"Your angles will decorate the church this year," Edmund Ripley had said. "I like them. More to the point, the Lord Almighty probably enjoys a bit of variety in Christian worship."

The following day had been less sanguine, to put it mildly. Able had followed the vicar's instructions to the letter about finding holly and ivy, which he had already agreed to use to deck the church from vestibule to nave to sanctuary.

"Ordinarily, Mrs. Ripley and Meridee perform this office, but I fear my wife is not equal to the task of greening the church this year," Mr. Ripley said, by way of apology. The vicar could blush, too, even though Mrs. Ripley's condition was precisely of his making, which made Able Six smile to himself.

The holly had been aggravating enough, making his hands bleed, but the larger issue of the ivy had ended his career in decorating before it even started.

The ivy was easy enough to find, even though Mr. Ripley's directions were vague to the point of nonexistent. Able had turned the directions into an exercise involving angles and titled it "Treasure Map," which meant his pupils could barely wait to start.

To his pleasure, the boys quickly found great patches of ivy and called for him to hurry with his knife and basket. He had begun his attack on the ivy when the whole plan unraveled. His hands began to burn, then break out in welts and start to swell. He tried to fight through the pain, then gave it up for a bad business. The countryside had turned on him.

Gerald and James commiserated, but could barely control their delight to be permitted to use a real knife, something their parents wouldn't have allowed, or so they told him. He supervised and did his best not to scratch.

The vicar had been properly appalled at the sight of his injury, but Mrs. Ripley seemed to find the matter amusing. She calmly slathered a pleasant-smelling, white ointment on his hands, all the while assuring him that he would not die.

"You are not taking this seriously," Able accused her.

"I suppose I am not," she said, coating a few spots on his neck that were starting to itch, too. "How wondrous that a man can survive Camperdown, the Battle of Cape St. Vincent, the Battle of the Nile, subsequent incarceration in a French prison and escape from the same, be thrown ashore to starve on half pay, and then succumb to ivy!" Her lips started to twitch, and she laughed.

What could a man do but laugh, too? "I suppose you will tell me that Meridee would laugh, too, were she here?" he asked, trying to sound indignant and failing.

His question dissolved Mrs. Ripley in more laughter, accompanied by the assurance that Meridee would indeed see the humorous aspect of a well-trained, dignified, handsome man with welts, spots, and ointment. "She would howl," Mrs. Ripley assured him. "Probably slap her knee."

Mercifully, by the time he went to bed that night—oh, God above, how he missed his chaste conversations with Meridee on the stairs—the swelling had retreated and the pain was mostly gone. He lay there as the smile left his face, wondering how soon he could quit the countryside. Meridee deserved better than him. What was he thinking, proposing to someone like Meridee?

Next day, he wasn't so certain he could ever leave. By noon, the redness was gone and he could bend his fingers again, so the vicar enlisted his help in distributing baskets of jams, jellies, and fancy bread to the worthy poor of his parish.

That was how Mr. Ripley had phrased it: the worthy poor. A man with a mind far livelier than most, Able asked what constituted the *unworthy* poor. When the vicar started to explain that women who birthed babies in the hedgerows might constitute the unworthy poor, as well as poachers and wife beaters, he stopped, embarrassed.

"Perhaps these people need help, too," Mr. Ripley said after a long moment of what must have been theological reflection.

You mean my mother, Able thought and felt no shame. Whatever events had brought Mary Whoever to his birth and her death in that alley behind St. George's Church had resulted in a life Able Six knew was worth living.

"The poor are poor, and worth has nothing to do with it," Able said, perhaps more forcefully than he should have. "They have hopes and dreams, too. I know they do, because I am one of them."

Mr. Ripley had looked at him seriously, then did a strange thing, a thing that touched Able's heart. He kissed the sailing master on his cheek. "I believe you are right, Master Six," he said. "I will not use that phrase anymore. After all, Christ was no respecter of persons, was He? Why should my church, my little vicarage so minuscule in the scheme of things, pretend otherwise?"

They distributed baskets at every hovel, regardless of worthiness, and returned home in remarkable agreement. A note to his patron requesting more funds to tend to the Christmas needs of all had gone out that evening to the lord of the manor, who controlled Mr. Ripley's living.

"We may not succeed this year, Master Able, but we will try," Mr. Ripley had said.

Able slept poorly that night, as his nearly visceral longing for Meridee Bonfort showed no signs of abating. Tomorrow evening, there would be caroling, followed by wassail in the vicarage. Maybe Meridee would at least send a letter.

He tried to relax—truly he did—even as he wondered if such a quiet, self-effacing woman could find a way to help him navigate the shoals of disaster during this time of near-war and national emergency. Had he asked too much of such a lady?

He knew he alone could live in poverty on half pay until the war resumed, but he wanted more. He could not afford a wife, but he wanted Meridee Bonfort. He had no home for her, but he wanted her watching for him out of an upstairs window as he returned from the sea. He didn't even have a bed for a wife, but he wanted one, and he wanted Meridee Six in it with him.

How had he gone from having nothing except a prodigious brain to wanting everything? When had the universe ever shifted in his favor? He sat up suddenly, resolved to quit this quiet country vicarage tomorrow. He had been well-fed and warm for several weeks. He had read most of the vicar's books and contemplated Christmas, however briefly. If the Ripleys chose not to pay him for his highly enjoyable service to their sons, he would understand, because he had not stayed to complete his tenure. He had enough coins to eke out bare subsistence until he collected his next half-pay cheque.

He went to the landing and sat there in his smallclothes, supremely dissatisfied with himself. He never should have accepted Lieutenant Caldwell's kind offer of employment, because now he hoped, where previously he had merely endured. If there was anything more treacherous than hope, he did not know what it was, and he knew everything.

No matter how distressed he was deep inside, in that

intimate place where only Meridee had been allowed a glimpse, Able taught his pupils in the morning with his usual flair. He admired their ability with fractions, when only weeks ago they had quailed at the thought of mere multiplication tables. Even Gerald, the more timid brother, sat sprawled in his chair with a certain confidence he had earlier lacked.

Able would have fared better if people had not come and gone all day from the vicar's study. Each ring of the doorbell set his nerves spinning. More than once, he casually leaned out of the schoolroom door, hoping against hope to see a lovely lady with striking blue eyes. Christmas was coming, and he began to understand the vicar's added work as parishioners came and went.

Able nearly sent the boys on their own after-luncheon walk, except that the sun had finally broken through, and James reminded him of his promise to show them how to use a sextant. Well and good. He had promised, and he confessed to himself his own eagerness to take the beautiful instrument outside and shoot the sun. There was no danger he could forget how to use this complicated instrument, but he felt his heart rise to just hold the thing again.

In a landscape flat and featureless, Gerald found a small rise. Able put his eye to the telescope and settled his elbow into his side, the better to prevent—Ah, but wait, the ground did not pitch or yaw like a quarterdeck. He could stand there and hold his lovely sextant.

It didn't take long to get latitudinal and longitudinal readings, do the math in his head, and determine precisely at what degree and minute they stood. Gerald and James were suitably impressed, then clamored for their own turns, which he happily supplied. They measured distance from a tree, then the height of the tree itself, until everyone was satisfied.

"We can do this at night, too," he assured them as they ambled home. "We can measure the lunar distance between the moon and, say, Orion's belt."

"Do you ever get lost, Master Six?" James asked.

I am lost now, he thought. "No," he lied. "I can find anything."

Nearly anything, he decided after supper, as he prepared to accompany the vicar and his sons caroling. Mrs. Ripley had been kind enough to let him watch her play five carols on the pianoforte that afternoon. He memorized the simple tunes immediately, but shook his head when she stood up and indicated that he play them. He knew he could because he had observed her, but the fun was gone.

They left the vicarage after dark in a disorganized gaggle of young parishioners and a few doughty older ones who provided the leaven of excellent voices to complement the enthusiasm of young singers. Mrs. Ripley waved to them from the door. The entire household had been tantalized all afternoon with the fragrance of wassail and Christmas treats. When they returned, Able knew he would enjoy the treats as much as the young ones because it was all new to him, this Christmas business.

First stop was the manor at the edge of Pomfrey belonging to the vicar's patron, Lord Peter Randolph, Earl of Pomfrey. They sang, and the bolder children who had been given the keeping of the alms basket stepped forward.

The earl did not disappoint, tossing in a number of coins

and stepping back so his footman could hand out warm pasties. When Lord Randolph nodded good night to them all and the butler closed the door, the children gathered around the alms basket with oohs and ahhs, as their parents looked on indulgently.

They traveled through Pomfrey, singing and collecting more alms for the poor, worthy or otherwise, and eating whatever their listeners chose to provide. Pomfrey was only a middling prosperous village, but the people knew how to keep up appearances. Master Able Six fell farther and farther back because he wanted to watch the children with their parents.

None of you have any idea how lucky you are, he thought. He would leave tomorrow before Meridee Bonfort returned. She deserved more than he could ever provide her.

Finally, he stood still on the path, unwilling to take another step. To his surprise, it began to snow. To his greater surprise, someone who must have crept up quietly put her arm through his. He started, then felt his entire body relax, because Meridee Bonfort had returned.

He stared at her, wondering how she had got to Pomfrey. Hadn't Mrs. Ripley told her to take a room in Plymouth and send a note the next day so they could fetch her? Why was she here?

He wanted to ask all those questions, but she was standing on tiptoe now, her hands already cupping each side of his face, reminding him that he hadn't bothered to shave this morning.

"You know your beard is too heavy to skip a morning shave," she scolded in her gentle way. "You need a keeper, and I am she."

He grabbed her up and kissed her, even though he had promised himself fifteen seconds ago that he would be gone by morning. She kissed him back, making small noises in her throat. Or maybe he was doing that; he couldn't tell. He couldn't even decide whose heart was beating louder.

He set her down for a moment, and it was his turn to take her face in his hands. "Was it a fool's errand?" he asked.

"No, Master Six, it was not," she said, turning her face toward one of his palms to kiss it, and then the other. "I did not go to fail."

"What . . . what . . . ?" He didn't even know what to ask her.

"You will be teaching boys from the age of six to sixteen all manner of arithmetic, geometry, and something called calculus at St. Brendan's School right in Portsmouth," she said, then rested her head against his chest. "I gave Captain Hallowell a black eye and . . ."

He grabbed her shoulders. "You did *what*?"

"He trod on my last and final nerve," she said with considerable dignity. Able saw how tired she was, and it touched his heart. "I'll tell you later. I went to St. Brendan's with him."

The woman of his heart gave him a kind and patient look. "You were wrong, though. St. Brendan's has nothing to do with Trinity House."

"I was *wrong*?" he asked, wondering if he heard her right.

"Completely," she replied. "St. Brendan's is . . ."

He swung her around, his heart overflowing with relief so unexpected he could barely contain himself. "I was wrong!" He set her down and stared into her astounded face. "Don't you see? I was wrong! Meri, maybe I'm a little bit normal, too!"

Her expression changed to one of surpassing compassion as tears welled in her eyes. She put her arms around his neck and pulled him close. "Maybe you are, my love," she whispered. "Even you can make a mistake or two."

He held her close in vast relief. Loving Meridee Bonfort was still the most wonderful thing that had ever happened to him. Coupled with the reality that even he could get something wrong now and then set his crowded brain at ease, not to mention his heart.

His practical almost-wife took him in hand. "All this mooning is well and good, Master Six, but you must hurry back to the vicarage with me. I promised I wouldn't keep Captain Hallowell waiting."

"Great merciful saints above, he is *here*?"

"Captain and Mistress Hallowell are sitting in the parlor with my sister as we speak."

She tried to put him into motion by tugging on his hand, but he held firm. "Tell me what you know first. St. Brendan's?"

She looked around as if the woods held French spies and moved closer until she was inside his boat cloak with him, which didn't upset him in the least. "St. Brendan's is a new school, rather a secret, established only three years ago by the Royal Navy. The idea is to train young men and boys for sea service."

"They already do that at sea as Young Gentleman and then midshipmen," he said, still mystified.

"And when did an orphan lad or a boy from the docks ever become a midshipman?" she asked, still whispering to throw off any spies. "No, Master Six, these are dockside lads willing to learn navigation and other skills *before* they go to sea, to serve as you do now, as warranted officers someday, if they are good enough."

"My word," he said in amazement and started walking at a fast clip, dragging Meridee with him.

"Slow down! That's better," she replied, hurrying to keep up. "It stands to reason, Able. Someone high up in the government—no idea who—decided to fund such a venture. At least, that's what St. Brendan's master told me."

He stopped again. "You spoke to the master?" he asked.

Meridee nodded. He saw the pride on her face. "I was frightened to death, but I told them how well-suited you were for such a task. I even looked Sir Horatio Nelson in the eye and said yes, you were a remarkable sailing master, but only one man, and wouldn't the navy benefit by that one man teaching mathematics to a whole generation of sailing masters?" She lowered her gaze modestly. "He agreed."

"Meri, you astound me," he said. "Nelson himself. You pleaded my cause before the master of St. Brendan's and Nelson himself."

"I did," she said, and he heard her quiet pride, which soon yielded to the bubbling enthusiasm he already knew was essential to his future well-being. "Do you know, Admiral Horatio Nelson isn't a great deal taller than I am? He told me such a diverting story about putting a telescope to his blind eye at the Battle of Copenhagen so he wouldn't have to obey an order!"

"Meridee Bonfort, where did Sir Horatio enter this story? Start from the beginning," he insisted.

Her eyes filled with tears. "A very handsome man on half pay walked from Plymouth to the home of Lieutenant Caldwell just as I happened to be dropping off some tatting for the lieutenant's mother."

He held her close.

Chapter Fourteen

They were married three weeks later, after Able's own quick trip to Portsmouth and St. Brendan's with his captain to be tested and tried and pronounced supremely fit to instruct. The wedding took place the morning after the third and final bann was called and two days before a Christmas that almost was lost in the shuffle, even in a vicarage. Meridee wore a green wool dress with a fine bit of lace at the collar, a serviceable garment that her sister said would be warm enough for a place as chilly as Portsmouth. Amanda Ripley had cried and kissed them both, and cried some more.

Meridee's nephews, solemn now and sad they were parting, gave them a paper sheaf full of Christmas angles. "Use them in your classroom, Master Six," Gerald announced.

"I will, lads," Able replied, his emotions barely held in check. "Thank you both. Mariners are a superstitious lot. Angelic angles will bring us good luck."

No one in the world had ever looked as handsome as

Master Able Six in his plain uniform with his black curly hair, his brown eyes, and his ivory complexion—gifts from an unknown father. His improbable Scottish accent when he spoke his responses so firmly made some of the less informed members of the congregation chuckle quietly, but Meridee didn't care.

There wouldn't have been a ring if Captain Hallowell hadn't taken Able aside the very morning before the wedding and handed him a filigreed bit of gold acquired somewhere considerably east of Greenwich Mean Time. It fit her thumb, which made everyone smile. Able whispered a promise to have it resized as soon as he could afford such an extravagance.

And that was the end of Meridee Bonfort Six's years in the country—and Able's month there. They spent a tumultuous, nearly sleepless Christmas Eve at The Drake in Plymouth, day one of a two-night stay, courtesy of that same Captain Hallowell, whose black eye had faded until it was scarcely noticeable. Officially husband and wife now, they woke bleary-eyed on Christmas morning to the sound of church bells.

"That's more noisy than birds in the country," her husband muttered and attempted to bury his face in her hair.

"You don't care for country birds and you don't like church bells, you heathen," his official keeper scolded, but gently. "What will satisfy you?"

His answer ended in a shriek from Meridee and then a pleasant sort of silence.

Someone—perhaps the captain again—had seen to it that meals were delivered to their room. Meridee discovered that onions did not agree with Able, but generously overlooked the matter.

Able told her something else that second afternoon, something he assured her he had never divulged to anyone. "Who would believe me?" he asked her neck.

She listened with her whole heart as he hesitated and stumbled, but finally came out with it.

"I have an early memory, Mistress Six," he said. "Quite an early one."

"Say on, Master Six," she replied, settling herself in the crook of his arm.

"I remember being cold and even getting stiff," he said, his eyes closed and moving about until she put her hand over them. "I was crying." He was silent a long moment. "Will *you* even believe this?" he asked.

"You know I will," she whispered and took her hand away.

"I felt someone's hand on my stomach and then my head, which was wet. A woman said, 'Grá mo chroí.' The next thing I remember is an old man wrapping me in a brown coat and taking me inside a church."

"My word," Meridee said in simple, quiet astonishment. "My word."

"I didn't know what it meant, but I knew what I had heard," he told her hair this time. "When I was seven, a little lad from somewhere in the country came to the workhouse. He spoke only Gaelic, so I taught him English. When he knew enough, I asked him what Grá mo chroí meant."

She felt her husband's tears in her hair and held her breath.

"'Love of my heart,' he told me." Her husband took a deep breath and another. "Meridee, she loved me."

Thanks to a generous wedding gift from Uncle Bonfort, Able and Meridee Six traveled in comfort in a post chaise to Portsmouth and still had quite a lot of money left over to start housekeeping, because Meridee understood domestic arithmetic.

To her delight, the master of St. Brendan's School included a furnished house in the bargain, and something more, which came in the form of a letter to her specifically, offering her, Meridee Bonfort Six, the position of house mistress to the youngest students of St. Brendan's.

The official letter made her blush, containing as it did a not-so-formal paragraph stating she and Master Instructor Six could enjoy their new house and their new marriage for two weeks with no little boys about. "After such time," the letter concluded, "you will manage four young scholars to begin with."

Following their brief-enough journey from Plymouth, they stood before the door of the two-story stone house on St. Brendan's Way, Portsmouth. After a huge sigh, Able took out the key the headmaster had given to him. He unlocked the door, pocketed the key, picked up Meridee Six, and carried her across the threshold. He set her down, kissed her soundly, then went in search of a lamp, or at least a candle or two, because evening was coming fast.

Meridee stood by the door, feeling surprisingly shy, considering her previous excellent days of indoctrination as wife of a man she adored and always would. "I will be the best keeper a genius ever had," she said softly.

She looked around at a quiet knock on the door, a knock low down on the wood. Curious, she opened it and felt her heart turn over.

There stood a small boy dressed in what she already knew was the uniform of a student of St. Brendan's. Next to him stood an older child.

"Welcome to our home," she said and indicated they come inside.

They did. She thought of another little boy, bewildered and frightened at his strangeness in a place where a child had no hope, unless he found it within himself. "Your names, please?" she asked.

"Jamie McBride," the older boy announced. "I am in my third year." She heard the pride in his voice. "I will be at sea soon."

"And your name?" she asked the little one, kneeling down to be on his level.

"David Ten," he told her.

She couldn't help her sudden intake of breath, then felt a firm hand on her shoulder. Her husband helped her to her feet.

"Are you two our welcoming committee?" Able Six asked. "Classes start tomorrow, promptly at two bells in the forenoon watch."

David Ten nodded. "Will we learn great things, sir?"

"The greatest," her husband said.

David looked up at the boy beside him. Through a film of tears, Meridee saw the fear in the child's eyes.

"Jamie says no one is beaten at St. Brendan's if they don't have a right answer, and we all go to sea when we have learned a lot."

Meridee leaned back against her husband and felt his shudder. She took his hand and kissed it, because she was his keeper.

"No one is beaten at St. Brendan's," Master Six said. "Anything else, lads?"

"Nay, sir. He's new. That's all he needed to know," Jamie McBride said. He touched his finger to his forehead. "Tomorrow, then, Master Six?"

"Tomorrow and every day after, until you go to sea."

For the further adventures of Able Six and Meridee Bonfort, please check:
www.carlakellyauthor.com

About Carla Kelly

What to say about Carla? The old girl's been in the writing game for mumble-mumble years. She started out with short stories that got longer and longer until—poof!—one of them turned into a novel. (It wasn't quite that simple.) She still enjoys writing short stories, one of which is before you now. Carla writes for Harlequin Historical, Camel Press, and Cedar Fort. Her books are found in at least 14 languages.

Along the way, Carla's books and stories have earned a couple of Spur Awards from Western Writers of America for Short Fiction, a couple of Rita Awards from Romance Writers of America for Best Regency, and a couple of Whitney Awards. Carla lives in Idaho Falls, Idaho, and continues to write, because her gig is historical fiction, and that never gets old.

Follow Carla on Facebook: Carla Kelly

Carla's Website: www.CarlaKellyAuthor.com

The Perfect Christmas

By Jennifer Moore

Chapter One

"I propose a Christmas at Waverly House." Archibald Montague Clawson, Lord Symons, stood on the plush rug of the drawing room, letting his gaze travel over his companions as he awaited their reactions.

The room became silent as his four closest friends glanced at one another in confusion. The Marquess and Marchioness of Spencer—or as he called them, Jonathan and Maryann—stared at him from their spot on the sofa. The couple raised their brows in unison, a synchronized movement that made Archie grin.

Jonathan's mother, the dowager marchioness, whom the group referred to as Mother Kathleen, lowered her knitting into her lap and tipped her elegant head in question.

Miss Jane Croft, Maryann's younger sister, was the only person whose quizzical expression thrilled his heart. She turned toward him, her brows drawn together thoughtfully above her large eyes—eyes that, like her sister's, seemed nearly too big for her face. She gave a small smile, which bent the bow of her pink lips into a most lovely shape, and closed her book, setting it atop a pile of volumes on the window seat beside her.

Archie had noticed Jane always kept at least one book within reach. He knew they provided an escape when the memory of a childhood tragedy brought on anxiety and attacks of panic. Books were her comfort. A thrill moved through him as he thought about the ancient, leather-bound volume of Apuleius's *The Golden Donkey* he'd found at an Oxford bookseller's shop. The book sat on his desk wrapped in gold paper and tied with a red ribbon—the perfect gift. It was just one piece of his Grand Christmas Scheme. He intended to present it to Jane in front of the candlelit Christmas tree on Christmas Eve.

Aside from the crackling of the fire, the silence in the drawing room grew so heavy that Archie imagined even the Egyptian-style statues that sat tall on either side of the hearth were staring at him with curious feline looks.

Finally, Jonathan cleared his throat. "I thought we had plans to spend the holidays with your parents in Ashford."

Archie dipped his chin. "Well, yes, but I hoped to modify the arrangements a bit. As you remember, the Holiday Ball will take place in Ashford on Christmas Eve, and you know how lively the festivities will surely be. Mother does love a good party." He shifted his weight to his other foot. He still hadn't broached the subject with Lady Bromley; he wasn't certain how she'd react to the news of her only son spending Christmas away. But he was determined to do this.

"I imagined the four of you might enjoy a smaller,

quieter celebration at Waverly Manor. Just for a few days, of course. We will continue to Kensington House on Boxing Day."

Though he didn't say it directly, he knew the others understood his implication. The late marquess, Jonathan's father, had died only six months earlier, and the family was still in mourning. Mother Kathleen, especially, had been devastated by her husband's death. She undoubtedly would not attend a large party, and even if she did make an appearance, the memories of having attended the same gathering in previous years with her husband would prove difficult, Archie was certain. Though he hid it well, Jonathan missed his father dearly as well and was prone to bouts of gloom that lasted for days. Besides his concern for Jonathan and his mother, Archie believed Jane, with her shy nature, would be much more comfortable with a small group of close friends than a gathering of strangers.

"That is very thoughtful, Archie," Maryann said. She and her husband exchanged a look, and she slipped her hand into his. "But isn't Chiddingfold rather out of the way?"

Archie shrugged. He'd only made the journey to the small country estate he'd inherited with his title a few times, but didn't consider the distance to be significant. "A minor detour is all—a few hours, at most—and the ride through the forest is beautiful, especially if it snows."

At the mention of the word *forest*, the others glanced toward Jane—or pointedly kept their eyes from her direction. Archie knew they all worried about her mental condition and feared another attack of panic might result from traveling through the forest, as she had the night her mother died. In truth, he felt a bit nervous himself, but still considered Waverly to be the best setting for his Grand Christmas Scheme to play out.

"The manor is not *in* the forest," he said, looking specifically at Mother Kathleen and Maryann. They were the most protective of Jane. "Just near it. It's a lovely estate with a large park and competent staff. I feel it will be an enjoyable place to spend the holiday before we journey to Ashford."

Kathleen's expression moved from thoughtful to understanding. "I think Christmas at Waverly is just the thing." She nodded. "A quiet celebration surrounded by those I love most . . ." She took a deep breath and pressed her palm to her breastbone. "It sounds splendid. Thank you, Archie."

Seeing the gratitude on Mother Kathleen's face, Archie felt even more confident about his idea.

"But *you* will miss the ball." Jane spoke in her quiet voice, then blushed when the others turned toward her. "And all your family's celebrations."

Maryann nodded. "That is true, Archie. Perhaps you would like to go ahead to Kensington House, and we could join you after Christmas. You should not forgo Lady Bromley's festivities. I hear they are very fine, indeed."

"I would not enjoy one moment of it. Not without all of you. My mother, as you know, is famous for our family's Christmas celebrations, and I intend to live up to her legacy. I'd not dream of letting my friends suffer without my superb party planning." He winked. "I am resolved to make this Christmas special, memorable. A new beginning for the people I care about."

He felt Jonathan's searching gaze, but didn't meet his eyes. His oldest friend was no doubt wondering what had brought on this proposal. Archie smiled to himself. *Proposal* was exactly the word. If things turned out the way he planned, next winter, *he'd* be the one sitting on the sofa, holding his wife's hand. He glanced at Jane, and his heartbeat sped up at the softness in her expression. More than anything, he was doing this for her. To give her the perfect Christmas. A taste of the joy the holidays could bring. Something that he knew had been lacking in her life for the past years.

Jane smiled at Mother Kathleen, lifting her brows slightly. The older woman returned her smile. Jonathan and Maryann glanced at one another, their eyes alight.

Archie grinned, rubbing his hands together. "Now that we are all agreed, shall we start planning? We shall have a Christmas feast, of course: roast goose, boar's head, venison, mincemeat pie, stuffing, potatoes, squash, cider, pudding..." He allowed his voice to trail off and grinned. "The cook at Waverly is magnificent."

Archie felt the excitement building in the room, and it only fueled his own enthusiasm. "And since we are combining our three families together, I would like each of us to choose a favorite Christmas custom—something specific to your home or childhood, something meaningful to you." He looked at each of his companions in turn.

"I thought you said it would be simple," Jonathan grumbled.

"This is important, Ren." Archie fell back on his friend's childhood nickname. He held up his forefingers for emphasis. "If *I* plan everything, it becomes *my* celebration, but with each of us bringing a tradition of our own, Christmas belongs to each of us." He circled his hands to illustrate the point.

"A lovely idea," Kathleen said. "And I choose for my tradition: making wishes as we stir the Christmas pudding."

Archie shook his head. "We did that weeks ago. The tradition must be something specifically for our celebration at Waverly."

Kathleen lifted her chin and tapped a finger to her lips. "Very well. I should like to collect garlands of ivy and branches of holly to decorate the house on Christmas Eve."

"A very good choice." Archie nodded. "The Chiddingfold Forest is just right for gathering holiday greenery."

"And don't forget mistletoe," Jonathan said, raising the side of his mouth in a smirk.

"You of all people have no need for mistletoe," Archie said.

"Hmmm," Jonathan pulled down the sides of his mouth. "You're right. I do not need a silly plant's authorization to kiss my wife." He bent down his head and kissed Maryann soundly to prove his point.

Archie rolled his eyes. "Ren, your custom?"

His friend pulled away from his blushing wife, grinning. "Singing Christmas hymns, and, of course, there must be a merry fire in the hearth."

"Christmas hymns, yes. And merry fire." Archie pretended to write a note on his palm. "The main hall at Waverly has a very fine hearth and a pianoforte. Mother Kathleen, you will accompany our little choir?"

"Of course."

Maryann scooted forward on the sofa, her eyes bright. "Mother used to build a cradle from sticks on Christmas Eve and tell the story of the nativity. Do you remember, Jane?" Seeing her sister nod, she continued, "I should like to do that."

"An excellent custom." Archie nodded in approval. This was shaping up to be a fine holiday, indeed. Exactly right for what he had planned. "And that leaves Jane." He stepped closer, then sat on the window seat beside her, not wishing to loom above her.

"I'm sorry, I don't know. I will think of something." She looked up at him with a shy smile. "What is your custom, Archie?"

"A grand Christmas tree in the front hall."

Jane blinked and cocked her head to the side. "A tree? Like Princess Caroline's?"

"Archie's grandmother came from Prussia as a young bride," Jonathan said. "The tree is always central to their family's celebration."

"A tree in the house?" Maryann wrinkled her nose. "It sounds so strange."

"A tree? Did you call it a *tree*? I'm afraid you are quite mistaken, Lady Spencer." Archie shook his head, closing his eyes as if her words were too painful to endure. "*Eine Tannenbaum* is not merely a tree, but a beautiful fir pine with thick boughs. At Kensington House, it stretches up to the very top of the great hall, filling the house with an evergreen scent. The branches are decorated with lit tapers, glass ornaments, and strings of berries. It is, in truth, the loveliest thing you can imagine." In spite of himself, he felt a pang, thinking of how he would miss his mother's party.

"It sounds beautiful," Jane said. "Could the Christmas tree be my custom, too?"

"Certainly." Archie twisted to face her. "I cannot think of another person I would rather share the tradition with." He promised himself this tree would be the most spectacular Jane, or anyone else, had ever seen.

"Thank you." Jane's gentle smile returned and, along with it, the pink in her cheeks.

Archie's fingers itched to tap her chin and raise her enchanting eyes to meet his own, but in present company, such an intimate act was out of the question. Instead, he clasped her hand as he turned to address the room. "Then it is decided. I will make the arrangements, and in one week, we set off for the finest Christmas Waverly Manor has ever seen."

Two hours later, Archie accepted Jonathan's offered glass of brandy and settled back into the leather chair of the marquess's drawing room. He rested his feet on an ottoman with legs carved into the shape of cobras and smiled as he remembered Mother Kathleen describing the chamber as an eerie mummy's tomb. She had complained about the late earl's obsession with Egypt for years, but with how deeply she mourned his loss, Archie didn't think she'd change the decor anytime soon.

And he was glad for it. The room held memories of summers and school holidays spent with the marquess's family. He smiled, remembering how, as boys, he and Jonathan spent hours studying the papyrus paintings with their golden hieroglyphics and the carved images of Egyptian deities.

Since their parents had been close friends, it was only natural that he and Jonathan should grow up together, especially since both had only sisters. He glanced at his friend, feeling at ease simply sitting in a memorable place with a person who was as familiar as he imagined any brother would be.

"Do you remember when we dragged the stuffed crocodile outside to the gazebo to frighten your sisters?" Archie asked.

"One of our greatest triumphs." Jonathan leaned back, settling an ankle on his knee. "Sending an entire garden party screaming into the house." He shook his head, letting out a sigh. "Please don't bring that up around Mother. I still don't think she's forgiven us."

"She'd forgive you anything, my good sir," Archie said. "That woman quite adores her son."

"Mother has a soft heart—much like yours. Both of you have a gift of knowing the right words and understanding what to do to ease another's heartache. It is something I envy." He was quiet for a moment, then he lowered his foot, leaning forward to rest his elbows on his knees. "Archie, I should be taking care of this family, not depending on someone else to do it. It is nice of you to forgo your holiday plans out of concern for our comfort, but it is truly not necessary. In all your twenty-six years, you've never missed your mother's Christmas party. Neither have I, now that I think of it. And I cannot bear to think of disappointing your mother in this way."

"Do not concern yourself on that point. Mother will have plenty to occupy herself. She will hardly miss either of us. And truly, I want to do it." He found it difficult to meet his friend's gaze.

Jonathan squinted, regarding him. "Is there someone you wish to avoid in Ashford? I get the impression you have a higher objective than playing Father Christmas for a family in mourning."

Archie swallowed over a sudden dryness in his throat. In all their years of friendship, this was the first time he felt nervous anticipating Jonathan's reaction. "I do have another motive." He took a fortifying drink, then leaned forward, setting the empty glass on the low table between them. "I intend to propose marriage to Jane." There, he said it. "I hope you, as her guardian, will give your blessing."

Jonathan gave a slow blink. He opened his mouth, then closed it, blinking again.

Archie would normally have thought the bewildered reaction amusing, but the anxiety of the situation overcame any inclination toward humor.

Finally, after a long moment, Jonathan seemed to find his voice. The sides of his eyes squeezed in a grimace. "Archie, Jane is—"

"Young? She is nearly nineteen." His voice came out sharper than he'd intended, even though he knew his friend's worry had nothing to do with her age. He braced himself for what he knew was coming.

"I know you care about her—we all do—but Jane is

delicate. She requires care and she's prone to . . . ah, bouts of—"

"She is not mad." Archie cut off his words.

"No, but she is also not a typical young woman."

"Do you think I don't know, Ren?" Archie glanced to the doorway, to make sure they weren't overheard, then lowered his voice anyway. "I was there when we found her, lost and frightened after escaping that horrible institution."

Jonathan shook his head slowly. "She didn't escape. If you were to ask her, she doesn't remember any part of that night. She suffered an attack of panic, took leave of her senses, and fled through London in a thunderstorm. That is what I'm talking about, Archie. She . . ." He stood and paced in front of the hearth, avoiding the gold painted sarcophagus in the corner. "Marriage requires two capable people, and Jane . . . is troubled."

"I know full well what I am undertaking." Archie felt a pain and realized his hands were tightly fisted, his nails biting into his palms. He forced them to relax, stretching his fingers out straight on his legs.

Jonathan rubbed the back of his neck as he stopped and faced Archie. "I know you care for her, and who wouldn't? She has endured more in her short life than any person should. Don't you think perhaps what you feel is more of a brotherly love? A desire to protect her? Pity, even?"

"It is not pity."

"Jane is nothing like any of the young ladies you've fancied before."

"Exactly right. And that is why I never married any of them." He'd expected some resistance on Jonathan's part, but the man's negative response surprised him. Archie breathed slowly and pushed away his frustration, knowing Jonathan rarely said anything without consideration. He was not being cruel, and part of Archie's anger came from realizing Jonathan's words held a hint of truth.

"I do feel compassion for what she has endured and continues to endure," Archie continued. "But that is not my entire reasoning. I love her, Ren. She touches something inside me that I didn't know existed before. I want to make her happy, to give her the life she should have—starting with Christmas. That is why I changed my holiday plans. Of course, the idea arose from a desire to ease your family's grief during the holidays as well, but it is especially for Jane. I intend to make our first Christmas together special." Archie held his gaze. He needed Jonathan to understand that he was in earnest.

Jonathan sighed, reaching down to fetch their glasses, then crossed the room to refill them. He handed one to Archie before resuming his seat. "I knew the two of you enjoyed each other's company, but I had no idea your feelings were so strong. Looking back over the past months, I realize I've been rather too caught up in my own concerns to see what was taking place beneath my nose." He took a slow drink, then nodded solemnly. "You, of course, have my blessing, and if you truly love Jane, I cannot think of a better husband for her."

"Thank you." Archie rested back into the chair, suddenly exhausted. He rubbed his eyes, grateful for his friend's understanding, as well as his honesty. "And I will make sure you and your family have an unforgettable Christmas."

"Don't worry yourself too much about perfection. You know how out of sorts you get when things don't go to plan." Jonathan spoke lightly, obviously trying to return them to their earlier good humor.

"That's why it will all go to plan. A simple holiday celebration with close friends and a romantic Christmas Eve marriage proposal." Just saying the words made his heart roll with nervous anticipation. He raised his glass toward his friend and grinned. "What could possibly go wrong?"

Chapter Two

Jane pushed aside the curtains and leaned forward to look through the window of the coach. Snow was still falling in the forest, making the late afternoon seem darker than the hour warranted. She looked to the sides, both ahead and to the rear, hoping to catch a glimpse of the men accompanying them on horseback, but the heavy flakes made visibility difficult. She felt sorry for Archie and Jonathan, as well as the coachman. At least the two footmen had been sent ahead to Ashford with the luggage they would not need until they arrived at the larger estate. Archie had told them there was no need for them to accompany the party the entire way. Waverly had its own footmen.

"Jane dear, move away from the window lest you take a chill." Mother Kathleen arranged the wool blanket that lay across Jane's lap, then sat back into her seat across from the sisters.

"We should arrive at any time," Maryann said. She patted her sister's hand, then gave the smallest wink. She knew how it frustrated Jane to be constantly coddled by Mother Kathleen.

The older woman meant well, and they were both grateful for her gentle care as Jane adjusted to her newfound freedom from the institution. Over a year earlier, fearing Jane's affliction of nerves would be discovered by society, her stepmother had insisted she be consigned to a suitably discreet home with other patients of varying degrees of madness.

The memories of that place turned Jane's stomach, and she did not permit her mind to dwell on them. Instead, she imagined their destination, feeling a tingle of anticipation at what awaited: *Christmas*. She'd not celebrated Christmas—not truly—since her mother died thirteen years earlier. Her stepmother had her own ideas of how to enjoy the holidays, and they involved keeping Jane as far away as possible from anyone who might notice her condition. She'd not been to a Christmas party since she was a child, and the idea of spending the holiday with her closest friends in a country manor surrounded by a snowy forest sounded utterly delightful.

Archie Clawson must truly be the kindest man on the earth. Jane's cheeks warmed in spite of the chilly air. In truth, he was the principal reason she so looked forward to the celebration at Waverly. And she knew it was silly. He was charming and handsome, perpetually cheerful, and genuinely kind—which explained his attentions to her. He paid attention to everybody. Somehow, Archie made the people around him feel important and knew precisely what to say to raise a person's spirits. Because of her ailment, Jane was unsure of herself and resigned to remaining in the background, but Archie always made a point to sit by her, talk with her. When it came to him, however, she wanted to be noticed.

Jane blew out a long breath through her nose. Archie would never consider her as anything beyond a friend. He was heir to an earldom—an important man who would sit in Parliament and make decisions that directed the country. She was commonly born, shy, and her mind was damaged.

Her spells of panic were rare, but they were enough to cause her parents and the local surgeon to declare her mad. The members of the marquess's household treated her kindly, but she felt as if they were constantly tiptoeing around anything that might upset her, just waiting for another spell to overtake her.

If anything, Archie felt pity for her, and in Jane's mind, that was worse than if he didn't care at all.

She shifted and brushed against her reticule. A fluttering started in her chest when she thought of what was buried inside: a small box that held a carved wooden nativity strung onto a ribbon. The man at the shop had told her the ornament was from Germany and meant to adorn a Christmas tree. She'd thought it just the right gift for Archie. Heat rose up her neck as she imagined giving it to him. Would he hang it on the Waverly Christmas tree?

The carriage bounced, causing Maryann's knees to bump into hers. Jane smiled at her sister and leaned forward to stretch her back. Her stomach complained, and she wondered how many hours had passed since they'd eaten the luncheon the innkeeper had packed that morning.

Are the men hungry as well? Surely they would stop soon. Closing her eyes, she leaned back against the seat, envisioning Christmas dinner at Waverly. At Maryann's insistence, Jane had packed her new ball gown. The dress was lovely, a daring red velvet trimmed with gold ribbons that made her feel beautiful. She imagined how she would have felt wearing it to the Christmas Ball in Ashford. Perhaps Archie would have asked for a dance?

Even though Archie hid his feelings well, she knew he was disappointed to miss his mother's celebration. A twist of guilt burned sour in her throat. It was selfish, she knew, but she felt glad they'd not be attending the ball. It pained her to think of him dancing and flirting with beautiful ladies in fine gowns. Of course it was inevitable that Archie would go to parties and dance with ladies once the Season began. He would eventually marry, and of course everything would be different then. The thought made her more miserable than it should. She resolved not to let her mind wander in that direction, to put aside her selfishness and be happy for him. And enjoy this Christmas. Because it was very probable that such a circumstance would not arise again. She was ready for a new start on life and excited for this opportunity to do it.

She breathed out a contented sigh as she thought of Christmas at Waverly—the crackling fire, the Christmas hymns, the tree, the lovely things Archie had described. It all sounded like a dream.

The carriage stopped, and Jane blinked her eyes open, realizing she must have dozed off. Outside, the night was dark, and it was so quiet. She glanced to the other women, then at the door as it opened. The cold wind that blew in took her breath away.

Jonathan stood outside, a strange look on his face. His brow was wrinkled as if he were troubled. Or perhaps confused. "We've arrived."

"Oh, I cannot bear one more second in this carriage," Maryann said.

Jonathan's eyes darted to the side, and he squinted. "Perhaps you should wait until the path is cleared."

Kathleen peered out. "I don't mind a bit of snow, and if I don't stretch my back, I fear I'll remain cramped the remainder of my days."

He nodded. "Very well. But beware, the snow is rather deep."

Jane took his hand as he and the coachman helped her from the carriage and into the snow. She sank nearly to her knees. Heavy flakes were still falling, catching in her lashes when she looked up.

She peered through the darkness, seeing nothing but falling flakes in the light of the carriage lantern. She couldn't see a pathway anywhere. "Where is Archie?" she asked Jonathan as he brought Maryann to stand next to her.

"He's gone to the house." He pointed with his chin, and Jane looked in the direction he indicated. Pulling her cloak tighter, she moved along the side of the carriage until she could see Archie's rapidly filling footprints. Using tromping steps, she followed his path away from the light of the carriage lantern, and squinted through the snowfall to see the dark shape of a large house. Was this Waverly Manor? She'd expected glowing windows, footmen clearing a path, and grooms hurrying out to tend to the horses. But the night was silent, noises muffled by the snow.

She hadn't gone far before a shape appeared in the snow, and Archie himself met her.

In the dim light, she could see his face was tight. "Everything is locked. I do not know why the steps are not cleared of snow. And where are the grooms and footmen?" He spoke in a strained voice, taking off his snow-covered hat and pushing fingers through his hair. "Was my letter lost? Certainly the entire staff . . ."

Jane laid a hand on his arm. "Perhaps everyone has retired for the night. Or they expected you later. It is all surely a misunderstanding."

Archie glanced down at his arm, then lifted his gaze to hers. He seemed to relax and, after a moment, smiled, though it appeared a bit forced. He put his hat back onto his head. "Yes. A misunderstanding is all." He blew out a breath that swirled white in the cold, then took her hand, wrapped it around his arm to nestle in the bend of his elbow. "I will inquire at the caretaker's cottage. But you and the other ladies should wait in the carriage. Your toes will surely freeze."

"My toes are quite snug in their boots." Truly, she had forgotten about the cold with her arm nestled so comfortably against him. "I have been sitting in the carriage for quite a long time, sir. If it's all right, I'd like to come with you."

He secured her arm more tightly and gave a warm smile. "I always welcome your company."

If her cheeks hadn't been frozen, the look on his face would have caused a blush.

The rest of the party chose to accompany them as well; apparently they were of the same mind regarding the appeal of remaining in the carriage versus trudging through the snow. Archie instructed Tom, the coachman, to care for the horses in the stables behind the house. He removed a lantern from the carriage hook, and the group set off.

The expedition took longer than anticipated, due partially to the difficulty of walking through the deep snow—especially for the women in skirts—as well as the limited visibility. If anything, Jane thought the lantern made it more difficult to see. The light seemed to reflect off the falling flakes.

Finally, exhausted and cold, they reached the cottage—a small stone house with glowing windows on the edge of the forest.

In answer to Archie's knock, the door cracked open, and a man's face peered out. He was short with a bulbous nose and squinting eyes. A thatch of wheat-colored hair was flattened against his head. When his gaze lit on Archie, his eyes opened wide. He stepped back, opened the door all the way, giving a bow. "Lord Symons, please come in. You'll catch yer death out there, ya will." He made a waving motion with his hands. "Hurry up, all of ya. You look near to frozen."

A wave of warm air wrapped around Jane as soon as she stepped inside. The cottage was tidy with well-used furniture, a fraying rug, and a crackling fire. At the moment, Jane thought it the most welcoming place in the world.

"Thank you, Simon," Archie said. "I'm sorry to disturb you so late in the evening, but we've just arrived, and the house is locked up. It appears quite empty. I fear there's been a mistake of some kind."

Before the caretaker could answer, an extremely pregnant woman entered from a back room. She regarded the group clustered in her house with some confusion, then seeing Archie, she bent in an awkward curtsey. "My lord, how nice to see you."

"You remember my wife, Eliza," Simon said.

Archie removed his hat, dropping a clump of snow onto the wooden floor. "Of course. How nice to see you again, Mrs. Cringlewood. And these are my friends, Lord Spencer, Lady Spencer, the Dowager Lady Spencer, and Miss Croft."

Eliza bowed again. "'ere, let me take them cloaks and hats, sirs and ladies." Eliza helped Kathleen unfasten her cloak, then motioned toward the sofa. "And you warm yerselves up, now. Simon, put another log on." She folded the cloak over her arm, accepted the other visitors' outerwear, and left the room.

Jonathan helped his mother to the sofa, and the other women joined her. Archie's jaw was tight, and his eyes darted around the room. He was worried, but Jane felt inexplicably calm. She trusted in her friends. Archie and Jonathan would know what to do.

Simon set some more wood onto the fire, then rose, scratching his chin. "I'm sorry, my lord, I didn't know you were visiting the property today or I'd have opened up the house for ye."

"I sent a letter a week ago." Archie plowed his fingers through his hair. "And where is the staff?"

"Gone 'ome for Christmas. With the master gone, I didn't see any reason . . ." His eyes darted nervously to his wife.

Jane thought if he was worried of a reprimand, he must not know Archie well. She didn't think him capable of chastising anyone.

"No, of course you didn't." Archie drew his hand down to rub the back of his neck. "Perfectly reasonable course."

An expression of relief relaxed Simon's face.

Archie clasped his hands behind his back. "I know it is late, but could you open the house and send to town for the staff? We are all very cold and hungry."

Simon fidgeted, shifting his weight back and forth. "My lord, I'm sorry, but 'twould take hours to gather the entire manor staff. And with this amount o' snow, longer."

Jonathan nodded. "He's right. We were lucky to make it this far ourselves. A sleigh might pull through, perhaps, but the hour is getting late. Best to wait until tomorrow."

Simon squinted in the direction of the manor. "I suppose Eliza and I could start the fires, take the Holland covers off the furniture, and find clean linens for the beds. But the pantry is not stocked, my lord." He hunched his shoulders and bowed his head.

Archie shook his head. "Your wife is in no condition to perform such labor, and with the late hour . . ." He puffed out a frustrated sigh.

An aroma came from the back room. Something was cooking. Jane's stomach made a noise, and she pressed her hand against it, praying nobody heard.

A moment later, Eliza returned. "I've some soup, if you'd like. Nothin' fancy, mind. But 'twill warm yer bones."

"It smells heavenly," Kathleen said, and Jane couldn't agree more.

"Come on into the kitchen, then." She led them down a few steps into a low-ceilinged room and indicated a scrubbed wooden table with a bench on either side. Jane sat, sliding over to make room, then nearly slipped off the end when Kathleen scooted in beside her, followed by Maryann. The men sat across from them, their backs against the stone wall.

Jane studied the kitchen. It was well used, just like the outer room, and very tidy. Eliza Cringlewood obviously took pride in her home. On one side of the room, their cloaks were laid over wooden drying frames, hats and bonnets beside them. Everything was clean and neatly in place. Curtains with yellow flowers hung over the window, the colors faded irregularly with the folds in the fabric, and above the table was a small painting of a seascape in a simple wooden frame. She saw a red ribbon tied around a sprig of mistletoe hanging over the doorway. Jane had come from a modest background, but her father had employed a cook, and they'd always taken meals in the dining room. She thought this humble kitchen was extremely cozy and liked the simplicity she saw around her.

Eliza stirred a pot hung from a metal arm over the hearth, then ladled soup into bowls. She set a basket of sliced peasant bread onto the table as well.

Jane inhaled. The food smelled delicious.

Eliza curtseyed again when she set a bowl in front of Archie. "I apologize, my lord. We've only simple fare, and no fancy dishes to serve such important guests."

"This is perfect, Mrs. Cringlewood. Thank you," Archie said and lifted a spoonful to his mouth.

"If ya please, my lord," Simon said, "I'll say grace first."

Once he'd finished praying, Simon bid them eat. He fetched a straight-backed chair from the other room for Eliza and helped her sit.

Jane was touched by the thoughtful gesture. Watching the couple warmed her heart. They were much like Maryann and Jonathan in the concern they showed for each other, even though their stations in life were so different. How would it be to have a partner to look after her—and whom she could look after in return?

"My lord, we've not much to offer," Simon said. "But the lot o' you are welcome to sleep here tonight." He glanced at his wife, who nodded her assent to the proposal.

"Your offer is very generous," Archie said, "but I'd not dream of imposing on you more than we have already. We'll either risk the road back to town and find an inn or make the manor habitable for the night." Archie rubbed his face again, and the room was silent except for the sound of wooden spoons scraping against crockery bowls.

Jane wanted to tell him the situation wasn't as bad as he thought. They were warm and safe, with two kind people caring for them.

Archie stared at a spot on the table, lines of worry pressed between his brows. He looked up, catching Jane's gaze.

She gave a smile.

Archie grimaced. *I'm sorry*, he mouthed.

She let her smile grow, hoping it looked encouraging. She reached across the table and squeezed his hand, then returned to her soup, surprised at herself for such a forward action. But it seemed important for him to know he had her support.

After a moment, Archie turned to their hosts. "This supper was just the thing for cold, weary travelers, Mrs. Cringlewood. You are a marvelous cook."

Her face reddened at the compliment. "Eliza, my lord." Archie dipped his head in acknowledgment.

"I concur. As fine a bowl of onion soup as I've ever had," Kathleen said, and the others chimed in their agreement.

Eliza's face grew even redder. She cleared her throat. "My lord, if ye'll permit a suggestion?"

"Yes, of course," Archie said.

"Th' gardener kept a cottage 'fore 'e moved into town to care for his mum," Eliza said. "'Tisn't grand like your lordship's used to, but perhaps 'twill do for one night . . ."

Simon bobbed his head. "Don' know why I didn't think o' it earlier. Much quicker to heat and put in order than the manor house."

"And where is it?" Archie asked.

"Just a little ways off, down near the pond in th' forest," Simon said. He stepped past his wife and opened a cupboard. "I've a key 'ere somewhere. . . ."

Jane felt the others tense at the word *forest*, and she knew her bouts of panic were the reason. She felt a rise of defensiveness inside. She was not going to succumb to panic. She'd not had a spell for months.

Archie grimaced, looking as if he were preparing to reject the idea. He looked to Jane and raised his brows, as if asking for her advice.

She couldn't imagine it was truly the case. She just must have been the person whose eyes he met first. Nonetheless,

Jane leaned forward, and he did the same. "I think it's a fine idea." She spoke in a quiet voice, even though the others could certainly hear everything she said in such a small space.

His eyes tightened as if he were uncertain.

"And it is only for one night. We'll make do," she said.

Archie brushed her hand with his fingers, and a small smile pulled at his lips. He looked at the others, whose expressions likewise conveyed their agreement. "Very well." He lowered his shoulders and gave a determined nod. "Simon, if you please, my coachman is in the manor stables. I'm certain you could reach him faster than I. Would you make certain the horses have sufficient feed and take some soup to him? He should be fine staying in the grooms' quarters tonight."

"Yes, my lord." Simon bowed his head and left the room.

"And, Eliza, if we might intrude on your hospitality a bit longer, we will await Simon's return and then set off for the gardener's cottage."

She nodded. "Yes, of course, your lordship." She left the room as well, presumably to help her husband don his outer clothing.

Archie turned back to the table, his brows pinched together. "I—"

"Do not apologize. I forbid it," Mother Kathleen said.

Archie's mouth snapped shut.

She rose, and the men attempted to stand, hunched beneath the low ceiling, their legs bent by the bench pressed against the wall. "I have enjoyed every moment of this trip so far, Lord Symons," Kathleen said in her most authoritative voice. "And I am determined to continue to do so."

She exited the room. Jonathan and Maryann followed.

Archie scooted along the bench until he stood, head bent forward beneath the low ceiling. He offered his hand, and Jane took it, sidling along the bench to join him.

She took a step toward the stairs, but he stopped her with a tug on her hand.

"You are certain the gardener's cottage will be all right?"

She knew what he was asking. Would the forest frighten her into having an attack? "It will be all right, Archie."

"How do you always remain so calm, Jane?"

She looked away, not meeting his eyes. "You know I do not, sir." Archie had seen her in the midst of one of her panic spells, and the knowledge was humiliating.

He stepped close, keeping hold of her hand and closing the distance between them, forcing her to tip back her head to look up at him. "This turn of events has made me angry and frustrated, but right now I feel calm. When I am with you, weight rolls off my shoulders. Somehow, you ease my troubles."

"I am glad that I can be of some use, then." She knew her answer sounded trite, but with him so close, she had trouble thinking. Her heart pounded so forcefully that she felt her pulse prickling in her fingers.

Archie's eyes flicked to the doorway overhead.

She glanced up and saw the mistletoe. Her breath caught, and the air between them felt hot.

His fingertips brushed her chin, and his eyes darkened as he studied her, bending forward.

Jane closed her eyes, every nerve tingling in anticipation as Archie pressed a very gentle, very chaste kiss . . . on her cheek.

She drew in a breath and opened her eyes, then smiled in an attempt to conceal her disappointment, even though her heart felt like it was shrinking.

What did I expect?

She scolded herself for her misplaced hopes and turned away, feeling childish at the tears that gathered in her eyes. For a moment, she thought she'd seen something different in Archie's expression, something more than simply friendship, but she was mistaken. She'd seen what she'd wanted to see. *I am a fool*, she thought. She pulled her hand free and hurried up the steps.

Chapter Three

The sound of knocking roused Archie from a fretful night's sleep. He rolled from the cot in the loft, rubbing his eyes and wincing at the feel of rough wood beneath his bare feet. Below, he heard voices, and so he dressed quickly, wishing he had hot water for a shave. With no mirror, he tied his neck cloth by feel alone, hoping he looked remotely presentable. What must his friends think of him after spending the night in this cold, dusty old house?

He moved to the edge of the loft and, seeing no one below, determined the voices must be coming from the kitchen area directly beneath him.

When he descended, he saw that Eliza Cringlewood and Mother Kathleen tended to a pot of porridge hanging over the fireplace, and Jane was placing bowls and cups on the round wooden table.

Jane looked up when he stepped off the ladder. "Good morning."

Her smile lacked its usual warmth, and Archie kicked

himself for his actions the night before. What was he thinking, acting so presumptuous as to kiss her like that? He'd quite obviously upset her but didn't know what to say to make it right. Telling her the kiss didn't mean anything would, of course, be a lie, and saying it had happened by accident was actually rather insulting.

"Good morning, Jane." He took two cups from her hands and placed them on the table. "Did you sleep well?" He grimaced, thinking of the small, dingy room with the straw mattress that she'd shared with Mother Kathleen.

"Quite well, thank you." She turned away toward the cupboards.

"Good morning, Archie," Kathleen said.

He would have to make another attempt to regain Jane's good favor at a later time. He turned toward the other women. "And good morning to you, Mother Kathleen, Eliza."

Eliza curtseyed.

"I hope we didn't wake you," Kathleen said. "We tried to keep quiet."

He put his arm around the older woman. "I am utterly ashamed that you were all awake and dressed before me. What kind of host am I?"

She rolled her eyes. "A tired man who spent the whole of the night making certain his friends were comfortable. I do not know how many times you and Jonathan trekked back and forth to the manor house for luggage and blankets." "Only a few." He yawned. The company had not gotten to sleep until well into the early morning hours, and he could not imagine how the others were awake so early.

The door opened, letting in a blast of frigid air and a burst of snowflakes. Simon entered, his cheeks and nose red and his arms full of firewood. "Brought ya some more wood, my lord." He closed the door with his foot and set the logs onto a pile beside the fireplace.

"Thank you. But that is beyond what we will need. Remember, we are leaving after breakfast."

"I'd not recommend a journey just yet, my lord. The snow's not stopped fallin' all night. Don' think a carriage will make it to town. Yer 'ere for another day, at least."

Archie's heart dropped, and he closed his eyes, taking a calming breath. *I have ruined Christmas for all of us.* The five of them could have been at this very moment warm, well-rested, and happily preparing for his mother's holiday party.

When he opened his eyes, he saw Jane and Kathleen looked particularly unaffected by the pronouncement, which was shocking to say the least. Maybe they assumed he and Jonathan would figure a way out.

"Come have some porridge, Archie," Kathleen said. "And thoughtful Eliza brought buttermilk as well." She waved away Eliza's attempt to lift the pot, taking the cloth from her, and wrapping it around the hot handle. Then she brought the steaming pot to the table and motioned for him and Jane to sit.

The Cringlewoods bid them farewell, promising to check on the horses and take food to Tom in the grooms' quarters.

Kathleen ladled porridge into a dish and poured in buttermilk, then sprinkled sugar over the top. Archie had always been impressed by the woman's self-sufficiency. She had grown up under very different circumstances than his own, and seeing her stir the porridge reminded him that she had not always been waited on by servants.

Jane stood and reached for Archie's bowl. "May I?"

"Thank you." He passed it to her, but she still avoided his eyes while she served him.

They ate in silence, Archie trying to come up with a strategy to get five people and their luggage, six horses, and a carriage driver out of Chiddingfold Forest. He devised and then dismissed scenario after scenario, feeling more hopeless with each attempt.

Jane's spoon clattered into her bowl, and she jumped up, startling him out of his pondering.

She hurried around the table. "Mother Kathleen!" In an instant, her arm was around the older woman's shoulders.

Tears ran down Kathleen's face.

Archie moved to her other side, offering a handkerchief. "My dear, what is the matter?"

She took the handkerchief and waved them away, wiping her eyes and making a very wet sniffing sound. "Oh, you must forgive a silly woman. Back to your breakfast, you two."

Jane looked at Archie, her brows pinched together in worry.

He lifted his shoulders, not sure whether to obey.

Kathleen waved her hand again. "I am not weeping out of sorrow. Please sit down."

They exchanged another uncertain glance, but returned to their seats.

After a moment, Kathleen took in a jerky breath and blew it out slowly. "Oh, what happy memories this morning has brought. The taste of the porridge, the smell of wet firewood and dusty stone walls. It reminds me so very much of my grandparents' house in Northumberland. My grandfather was a tailor, you know. And their little cottage was very much like this one." She dabbed her eyes again and smiled sheepishly. "I did not mean to be such a watering pot."

"This cottage is very pleasant," Jane said. "Simple and quiet."

Well, that, at least, was true: plain wooden utensils, shabby furniture, and no happy chatter of family members or servants preparing for a party. In the air hung the odor of dust and mildew instead of anticipatory smells of a Christmas feast. It was, indeed, simple and quiet. He didn't consider the observation to be a positive one.

In a moment, Jonathan and Maryann joined them, wishing all a good morning. Jane scooped porridge for the two.

"Sleep well?" Archie asked.

"Like a baby," Jonathan poured buttermilk onto his porridge and smirked. "Once my feet thawed."

"Well, you shall have plenty of time to warm up." Kathleen smiled and passed the sugar dish. "The roads are impassible. We will be here at least another day."

"Oh." Maryann smiled at her husband. "Well, I was not looking forward to another carriage ride anytime soon. And it is quite cozy in this little cottage with the fire crackling and the snow falling outside the windows."

"I agree," Kathleen said. "And, Jonathan, have I told you about your great-grandfather in Northumberland? His son, your Uncle Bernard, was a Jacobite supporter and lost a foot in one of the border skirmishes . . ."

Archie's mind drifted from the conversation. He couldn't push away the anxious feelings tying his stomach in knots. Jonathan laughed at something Maryann said, then took another bite of porridge. The Marquess of Spencer—one of the most influential men in the country—was sitting on a hard chair, shoveling gruel with a wooden spoon when he should have been in a fine dining room, eating a delicious breakfast prepared by a master chef.

"It can't snow forever."

Archie hadn't realized Jane had moved her chair closer to him.

She spoke quietly, leaning to the side, so only he could hear. "Do not worry. We will still carry out all of the Christmas customs. Just on a smaller scale." She tipped her head to the side, looking up at him. "Do not be troubled any longer. We are all enjoying ourselves, yet I can see you are frustrated."

In spite of his worries, his tension eased at her words, or perhaps it was her closeness—he never could decide how she managed to calm him.

"I wanted to give you all a special Christmas," he said. He heard a whine in his whisper, but it was true. "Christmas shouldn't be like this. It should be exciting and splendid and . . ."

"You will see, the holiday will be special, even in a simple cottage," she said. "Spending time with those we care about makes it so."

He turned to watch the others, surprised to see them comfortable and happy. He slid down in the chair and leaned back so his head was near hers. "Miss Jane Croft, how is it that you are so wise?"

"I do not believe I have ever been called wise."

"Well, that is a travesty. You are one of the wisest people I know."

She remained quiet for a time, and he glanced over at her.

"Thank you." Her gaze locked on his, just for an instant, then dropped.

He leaned closer so their arms touched. She did not pull away. Archie hoped it meant he was forgiven for his actions the night before. He considered what she said. Could they truly enjoy Christmas in this place? It would certainly be one they'd remember. Would it be a fond memory? Or spoken about with dismay for years to come?

When the meal was complete, the women took the bowls and cups away, washing them in a large wooden basin that must have been filled with melted snow.

"Come, Archie," Jonathan said, indicating the area before the kitchen fireplace. "This is the warmest spot in the place. Let's move the sofa and chairs closer."

Closer consisted of just a few steps from one end of the room to the other. They pushed the table against the wall and carried the sofa and two soft chairs across the room, arranging them before the fire in a crescent shape.

Mother Kathleen swatted the patched cushion of the sofa a few times, raising a cloud of dust, but she sat anyway, unrolling her knitting and counting her stitches to resume.

Jane sat in a chair, and Archie took the other on the far side of the room. Jonathan and Maryann nestled into a corner of the sofa, his arm around her shoulders.

"Is everyone warm?" Archie asked.

"Very comfortable," Kathleen said.

The others nodded their agreement.

"Well, should we play a game, then?" Archie said. "The space is a bit cramped for charades, but I suppose we could devise another sort of guessing game."

None of the group looked very interested in the idea. With the darkened sky and the long night, he thought they all must be rather tired.

"It is so nice to just sit quietly," Maryann said. "Perhaps someone could tell a story." She leaned against her husband's shoulder. "Or, Jane, will you read to us?"

"I have a book," Jane said. "But I think it is rather dreary for Christmas Eve."

"What is it?" Maryann asked.

"A new book written by an anonymous author: *Frankenstein*."

"I've heard of it," Jonathan said. "And I think you're right. Hardly the thing for Christmas Eve." He made a motion with his eyes toward his mother, and they all understood Kathleen would probably not care for a dark tale. "Do we have any others?"

Archie waited, hoping someone would devise a game or perhaps conjure a book, but none of them came forward. Finally, he sighed. "I have a book."

Jonathan twisted to look at his friend. "You?"

Archie didn't take the bait and engage in the teasing

banter his friend expected. He felt heavy as he climbed the ladder to the loft, then returned with the book wrapped in golden paper. His dream of finding a special moment to present it to Jane in front of the Christmas tree puffed out like a candle's flame.

"It is actually for you, Jane. I meant it to be a Christmas gift, but it seems we have need of it early."

Jane's face lit up, and she smiled. She tugged on the bow, untying the ribbon, then tore the paper free. "Oh, Archie." She ran her hand over the embossed leather. "It's beautiful." Turning it, she read the title, printed in gold letters on the spine. "*The Golden Donkey* by Apuleius."

"I know you're interested in classical works. The man at the book shop said this is a very good translation."

She pressed the book to her chest. "This is such a thoughtful gift." Her eyes were soft, and the look in them nearly brought him to his knees. She held his gaze for a long moment, then blushed and looked back down at the book. "I have heard the story is rather scandalous."

"I remember quite enjoying it at university." He shrugged and returned to his seat, trying to act as if his heart hadn't melted into his boots at her reaction.

"Scandalous is the preferred genre for students," Jonathan said.

"I, for one, could do with a bit of a scandal." Kathleen smirked, her eyes still on her knitting. "I should like to hear it."

Jane smiled. "Very well." She opened the book and turned slightly to allow the firelight to illuminate the page.

Owing to Jane's shyness, she had only read for them a

few times—always short passages in a soft voice—but today, Archie saw something different.

As she recited the story, her confidence grew. She sat tall in the chair with a straight back and lifted chin, holding the book before her. Her words were sure and strong. The inflections and cadence of her voice added nuance to the story and, at times, humor. The party burst into laughter more than once and listened raptly as she told the story of Lucius and his experiments with magic that eventually led to his being changed into a donkey.

After a particularly bawdy scene, the group's laughter forced her to come to a stop. Jane's face blushed a furious red, but her eyes were bright and an adorable smile pulled her lips. She caught Archie's eye and winked—something he'd never seen her do before. Perhaps Jane wasn't the timid young lady they all assumed. Perhaps she just needed an opportunity to display another side of herself. Archie wondered if they had all been so careful not to upset her that she felt smothered.

She continued to read, and his affection for her increased with every word.

After she'd read for the remainder of the morning, Jane came to a stopping point and closed the book. "I am sorry, we will have to hear the rest another day. My throat is raw."

Archie jumped up, applauding. "A marvelous performance, Jane!"

"Hear, hear," Jonathan said, rising as well.

The ladies stood. "If only I had roses to toss onto the stage," Maryann said, grinning.

"Utterly shocking tale," Kathleen said, smiling. "I enjoyed it very much."

Jane swirled her hands, raising her arms and bending into an elaborate curtsey.

Archie didn't think he'd ever seen her smile quite so brilliant. She practically glowed at the attention. He again wondered if they had been mistaken in their manner of caring for her.

Once the applause ended, she stepped toward Archie. "You were correct, Archie. You really are a marvelous party planner."

Her face was flushed and her eyes bright. Archie did not think it improper at all at that moment to embrace her. "I have never heard an old Roman tale performed so gloriously," he said, keeping his voice low, though the others were only feet away.

She drew back but remained in the circle of his arms. Her hand rested on his arm, a few inches above his elbow, the other clutched the book. "Thank you, Archie. For the gift and for the chance." She shrugged, giving a small smile. "I—Thank you."

His skin felt hot beneath her touch. Had she always had those few freckles on the bridge of her nose? How was a man expected to remain coherent with her gaze trained upon him? Her eyes were the most perfect shade of blue—nearly gray that darkened slightly at the edges—and at the moment, they were focused completely on him. His collar seemed to grow tighter. Where was the blasted mistletoe when he needed it?

Hearing the sound of furniture scraping on the floor, Jane released his arm and turned, the spell broken.

Jonathan and Maryann moved kitchen chairs out of the way as Kathleen carried a covered basket toward the table.

She lifted the cloth and peered beneath. "Shall we see what our considerate Eliza Cringlewood left for luncheon?"

With Jane's help, she laid the victuals on the table: a block of cheese, a loaf of bread, and a portion of ham. A simple meal, to be sure. Archie wrinkled his nose, thinking again of the fine meals he'd expected to give his friends.

Kathleen pressed her hand to her chest. "Oh, bless them."

Hearing her words, Archie felt a swell of shame at his reaction. The Cringlewoods had undoubtedly given the best they were able, and none of the others seemed disappointed by the meager offering.

Maryann looked in the kitchen cupboards and only found one knife. "I suppose I shall start slicing. Jane, will you fetch the plates?"

"Wait," Jonathan said. His mouth lifted in a smile. "Only the bread and ham. I have a better idea for the cheese." He crossed the room to his sleeping chamber and returned with an armload of blankets. A moment later, they were spread over the floor in front of the fire.

Archie's own smile grew. "Just like at Oxford, eh, old boy?"

Jonathan nodded. He searched through the kitchen and, in the end, looked through the wood pile, pulling out a handful of long, thin branches.

Archie brought the plates of sliced ham and bread and the lump of cheese. "What are you waiting for?" He knelt on the blankets, setting the plates next to him, then jerked his head to the side—a signal for the others to join him.

Jonathan removed his coat and sat before the fire,

wearing only his shirtsleeves. "I hope you don't mind my attire," he said, loosening his neck cloth. "The hearth gets dratted hot."

"Eating luncheon on the floor is hardly the time to be worried about propriety," Maryann said. She sat with her feet to one side, adjusting her skirt over her legs. Kathleen knelt beside her.

Jane sat beside Archie.

Jonathan distributed the sticks, keeping two for himself. "Now, the trick is in the timing. You want the bread toasted, the ham hot, and the cheese soft and warm, but not fully melted. When it is done right and all are ready at the exact same time, the result is—"

"Exquisite," Archie said.

Jonathan nodded. "Exquisite." He handed a slice of bread to Archie, picked up a slice of ham, and broke off a chunk of cheese. "It works best with a partner." He swept his hand toward the flames with an exaggerated gesture, holding his two laden sticks in one hand, spacing them between his fingers so the ham and cheese didn't touch. "Allow us to demonstrate."

Archie poked the end of the stick through the bread and extended it. He glanced at his friend and saw his nod, and a flood of memories crashed over him: sitting on the rug in a chilly Oxford student's apartment; all the hours of conversation, the laughter, the grand ideas; discussing theories, coursework, and ladies; complaining about professors.

Jonathan was the Earl of Rensfield then—an ambitious young man, a serious person by nature—but now Archie could see the toll this past year had taken. With his father dead, the responsibilities of a great house sat squarely on Jonathan's shoulders. He was a member of an important parliamentary committee and had a new wife, grieving mother, and troubled sister-in-law to care for. Now he often seemed heavy-burdened.

Yet today, Archie caught a glimpse of the younger man. He was relaxed and untroubled here in this simple cottage. Perhaps taking the time away from society, his house, and government duties, and being able to focus on his family was good for a man.

Jonathan twisted his wrist, adjusting the angle of his sticks to cook the cheese and ham evenly.

Archie turned the bread around to toast the other side, careful not to burn his fingers. The stick was every bit as effective as a long-handled fork, but it didn't grow hot as a metal utensil did when held over a flame. He'd learned that lesson the hard way.

At length, Jonathan held out his sticks, and Archie removed the toasted bread, folded it, and used it to slide off the ham, then the soft cheese, smashing it between the two halves until it pushed out the sides.

"A masterpiece," Jonathan said.

"As fine a creation as I've seen, sir." Archie grinned and gave the toasted sandwich to Kathleen.

"Shall we allow these apprentices to try?" Jonathan made a show of sizing up Maryann and Jane.

"Yes, please." Maryann reached toward the cheese.

Jonathan stopped her hand. "Patience, my dear. Patience is essential, or you end up with cheese overcooked on the edges and cold inside." He shook his head as if this were an unbearable travesty.

"Bread that is too soft or chewy ham," Archie added. "Creating a toasted sandwich requires more refined skill than one would assume."

"I don't know if they're ready for such an enormous responsibility." Jonathan sighed. "Perhaps a few years of training and they just might—"

Maryann swatted his arm. "Enough already. We'll starve before the two of you finish expounding on your staggering talent."

Archie chuckled and handed Jane a slice of ham, helping her fix it in place on her stick. He held his hand over hers, guiding the piece of meat to just the right spot where it wouldn't cook too quickly, but would be warm and just a bit crispy when the other ingredients were ready.

She looked up at him, hand in his, firelight flickering in her eyes, and smiled. "Everyone is so happy today. I'm glad you brought us here, Archie."

"It has been a fine day." His neck cloth was loosed, but still he felt a difficulty breathing. How did this woman have such an effect on him?

"More than a fine day," She shifted her legs, leaning slightly against him. "One of the best days."

Archie tipped his head to rest on hers, and at that moment, everything felt right with the world.

For the next hour, the five sat like children before the fire, the quiet broken only with calls of, "My cheese is ready to drip! Who has a bread?" "My ham is done." "Here's a bread, does anyone have a cheese?"

Archie watched his friends taking part in an activity he would never have anticipated, and his heart was soft. His worries about Christmas eased, albeit slightly, and he allowed himself to enjoy the moment with people he loved. Not the least of whom was the excellent ham-crisper leaning against his arm, sending a jolt of awareness through him each time she moved.

Finally, the food was gone, and their bellies filled.

Kathleen returned to the couch and took up her knitting. Jonathan slid back to rest his shoulders against a chair as he munched on a sandwich. Maryann sat curled up beside him, her head on his chest.

Archie shifted, resting his hand back on the blanket behind Jane.

Jane stretched and yawned, giving him a smile. "If I remain here, I will fall asleep." She stood and walked toward the couch.

Archie agreed wholeheartedly. He wouldn't mind a nap himself, and without permission, his mind conjured the image of an early afternoon nap with Jane's soft figure curled up beside him. He was still dwelling on this pleasant thought when he heard Jane's gasp.

She moved to the window, then turned to the group with a smile. "Come look outside. It has stopped snowing!"

Chapter Four

Jane stepped through the cottage door onto the small porch and stopped, enchanted by the sight before her. "Beautiful," she breathed.

The air smelled clean and crisp. Above, the clouds had separated enough to allow sunshine through, and all around, the earth looked as if it was covered in a thick, white blanket. Forest branches hung heavy with their loads, and the ground was pristine, save for a few trails of animal tracks crisscrossing over the soft snow.

"I don't believe I've seen this much snow since I was a girl," Kathleen said.

"It feels like we are the only people on the earth," Maryann replied. "It's so peaceful."

Jane pulled her cloak tighter, glad that she wore thick boots and mittens. Though the sun shone through thinning clouds, the air was still chilled. She shivered and hoped once she started moving, her body would warm up.

The group set off through the thick powder, Archie in the lead. He pulled a sled he'd borrowed from Simon. It had a sort of wagon box attached, apparently used for excursions into town or hunting trips. He had also procured gardening shears and a small hand ax to assist with their task of gathering Christmas greenery. Was the wagon large enough to hold a tree?

Jane sank with every step, then pulled her foot from its pit and sank again. Glancing at the group, she saw the others did the same. Walking took an enormous amount of effort. The women's dresses and cloaks were cumbersome and grew heavy when snow stuck to them. She held her skirts as well as she could, but short of throwing them over her shoulder, they were destined to be a burden. But Jane wouldn't complain.

She was thrilled with their outing. Searching for greenery and a Yule log as a child was nearly a forgotten memory. She was surprised at the swell of anticipation. She almost felt giddy. But as she glanced ahead at Archie's broad shoulders beneath his cape and his hair curling over the back of his collar, she thought perhaps a portion of her enjoyment came from the man leading the excursion. If she were to be honest, his presence accounted for more than just a portion.

Archie made her happy—it was simple, really.

When she spoke, he listened. He complimented her and was genuinely interested in what she said. While the others watched her carefully, babied her, and seemed as if they were just waiting for her to succumb to another attack, Archie was her friend. He'd never treated her as if she were mad. And there were moments when . . .

She shook off her silly thoughts and reminded herself that Archie acted the same to everyone—equally happy, equally considerate, and equally kind—which was the reason people sought his presence. Putting too much significance on his particular attentions to her would only lead to heartache later.

That lesson had been painfully obvious the night before when he'd given her the disappointingly brother-like kiss. But try as she might, she could not prevent her thoughts from turning to his expression when he gave her the book. The considerate gift showed he knew her well. He had laughed and complimented her when she read and made her feel so sure of herself. He'd sat close beside her as they toasted cheese, and how could she forget his embrace? It was all so confusing. Her feelings for Archie grew deeper with each passing day, and last night she'd thought there could be more to his. But she was mistaken.

The surrounding snow muted the sounds of their boots scuffing through the powder, and the group walked in silence. Jane wondered if the others felt the enchantment of the fresh snowfall or if they were just quietly struggling to wade through it. They moved along the edge of the forest where the trees were well-spaced. Large, snow-covered boulders dotted here and there along the slope.

Jane wondered why they weren't walking directly into the forest. It seemed a much smarter course to search for greenery where there were more trees.

Reaching the top of a gentle hill, Jane looked back and saw the cottage by daylight: a humble stone structure set between a frozen pond and the deeper forest. Gazing beyond, she could see the smoke from the Cringlewoods' home, though she could not see the house itself through the trees.

Archie stopped after a moment, then looked up at a tree, scratching beneath his ear. He turned to the others with brows drawn. "This is the direction Simon pointed us in, but it appears holly trees look exactly like all the other trees when they're covered in snow." He turned, taking off his hat and squinting as he looked up through the branches. "I'm not exactly sure how—"

His words halted when a shower of snow dropped on him. He shook himself, brushing piles of powder from his shoulders.

From the corner of her eye, Jane saw Jonathan move again. He hurled a ball of snow into the tree, and another branch released its load down onto Archie.

"Jonathan!" Maryann said, the reprimand she'd obviously intended at odds with the amusement in her voice.

The marquess grinned. "I'm just offering assistance, my dear. Archie needed a way to identify the trees beneath their covering of snow. And I obliged him by solving the prob—"

A mass of snow exploded on Jonathan's chest, spraying over the entire group.

"Now, see here, sir," Jonathan called, grinning. He scooped up another mass of snow, and cocked his arm to throw it.

Archie was already prepared and let another shot fly.

The women scampered away from the two men who had, without warning, reverted back to their boyhood. Yells and taunts sounded through the quiet woodland behind them as Archie and Jonathan continued their snow battle.

"Oh, really." Maryann folded her arms and huffed. "Acting like chil—" She gasped when a clump of snow hit her, then whirled around to find the culprit.

Another hit Jane. The sisters shared a confused glance, looking at the men who were engaged in their own match and couldn't have hit them from such an angle. They both turned to see Kathleen wearing an enormous grin.

She was forming another handful of snow into a ball.

"Mother Kathleen!" Maryann looked at her, disbelieving. "You—"

Kathleen threw the snowball, barely missing the brim of Maryann's bonnet.

Jane and Maryann both snatched up snow and began to fight back, shrieking and laughing when a cold projectile hit them, then retaliating at both the older woman and each other.

Archie and Jonathan must have heard their shouts, because they halted their battle and started toward them. Both men had lost their hats.

Archie's hair was damp and falling over his forehead in curls. He smiled widely. "I would not have supposed you proper ladies capable of such mischief."

"Archie, watch out for Mother Kathleen! She's an excellent shot," Jane panted.

He raised his brows in a surprised expression and opened his mouth to respond when Kathleen hit him. Snow sprayed on his shoulder, over his face, and into his mouth.

He laughed heartily. "It's the sweet ones you have to watch out for. They're the most devious." Wiping off his cheeks with the back of his sleeve, he grabbed Jane's hand and pulled her across the field to duck down behind a large mound of snow that was likely a buried boulder.

Jane's heart was beating from the physical exertion, and she breathed heavily, her breath swirling out in white puffs. "Are we hiding?"

"Hiding? Never." Archie crouched down and started compressing snow into balls, making a pile. He glanced around the rock and pulled his head back as a snowball flew past. "It looks like the enemies have joined forces. I'll build up the defenses, and you work on artillery." He smiled eagerly, his eyebrows bouncing, and he started packing snow up along the side of the rock to make a wall.

Jane knelt and patted the snow into balls, building up the pile he'd begun. His enthusiasm was contagious, and she couldn't help grinning, even though this activity bordered on the ridiculous.

She glanced up at him, and he met her eye, giving a wink that warmed her insides. She turned back to building snowballs. "Archie, we could hide in the forest."

He darted a glance at her, then shook his head. "What's the Artillery Battery Unit's report?" he said, packing more snow onto the wall.

"Ah." She assessed her pile. "I've about thirty snowballs . . . Sergeant."

"Sergeant?" Archie huffed, looking offended.

"Lieutenant?" Jane offered.

"Much better." He gave a satisfied nod. "Thirty is good, but far from enough. Keep packing, Private."

"Private?" Jane imitated his injured tone and expression.

He grinned. "We can't both be lieutenants, Jane. Someone must be the superior officer."

"Then you may refer to me as General, sir."

His eyes opened wide, then he burst into a laugh. "Excellent." He gave a salute. "Brilliant idea, General." He returned to working on the fortification, still chuckling.

Once the wall stretched a few yards, Archie moved in a crouch to the rock, pressing his hands and chest against it as he peeked ever so slowly out onto the battlefield.

He pulled back, squatting down in the little space next to Jane. Looking over the pile of snowballs, he nodded. "Fine work, General."

"Thank you, Lieutenant." She nodded in what she thought was a commanding manner. "And what of our enemy?"

He moved back to the rock, glanced over, and then reached out an arm, beckoning for her to join him. He held her shoulders, moving her in front of him.

Jane pressed her hands to the rock and, following his lead, peeked out at the hillside, trying for all she was worth to concentrate on the snowball battle and not Archie's hands on her shoulders or his warm chest against her back. The battlefield was empty.

"Where did they go?" she whispered.

Archie leaned forward beside her ear, and she shivered when his warm breath caressed her cheek. She wished she weren't wearing her dratted bonnet. He motioned to the trail of prints that led to another large rock about twenty yards away. "They've taken cover, probably building up their own battlements."

"What do we do? Attack?" She prayed that he would insist they remain here, and perhaps in this very cozy position.

"Well, battle strategy is ultimately up to the general, but we've strong defenses and a fine storage in the artillery battery." He moved back, and Jane immediately felt cold without him pressed against her. "If you command an attack, I will, of course, follow orders."

"I would rather stay here a bit longer." Her cheeks heated with a blush, and she turned her gaze downward.

Archie remained silent for a moment. When he spoke, his words came slowly. "A fine strategy, General. Wait and draw them out into the open, thus giving us the advantage." She glanced up and saw his eyes were squinting thoughtfully.

Jane's blush deepened, feeling even hotter in the cold air. "But if you think we should go, by all means . . ."

He put his hands back on her shoulders, pulling her down so they sat with their backs against the rock, his arm around her. He pulled her closer, resting her head beneath his shoulder. "I would rather remain as well." His voice was a rumble beneath her ear, and in spite of the snow, heat spread through her, pooling in her stomach, warming her cheeks and neck.

The emotions she feared to reveal sprang to the surface again, leaving her supremely blissful and, at the same time, uneasy. She was unsure how to respond. Was Archie treating her as a treasured younger sister? Or did he feel pity for her? She remembered the cold sting of disappointment from the night before and couldn't bear to hope.

With enormous reluctance, she pulled herself away from her companion's warm chest and twisted around, trying to speak lightly. "Perhaps we could escape through the forest, Lieutenant?"

Archie darted a look to the side, but not before she saw something in his gaze. Worry? Guilt?

The realization hit her, tightening her throat. "You want to keep me from the forest. That is why we walked in this direction." She fought to keep her voice steady. "You fear I will have a spell." Jane blinked, her lips trembling.

"No, of course I don't." He grasped her arms, perhaps fearing she would run. "I just don't want to put you in a situation where you might."

"Archie, you think I am mad." She whispered the word—a word she'd heard others use regarding her for years, but had never spoken herself. She pushed her wrist against her chest as if to dull the pain inside. "You, of all people."

"Of course I do not. Jane, I swear to you—"

A snowball hit the rock beside him.

They both jumped then, ducking their heads, staring in the direction from whence it came. A flash of black fabric in the trees indicated Mother Kathleen had crept around to the forest behind them. *How had she moved so quietly?*

"They're flanking us, General." Archie's brows were raised, his voice sounding hopeful, as if he might pull her back into the game.

From the hill behind them, they heard the sound of Maryann giggling. Jane moved to rise, but he held on to her arms. "Jane, please believe me."

Words would not come, and she could only shake her head. Though the others looked at her with worry in their gazes, she'd always thought Archie was different, that he saw beyond her disorder.

"On my count," Jonathan yelled. "One. Two. Now!"

The three attackers lobbed their snowballs high above the fort. Jane understood their plan an instant too late.

"Take cover!" Archie pulled her toward him just as a shower from the tree above buried the two in snow.

For a moment, there was silence, then their opponents cheered.

Jane raised her head, brushing powder from her bonnet and shoulders. Archie had protected her face from the worst of it, but the cold still bit her cheeks. She pulled away from his embrace and rose, shaking her skirts.

"And thus falleth the impregnable snow fortress." Jonathan spoke with his hand over his heart, a look of mock solemnity in his face.

Archie sat back in the snow, clumps of powder clinging to his hair. He raised his hands in surrender. "Well, General, we fought a good fight, but they had the advantage of a superior spy." He looked up at Jane, his expression wary, but his words light, probably for the benefit of the others.

Kathleen laughed and clapped her gloved hands together. "Oh, I haven't had so much fun in ages."

Jonathan put his fists on his hips. "Mother, I'd never have believed you capable of such mischief."

Jane reached out a hand to Archie. "You fought well, Lieutenant."

He grasped her hand, pulling himself up. "As did you." He pulled a clump from the hood of her cloak, dropping it to the ground.

Jane felt an uneasy heaviness between them. Her heart ached, and she wanted nothing more than to return to the little cottage to hide away in her bedchamber and let her tears flow.

"Well, that's interesting," Jonathan said.

The pair turned to where Jonathan and Maryann stood outside the snow fort. He was looking up into the branches of the tree above them.

"What's interesting?" Archie asked.

"I believe it's mistletoe." He pointed. "Yes, I'm certain of it. Up near the top branches." He looked down at Jane and Archie, a smirk on his lips. "And what do you know? It's hanging directly over your stronghold. Seems a pity to waste it."

Jane realized she and Archie were still holding hands. They stood close. She glanced at him just as he tightened his eyes in a glare, directed toward Jonathan. He shook his head and yet hardly moved it. The gesture was so fleeting; it was obviously intended to be unnoticed by anyone but his friend.

Jane looked away quickly, hoping he didn't realize that she'd seen. Her heart compressed. *I am a fool,* she thought. *I've made him ill at ease with the thought of kissing me.*

She glanced at Archie and saw that his neck and ears were red. His expression was a grimace of apology. "You don't have to, Jane."

Her heart shrank further into a painful little rock. She could feel the others watching. "Oh, mistletoe." She forced cheer into her voice. "How nice." She placed a hand on Archie's shoulder and rose up onto her toes, giving him a quick peck on the cheek.

She turned without looking to see his expression. "You found mistletoe, Jonathan. Now we need to locate some holly." Jane kept her voice light to disguise the growing ache in her chest.

"Yes," Maryann said. "It will be dark soon, and we've still gathered no Christmas greenery." She slid her arm through her husband's, and the two started back up the hill.

Jane stepped out of the ruined snow fort and joined Mother Kathleen, linking arms with the older woman. She did not allow herself to look back, not when, for the second time in as many days, an encounter beneath the mistletoe had brought her to tears.

Chapter Five

When they returned to the cottage, the night was near to full dark. Archie released the sled's rope and rubbed the ache at the base of his back. He was cold and wet and exhausted. He assumed the others felt much the same. He opened the door and was greeted by a blanket of warm air carrying a savory aroma. How could a mere smell raise his spirits? His mouth watered.

Bless you, Eliza Cringlewood.

The caretaker's wife unbent from stirring a pot over the fire and curtseyed as the group entered. "Welcome back, my lord, Lord Spencer, and ladies."

Simon joined her, giving a small bow. "I 'as nearly ready to go looking for the lot of ya. Worried ye'd gotten yerselves lost."

"Your concern is appreciated," Archie said. "But as you can see, we are all safely returned." He nodded toward the caretaker, then turned, looking for Jane through the commotion of his companions shaking off snow and removing wet outer clothing. He needed an opportunity to speak to her alone.

She stood behind the others in the corner, untying her bonnet.

Archie moved through the group to join her. "Jane."

She didn't answer, unfastening her cloak without lifting her gaze. He moved behind her and took it from her shoulders. She shivered. The heavy garment was cold and wet. Archie feared she might catch a chill. "Come closer to the fire."

He touched his hand to her lower back, putting a bit of pressure to coax her forward.

"Thank you." Her voice was soft, but he could hear the hurt in it. She wrapped her arms around her middle but didn't move from her position.

Archie stepped around to face her, wishing for even the smallest bit of privacy in this wretched cottage. He settled for turning his back to the rest of the group. "Jane, I'm sorry. Please believe me. I never intended to hurt you."

"You've no need to apologize." She turned to slip past him. "I know you meant well. You care about me, just like the others." She paused, her eyes moving to his. "I suppose I was just surprised. I thought—"

Archie caught her arm. "You thought what?"

She shook her head. "It is nothing."

"Jane, please."

She started to turn away but hesitated, once again fixing him with her perfect, blue-eyed gaze. "I thought you felt differently." Sorrow filled her eyes, and she seemed to wilt. "Sometimes, with you, I can almost forget." Her voice was quiet. She moved past, pulling away her arm.

Archie's stomach sank. He stood, holding her dripping cloak, and watched as she joined Kathleen near the hearth.

The older woman put an arm around her shoulder, moving Jane back a few steps as if worried she was standing too close to the fire.

Jane didn't protest, but stood silently, letting Mother Kathleen fuss over her. Archie saw no trace of the confident woman who'd directed him to refer to her as "General" in their snow fortress. Could this be the same Jane whose eyes gleamed with mischievous mirth as she winked after reading aloud Apuleius's shocking tale?

How must she feel with everyone walking about as if on eggshells, worried that she might suffer another attack? Did she think they all watched her, just waiting for panic to overtake her? How would it be to feel as though one's friends didn't trust her sanity?

Archie's unease grew. He'd been every bit as guilty as the others, pitying her, watching out for her, fearing what might set her off. He cared for her—of course he did—but he never fully trusted her capability. His mouth tasted sour, and a wave of shame flowed hot through him. He was an arrogant fool to believe all Jane needed was a man to protect her, to watch over her, and keep her safe from herself. When, in truth, it wasn't what she needed at all, not really. Jane Croft needed someone to believe in her. To see past her loveliness and frailties and just *trust* her.

He hadn't been that person at all.

"It smells divine in here." Kathleen made her way to the hearth. "What have you made, Eliza?"

"Rabbit stew, my lady."

Kathleen smiled. "Just the thing to warm us up."

Simon put a worn woolen cloak over Eliza's shoulders

and held his arm around her waist. "I best be getting my wife home."

Kathleen nodded. "Yes, you look very tired, my dear."

Archie looked closer. Eliza's face was pale. She did look tired. And yet here she was, preparing their supper. He stood aside, opening the door for the couple, then followed them out, closing the door behind him. "Simon, Eliza, I cannot tell you how I appreciate your efforts on our behalf." Knowing what a sacrifice it must be to unexpectedly care for them, especially in Eliza's condition, filled him with a gratitude he'd rarely felt. While he'd experienced the generosity of others, it had never felt as if the other party had sacrificed so greatly for him. His thanks felt extremely inadequate.

"'Tis our pleasure, my lord," Simon said.

"I didn't once consider how our surprise arrival might have affected your own holiday plans, and yet you've shown us the most thoughtful care. I truly don't know what we would have done without your generosity." And, indeed, he did not. Stranded as they were, without the couple's assistance, they'd likely have spent the last twenty-four hours cold and hungry in the stables.

"Thank you." Eliza dipped in a curtsey, her eyes wincing in pain.

Archie experienced a moment of helplessness, wishing he knew how assist her. "Will you—Are you able to walk? I'm sorry, I've no carriage to offer."

Simon tightened his arm around her waist. "Don' trouble yerself, my lord. A strong'un is my Eliza. She'll be right as new in the morning."

"Yes, well, I'm glad to hear it." Archie scratched behind his ear. "That brings me to another concern. I hate to impose on you further, but Christmas supper . . ."

"Not to worry. I've a fine goose," Eliza said. "The bird's rather on the small side, but Simon brought in some fowl this morning."

"And Eliza's been preparing ever since ye arrived: stuffing, pudding, potatoes, squash, mince pies." Simon's grin shone in the dark. "'Twill most certainly be enough for all."

Archie's throat tightened at the sight of these two good people and their selfless actions. His family had always taken special care of the poor at Christmastime, and he realized he'd never been on the receiving end of that type of charity. He felt extremely humbled. He swallowed hard, finding himself unable to speak for a moment.

"O' course, I realize your lordship is used to much finer foods—venison and roast beef and such." Eliza twisted her hands, apparently mistaking his silence for disapproval. "I'm afraid—"

Archie shook his head, clearing his constricted throat. "Eliza Cringlewood, I forbid you to apologize." His voice sounded rather choked, and he blinked at the moisture in his eyes. "You have done more than I had any right to expect, and I cannot begin to thank you." He stepped forward and took each of their hands, feeling the strongest urge to embrace these good people, but resisted, knowing it would only make them more uncomfortable. "I wish I knew how to repay your generosity."

"'Tisn't necessary, my lord." Simon said. "Happy to help, we are. After all, it's Christmas."

Archie pinched the bridge of his nose. Once he'd regained a bit of his composure, he spoke. "Please, you will join us for Christmas dinner?"

The two looked at each other, then at him.

"I would consider it an honor," Archie said.

"Thank you, your lordship," Simon nodded his head solemnly. "Now, if ye please, Eliza needs to rest."

Archie stepped inside a moment later and saw Kathleen and Jane were preparing the table.

"Oh, look, Jane." Kathleen pulled a loaf-shaped pan from the basket. "Bread pudding."

Jane didn't say anything. She nodded, then fetched more plates from the cupboard.

"Are you feeling all right, Jane dear?" Kathleen asked.

"Yes. Thank you," Jane responded in a quiet voice.

Archie's chest was tight. He crossed the space and took the plates from her, trying to catch her gaze as he set them on the table. After a moment, he resigned himself. Regaining Jane's trust wouldn't come easily.

The rabbit stew tasted every bit as good as it smelled. Eliza had brought peasant bread and honey, and the bread pudding with clotted cream could have competed with the creation of any chef in London. Archie would never have believed such simple fare could taste so delicious.

As they ate, Archie told the group about the Cringlewoods' preparations for a Christmas feast and his invitation for the couple to join them.

They discussed the best way to arrange the furniture to

accommodate the larger party. Kathleen assigned the men to fetch tablecloths and dishes from the manor, as well as some chairs and another table.

Jonathan looked as if he'd protest, but Archie agreed. If they were going to do this, they'd do a fine job of it, in spite of the inconvenience. Besides, the sled would make the trips much easier.

Maryann reminded the men to invite Tom from the stables as well.

Jane remained quiet throughout the meal. From her expression, she seemed to be listening closely, but did not contribute more than a few comments, despite Archie's attempts to draw her into the conversation. When the meal was finished, she excused herself, then returned a moment later holding a small package.

"If you please." She spoke quietly, her eyes meeting each of theirs, then dropping to the wrapped parcel in her hands. "I have been thinking of the Cringlewoods and how very kind they've been to us. I wanted to do something. To give them a Christmas gift."

"A fine idea, dear," Kathleen said.

Jane held up the package. "Maryann, I purchased these rabbit fur mittens for you, but if you don't mind—"

"Eliza could use them more than I," Maryann finished for her.

Jane nodded. "Yes."

"Very thoughtful of you," Maryann said. "And I have a contribution of my own." She hurried from the room and returned with a package as well. "Jonathan, I'd intended this scarf for you, but Simon . . ."

Jonathan nodded. "I heartily approve."

Kathleen jumped up. "And I have just the thing." She hurried into her bedchamber and returned with her own package. "I knitted this blanket for Miriam Pemberley's new baby, but I'm sure she would not mind waiting a few more weeks for another."

Archie's heart warmed. Jane felt exactly as he about the Cringlewoods, yet instead of simply wishing she could do something in return, she'd taken action.

Jane beamed as she looked at the pile of gifts. "Oh, yes. They will be so happy. Can we deliver them tonight?" She clapped her hands together. "What if we knock on the door and hurry away before they answer?"

"Jonathan, you and Archie can deliver the gifts while we decorate the cottage." Kathleen started to gather the dishes from the table. "Jane and Maryann, if you please, will you bring in the greenery from the sled?"

Maryann started toward the door, but Jane remained where she was. "I'd hoped to deliver the gifts as well." Archie could see her hands clenched behind her back.

Kathleen and Maryann exchanged a concerned glance, then looked at Jane. They both stepped toward her. Jane winced as if bracing herself.

"My dear," Kathleen said.

"Jane," Maryann began.

"Absolutely!" Archie spoke up before the others could finish. "The proposal was Jane's, and she should be the one to execute the plan."

The entire room turned toward him, alarm on their faces, save for one whose expression shone with gratitude, and hers was the only one that mattered to Archie.

"But, Jane, are you certain you should go into the forest?" Maryann asked.

She nodded. "Yes. I will be all right. There is nothing to fear. Not when Archie is with me."

Their cloaks weren't fully dried, but Archie grabbed them anyway. He didn't think anything could chill him after Jane's declaration of confidence in him. And he wanted to leave immediately, before anyone talked her out of going.

Once they were bundled again in their outerwear, the pair stepped back into the snow. Jane stopped at the sled and pulled off bits of holly, tucking them into the ribbons on the gifts. She held the packages against her and smiled at Archie.

"Shall I carry the parcels?" he asked.

She shook her head. "I'd like to bring them, if it's all right with you."

"Very well, then." He lifted a lantern, and the two set off. Archie felt most ungentlemanly walking through the dark forest without taking her arm or carrying her load. But he could feel Jane's resolve and knew that, though it was a small errand, to her it signified much more.

He held the lantern high and kept pace with her. The pathway was marked by the Cringlewoods' footprints as well as his own, but it was still far from an easy walk. The snow was deep, and in the cold of night, a layer of ice covered it, making it not only difficult to step in and out of the uneven pathway, but slippery as well. He rested a hand at Jane's waist, ready to catch her if she should lose her footing.

Above them, branches swayed as the wind howled. The lantern's shadows played off the moving trees, and Archie found himself jumping at every sound—whether startled himself or worried the noises might frighten Jane, he wasn't certain.

Jane walked in silence, and he glanced at her each time she paused or changed her breathing. He strained his ears and tightened his nerves, wondering if, at any second, Jane would have an attack of panic and drop the parcels and run off into the woods. Would she weep? Call out? Would he have any warning?

"I am all right, Archie," she said after they'd walked a few minutes. "You do not need to be so tense."

"I am not tense."

"Your knuckles are white, and your jaw is clenched." She hugged the parcels closer, cutting her eyes at him. "I can do this."

"Jane." He held on to her elbow, stopping her. "I know you can. I would never have recommended that you make the trip if I didn't believe you to be capable." He waited for her to lift her gaze to his. "But believing in someone does not free you from worrying about them."

"You pity me." Her face looked so hopeless he wanted to gather her in his arms.

"Jane, I feel concern, but it is not pity." He took a breath. "You are one of my dearest friends. I care for you."

"The others care—Kathleen, Jonathan, and Maryann—but . . ." She winced. "I do not mean to be unappreciative. They have been nothing but good to me, but I know they don't trust me. I have to try, Archie. Push myself to do things I fear, otherwise—"

"Otherwise, you will never know what you can do."

She nodded, lifting her chin, even though her bearing looked far from confident. "I am stronger than any of you think."

"Being strong doesn't mean you have to do it alone. I will help you. And when you feel as if you can't be strong anymore, I will be beside you, ready to catch you."

A tear slipped from her eye, and she bowed her head. "Thank you."

When they reached the cottage, light still shone beneath the shutters. Jane set the packages on the porch, arranging the bows and sprigs of greenery. She stepped back, apparently satisfied with the presentation. "We should extinguish the lantern," she whispered.

Archie blew out the flame, and they were plunged into darkness.

Jane gasped, and he moved closer, taking her hand. The moon gave a soft glow, and within a few moments, his eyes adjusted enough that he could make out the shapes of trees and even see the shadows of the footprints marking the path.

"Would you like to do the honors?" Archie spread his hand toward the door.

She nodded. "Are you ready to run, Lieutenant?" Though he could hardly see her face, in her voice, he could hear an excited smile.

He gave a salute.

Jane knocked, then spun, running along the path, her feet making a crunching sound.

Archie stayed directly behind her. When he heard the sound of the door opening, he pulled her behind a clump of bushes, spinning and crouching down so they could both see.

A splinter of light shone on the snow, then grew into a rectangle. Simon Cringlewood stood in the doorway. He took a step forward, looked in both directions, then down. His face was shadowed, but Archie thought he could see a smile on the man's face. Simon stooped, lifted the packages, and called over his shoulder. "Eliza, you'll not believe this. Father Christmas 'as come."

When the door closed, Jane clapped her hands. "I wish we could see what was happening inside right now, don't you?"

He grinned at the delight in her voice. "I do."

She rose and started along the path. "I can see quite well now. I don't think we need the lantern after all."

He walked beside her, enjoying the quiet and the pure pleasure that came from doing a good turn for someone who genuinely deserved it. Glancing to the side, he could see that Jane was pleased, even though her face was shadowed. Her happiness showed in the way she walked, the set of her shoulders, the lift of her chin. Her silhouette reminded him of the laughing woman of earlier today.

As they continued, the path led through a particularly thick section of trees. The wind sounded louder, and the air felt colder. He glanced again at Jane as her shoulders hunched slightly.

"Jane?"

Her hand slipped into his. "I am all right. I can do this."

"I know you can." He squeezed her hand, feeling her small fingers through their thick gloves. He thought of their first walk through the darkness when the carriage had arrived and the manor was deserted. He'd felt worried and anxious, but Jane's soft touch had brought reassurance. He hoped their connection now provided her the comfort she needed.

She leaned closer to him as they walked. Her breathing was quicker, but she kept her pace steady—well, as steady as possible in the uneven snow. And before long, they could see the glowing windows of the cottage.

Jane relaxed, and Archie let out a breath he hadn't realized he was holding.

At the door, she stopped, turning toward him. A slice of light shone from inside, giving her face a soft glow. Her pretty lips bent in a gentle smile, but it was the look in her eyes that brought him up short. It was warm and grateful and . . . trusting. He couldn't have put words to the expression if he'd wanted to. And he found he didn't need to.

He gazed back, hoping his own eyes would convey the depth of his feelings. How deeply he cared for her, worried for her, ached for her pain, and delighted in her victories. How he'd not completely realized what it was to love a person until today as he watched her feel pride in herself.

She stepped forward, her arms going around his waist and laid her cheek against his chest.

Archie held her in a tight embrace. Her body was soft and warm against his, and he noticed how nicely she fit in his arms. He cupped her head and decided it was exactly the perfect height to rest his cheek on. Tightening his arms the slightest bit produced the welcome effect of moving her head to lean into the hollow beneath his shoulder.

She belongs here.

"Thank you," she whispered.

Chapter Six

Jane entered the cottage in a state of extreme contentment, still warm from Archie's embrace. But her happiness went much deeper than simple enjoyment of his physical closeness. She'd stayed in the shadows for so long, worried about people discovering her condition and worrying herself about losing control of her mind. She could hardly remember a time when fear hadn't been forefront in her thoughts. But today had been different. For a few brief periods, she'd felt free, completely able to act as her nature dictated, instead of tempering her reactions lest exerting herself brought on another spell.

And she attributed it to Archie. His belief in her had given her confidence she'd not felt since . . . possibly since she was a young child.

She smiled and stepped forward as Archie helped her remove her cloak. His fingers brushing over her shoulders sent a tingle over her skin, eliciting a sigh. Even as she tried to talk herself out of it more times than she could remember, she was falling deeper in love with Archie Clawson with every passing hour.

But, of course, it was all foolishness. She had only to remember the fiasco of the kiss in the Cringlewoods' kitchen the night before and Archie's face when Jonathan had pointed out the mistletoe to know that her feelings were one-sided. Archie certainly cared for her, but his affection was friendly, not romantic.

Yet there were times when she imagined she saw something in his eyes, felt there was more to his attentions. She sighed again, this time frustrated at her imagination. Perhaps she only saw what she wished to see. She untied her ribbons and slid the bonnet from her head.

Maryann and Kathleen hurried toward her with worried expressions, and Jane drew back, bracing herself and feeling her defenses rise into place.

Archie put an arm around her shoulders, giving her a squeeze. "I am pleased to report a successful mission." He spoke in a loud voice to the entire room.

His words stopped the others before they could fuss over her, and she felt a wave of relief at his intervention. She looked up, giving him a grateful smile, then turned to face the room. "Yes, a very successful mission." She liked the feel of the two of them acting as a pair.

"And all credit goes to the general, here. This young woman is quite adept at the role of Father Christmas, I'll have you all know."

"Not *all* the credit." Jane gave a small smirk, turning her head so only Archie could see. "I'd not have managed without my very skilled lieutenant."

He returned the teasing expression, and she felt a thrill at their private joke.

"I am glad you are safely returned," Kathleen said.

"Oh, it truly looks like Christmas." Jane only now noticed the holly and ivy adorning the corners of the windows and decorating the hearth. She spun, taking in the entire cottage and its new festive appearance.

"Funny how a few leaves and twigs can brighten up a place, wouldn't you say?" Maryann took the cloaks and head coverings.

"It's splendid."

Jonathan was sliding the kitchen table to the side, and Archie moved away to assist him.

Maryann returned to her sister, taking her hand. "Are you truly well, Jane?" She spoke in a soft voice, and Jane felt guilty hearing her sister's concern and seeing the worry in her eyes.

"Completely well," Jane said.

Maryann squeezed her hand. "You've been different on this trip—happier. More like the sister I remember."

Jane smiled. "Perhaps I am getting better."

Maryann opened her mouth as if she would say something, but stopped when Archie spoke.

"What's the consensus?" Archie asked, standing in the space before the fire and motioning to the sofa and chairs. "Furniture? Or should we spread the blankets again?"

"I, for one, enjoyed sitting on the floor," Kathleen said.

"Agreed." Jonathan nodded. "If the other ladies are of the same mind, I think the blankets are much more appealing than the lumpy furniture."

The others concurred, and the group set about moving furniture and spreading blankets. They settled onto the floor, returning to their earlier positions, and the men removed their coats.

"I could permanently adopt this practice," Archie said, pulling off his neck cloth and loosening his collar. "Perhaps I could convince Mother to amend the holiday fashion policy."

He rested an arm on his bent knee, the other leg tucked beneath. The sight of him so casually dressed made Jane's breath catch. She had no brothers and had never experienced a man behaving so informally. His collar loosed, she could see the dip where his neck met his chest, and blushed, hoping no one else noticed her glance.

Archie appeared utterly at ease, and sitting beside him on the floor with their arms nearly touching seemed intimate. She felt special, knowing the memories from their time in this little cottage in Chiddingfold Forest were something that they shared—something that belonged only to the five of them. She wondered for a moment where they would be next Christmas. Would she be invited to Ashford to attend Lady Bromley's Christmas Eve ball? Even if she was Archie's guest next year, the experience wouldn't be the same. He'd be obligated to his family and friends, spending time with them, planning the festivities, and acting as host with his parents.

And she . . . Jane tried to imagine what the coming year would mean for her, but came up short. She had no future plans of her own, and that knowledge felt extremely discouraging.

Archie bumped her arm, shaking her from her reflections. She realized she was staring at the blanket, running her fingernail along a seam. When she looked up, he was holding a large earthenware mug toward her.

"Tea?"

She took the mug, inhaling the hot steam and comforting smell. "Thank you." When she glanced back, she saw Archie still watched her. He cocked his head and lifted his brows.

She smiled. "Excuse me, my mind wandered."

"Somewhere nice, I hope."

Taking a sip of tea, she shrugged off the question.

Archie watched her a moment longer as if to ascertain that everything was all right, then he scooted forward on his knees and placed more wood onto the fire. It spewed and crackled with the new logs. "Well, it isn't a roaring fire, exactly, and I am a bit disappointed that we haven't a Yule log, but the requirement was for a *merry* fire. And I'd consider it merry, wouldn't you?"

He spoke loud enough for the group but watched Jane as if her approval was the one that mattered.

She pushed away her thoughts, determined to focus on the here and now. Pursing her lips, she contemplated the fire for a moment and tapped her chin. "I think one more branch, a smallish one. Yes. That one there."

Archie placed it onto the fire where she directed, and Jane gave a nod of approval.

"Now that is what I call a merry fire," Archie said.

"I have never seen merrier," Jane agreed solemnly, then smiled.

He smiled back and stood before the hearth, facing the room. He cleared his throat, and the others grew silent.

"Thank you, each of you," he said. "Thank you for being here with me for this . . . ah, unconventional, yet very special Christmas."

Jonathan raised his mug. "Hear, hear."

"Special, indeed," Kathleen said, and the others lifted their tea and voiced their approval.

Archie clasped his hands behind his back. "And now, I yield the floor to Maryann for our Christmas program, along with my apology for the lack of a Bible or a pianoforte."

Maryann stood. "No apology necessary."

Archie inclined his head and moved back to join Jane, sitting a bit closer than he had before. He rested back on his hand, leaning so he barely brushed against her shoulder.

Jane was tempted to rest against him. It would be quite easy to do. With her legs tucked to one side, she was already slightly off-balance. She glanced up at him and saw him watching her thoughtfully.

Maryann told the story of the Lord Jesus's birth from memory. While Jane quite loved the scriptural account, her sister's words gave the story a simple beauty that touched her heart. Between segments of the narrative, Maryann paused and Kathleen led them in an appropriate Christmas hymn.

The music was beautiful, even with only the five of them singing. Kathleen had a lovely soprano voice, and Maryann a warm alto. With the men's low tones, she thought the angels themselves could not have sounded lovelier on that Christmas Day of old.

As they sang about shepherds watching their flocks by night, Archie took Jane's hand, holding it in the small gap between them. He ran his thumb over her knuckles and made gentle circles on the back of her hand.

Jane's mind emptied, her entire consciousness centered on Archie's touch. She glanced at him, but he continued to sing as if he'd not noticed what his hand was doing. Was he utterly unaffected? Jane's hand grew warm as if the stroke of his finger left fire in its wake and sent heat over her skin. Her breathing became uneven, and she stumbled over the words of a hymn she'd sung since she was a child.

She could feel a mighty blush moving up her neck and onto her cheeks. Perhaps the others would attribute it to her closeness to the fire.

Feeling bold, she allowed herself to relax, just slightly, until the back of her shoulder brushed against Archie's chest. She braced herself for him to pull away, but instead, he moved closer, pressing against her.

Jane's heart sped up, her blood pumping in her ears. She could feel his chest vibrating as he continued to sing. How could she possibly feel so safe with a person yet, at the same time, have trouble catching her breath?

She glanced around the room, the euphoria of cuddling against Archie blending with the spirit of the music and the love she felt for the people in the cottage. *This is how Christmas is supposed to feel*, she thought, a swell of gratitude making her heart soft.

"Magnificent," Jonathan said when the song concluded, his face filled with genuine contentment.

Maryann brought out a bundle of sticks. Four were tied with string, forming crosses. These she placed carefully on the floor and laid the other sticks along the edges, constructing a primitive-looking cradle.

Jane let out a soft breath, curling her fingers around Archie's while she watched.

As Maryann continued with the nativity story, the memory of their mother telling the same story as she built a simple manger quite overwhelmed Jane. Her throat tightened, her eyes itched, and, without any warning, a sob wrenched free from her throat. She clapped a hand over her mouth but could not stop the flood of tears and weeping that burst forth.

"Jane," the others said in unison, their voices tinged with worry. She shook her head, embarrassed and not wishing to ruin their Christmas Eve, but unable to speak, let alone hold back her tears.

Archie knelt before her, his hands on her shoulders. "Jane, what is it?" His voice was deep with worry.

She shook her head again, humiliated by the scene she was making. "I am sorry," she finally managed to choke out. "I just . . ."

Maryann hurried toward them and slid an arm around Jane. "Dearest, what is the matter?"

Jane swallowed and tried to hold down her ridiculous bout of tears. "I—I just miss Mother." Her voice was choked and gasping.

"Oh, Jane." Archie lifted her chin.

She pulled away, not wanting him to see her in such a state. Her eyes and nose were dripping, her breath came in gasps, and she was completely unable to get control of herself. "I'm so sorry," she choked out again.

"No. Do not apologize. Jane, you have every right to weep." The concern in Archie's voice brought on more tears. What was wrong with her?

"Come," Maryann tugged on her arm, pulling her to her feet. "Perhaps you should lie down."

Jane nodded and allowed herself to be led into her bedchamber. Her sobbing was becoming exhausting.

Maryann held her, speaking in a low, crooning tone, but Jane could not make sense of her words over the sound of her weeping and sniffing. She didn't think she could have possibly been more humiliated if she'd tried.

Maryann sat quietly, holding Jane until her tears dried up. She lit a candle and helped Jane change into nightclothes.

Once she'd convinced Maryann that she just wanted to sleep and would call out if her sister was needed, Jane was left alone in the dark room.

She lay down beneath the blankets, feeling wrung out physically and emotionally spent. She wondered what could have possibly brought on such a bout of weeping. She couldn't remember ever crying like this. Not even when her mother died. Or when she'd been left in the institution.

As she considered the incident, she realized that over the years, her attacks of panic had not only made everyone around her watchful, but she'd also been cautious about allowing herself to feel anything too strongly. She didn't mourn her mother or give her emotions any free rein, afraid of what could happen. Instead, she held them tightly, hoping to fend off the panic spells. The feelings bottled up inside for years had, for reasons unknown to her, decided on this moment to erupt in a torrent of tears.

They couldn't have picked a more inconvenient time. Her chest heated as she remembered the feel of Archie's hand and the closeness of sitting beside him on the blanket. She didn't imagine such an opportunity would arise again.

What must the others be thinking? She didn't hear the sound of singing or laughter. Undoubtedly, her fit of tears had put a damper on the cozy celebration.

"I have ruined Christmas for everybody." She muttered the words aloud, feeling even more miserable. Had it been only two days earlier that Archie voiced the same sentiment? She curled up beneath the blanket, bending her arm under her head. She hoped by now he realized how untrue it was. What he considered to be a misfortune had, for each of them, proven to be exactly what they needed.

Jonathan was happier than she'd ever seen him, enjoying time with his wife and mother instead of worrying about Parliament and his estate. She thought of his face as he sang the Christmas hymns. Though he'd surely imagined it differently when he'd requested that particular custom, no fine pianoforte and roaring fire could have brought about such a tender moment.

Maryann's presentation of their mother's tradition had been perfectly delightful—a beautiful tribute to a woman they loved and missed. Jane had seen the love in her sister's face as she recounted the story with her mother's custom of the cradle.

Kathleen seemed a new person in this funny little cottage. First, as she'd been overcome with childhood memories at breakfast, and then again as they'd gone to gather holly and ivy and she'd participated in the snow battle. Being away from home and finding a distraction from the pain of losing her husband had given her a chance to heal, Jane thought.

And Jane herself experienced healing moments, feeling

brave as she read for the group and journeyed through the darkened forest. She felt different. Not that she thought she had overcome her episodes—they'd probably never completely leave—but somehow, she was stronger. As if she could endure them, knowing she had people who loved her to help when the panic grew too great to manage alone.

They'd all been touched by this Christmas in spite of—or rather, because of—their singular circumstance.

They'd each celebrated their traditions, albeit in a different way than anticipated.

Their traditions. She sat up. Each of their requests had been granted, except for Archie's. He had no Christmas tree. How had she forgotten? She pulled her knees to her chest, wrapping her arms around her legs and feeling a sinking inside. She'd been so caught up in her own bruised feelings in the snow fort that she'd not remembered his custom. Archie had never celebrated Christmas without a tree, and he hadn't mentioned the lack once.

The tears she'd finally managed to stop threatened to reappear. She pressed her hand over her mouth, knowing one sniffle would bring her sister running back into the room.

Archie had planned and worried and done all that he could to make this Christmas special for them, but nobody had done the same for him. It was his Christmas, too. And nobody loved the holiday more than Archibald Clawson.

Jane lay back onto the pillow, devising a plan. Somebody had to find a Christmas tree for Archie. He'd given them all a lovely Christmas. Was she brave enough to do the same for him?

Chapter Seven

Archie glanced at Jonathan in the growing morning light. His friend trudged beside him through the snow, his breath coming heavy in white puffs. Each of them held on to a limb of the tree they were dragging.

"I'd never have guessed such a small tree would be so much work," Jonathan said. "Or so heavy."

"Don't pretend you aren't enjoying playing the part of the rugged woodsman. Maryann will undoubtedly be impressed."

"Chopping down and hauling a frozen tree through two feet of snow in the predawn woods isn't how I planned to spend my Christmas morning," Jonathan muttered. "I can't even put into words how much I'd rather be in a warm bed with my wife."

Archie grunted as they tugged the tree through a thick growth of underbrush. "I wager any married man would say the same."

"Speaking of impressing ladies, how goes it with Jane?

You never did explain to me why my suggestion of a mistletoe kiss in your snow fort should elicit such an adverse response."

Archie blew out a cold breath. "I don't know. I can't figure her out for the life of me. Sometimes, I think she welcomes my attentions. She seems happy to be with me. But then there are other times . . ." He glanced to the side. "I kissed her in the Cringlewoods' cottage—a very pure, gentlemanly kiss—you know, in order to see how she'd respond."

"And?"

"And it didn't go well. She ran away, upset." He turned to the side and used two hands to pull the tree through another thicket, wishing Simon hadn't come early and taken away the sled. But he supposed the man was using it for Christmas-related errands, and he could hardly fault him for that. *He could have at least left the ax*, Archie thought. But luckily, Archie and Jonathan had managed to find one in a groundskeeper's shed.

Once the tree was free, they continued onward.

"I just wish I understood what she was thinking," Archie said.

"Ha!" Jonathan barked out a laugh. "I'd wager that very statement has been said by every man throughout history."

Archie gave him a wry grin. "Why must women be so complicated?"

Jonathan shrugged. "I suppose that's the challenge. But in my experience—"

"You've been married for nine months, Ren."

"Yes, I have. And how long have you been married?"

Archie rolled his eyes. He had a point. "Continue."

"In my experience," Jonathan repeated, "I've found women to be less complicated than we assume."

"You must need more experience."

"Just tell her how you feel. Don't try to decipher her expressions or body language. And never assume anything based on what she says when she's upset. That's where you get into trouble. And trust me, it's not worth it." He pretended to shiver in fear. "Talk to her—plainly—and then listen."

"If it were so easy . . ."

Jonathan stopped walking and put a gloved hand on Archie's shoulder. "Oh, I didn't say it was easy. It's never easy. But I'm giving you the best chance at success." He turned back and lifted his side of the tree.

But what if Jane refused him? What if he told her how she felt and Jane didn't return his love? The thought was like a hole in his heart. "Is a grown man supposed to feel terrified by the very idea?"

"Absolutely terrified, or you're not ready." Jonathan smirked.

"I suppose I'm ready, then."

Jonathan nodded in approval. "Best of luck to you, old boy. I know none of this has come off as you expected."

"It's true." Archie kneaded his hands for a moment, trying to release a cramp from clutching the branch so tightly. He thought of his imagined proposal beneath the Christmas tree in Waverly House's great hall after a lovely Christmas Eve supper. He'd planned to give Jane the book then, to steal a kiss in the candlelight as they admired the sparkling tree and drank mulled cider from delicate china cups. "Not one blasted thing worked out as I'd hoped."

Jonathan rolled his shoulders. "It may not have felt like it to you, but this Christmas was just what my family needed." He turned more fully toward Archie. "I don't know how Mother would have survived a house party or a ball this year. But here, away from crowds and memories and society, she's been a new person. And Maryann has been so happy."

"Very likely because her husband's been happy, as well." Archie grabbed on to the branch again.

Jonathan considered for a moment, then grasped the tree, pulling it forward. "I suppose I have."

In the early morning light, Archie saw a thoughtful smile bend his friend's mouth.

They continued in silence, each lost in his own thoughts until they reached the cabin.

"Shake off as much of the snow as possible before we bring it inside," Archie said.

They lifted the tree upright and brushed off the branches, sending showers of snow into powdery piles. He opened the door and stepped inside, pulling the tree in behind him.

"Oh, thank goodness you're back." Maryann rushed toward him, followed closely by Kathleen.

Something in her voice sent an uneasy tingle up Archie's spine. He looked closer at her and Kathleen. The women were crying. "Has something happened?"

Maryann grabbed his arm. "Jane's gone."

The uneasy tingle grew.

Jonathan stepped around the tree, closing the door behind him. "What do you mean, 'gone'?"

"When I woke, she was nowhere to be found," Kathleen said. "We've searched the cottage."

"She must have had another spell," Maryann settled into her husband's embrace, looking frantic. "Brought about by her weeping last night."

"We'll find her," Jonathan whispered to his wife.

Panic jumped over Archie's skin in prickly bursts. How long had she been gone? She could be cold, lost, hurt . . . He leaned the tree against the wall and strode back outside, Jonathan following. The men's footprints from this morning were clear in the snow, but aside from the trail the company had made on their outing the day before and the path toward the Cringlewoods', there were no others.

"Find Simon." Archie pointed toward the woods. "He may have seen her, or at least have an idea of where to look." Archie started along the other path. "I'll search in this direction."

Jonathan nodded and started toward the Cringlewoods' house.

Archie moved as quickly as he could through the deep snow, nearly at a run. His mind spun with scenarios. When had she left? Was she dressed in her nightclothes, as she'd been when she went missing last spring? He thought of that night, how they'd found her wet and afraid and with no memory of how she'd come to be there. But here in the freezing snow, the danger was so much worse. His breathing grew ragged and his thoughts frantic. If he didn't find her soon . . . The alternative was too painful to imagine, and he couldn't allow himself to dwell on the thought.

He moved up the hill, following the footprints past

where the snowball battle had taken place. *Oh, Jane, where have you—*

He stopped, hearing voices. With a fresh burst of energy, he reached the top of the hill and looked between the trees beyond.

Simon Cringlewood was pulling the sled. Tied to it was a freshly chopped pine tree. But Archie didn't focus on Simon for longer than an instant when he realized Jane walked beside him.

When she saw him, she raised her hand, a wide smile spreading over her face. "Happy Christmas, Archie!" she called. "We've brought a tree!"

"Happy Christmas to ya, yer lordship." Simon gave a small bow.

Archie drew in a breath; the relief at seeing her safe and warm, bundled in her cloak and mittens, filled him so strongly that he thought his insides would melt. He sprinted down the hill and pulled her into his arms. "Jane. I was so worried. When I returned and they said you were gone . . ." He held her tighter, wanting to reassure himself that she was here and unharmed.

"I hoped to be back before anyone was awake. But finding just the right tree took longer than I expected, then Simon had to chop it with the ax and tie it to the sled."

Archie still did not trust himself to speak.

Jane wriggled out of his grasp and stood back, studying him. "Archie, what is wrong?" Her eyes rounded with realization. "Oh my. You feared I'd wandered off."

He nodded, worried how she might receive the affirmation.

"I did not even consider," she said, her brows pinching together. "I thought I left early enough to return before everyone awoke. I—Oh, I am sorry, Archie."

"Shall I continue on to the cottage, Miss Croft?" Simon pulled on the sled's rope.

"Oh, yes. I suppose we all should."

Simon started off, and they followed. Archie was torn between wanting to walk slowly to extend the time they had alone and knowing he needed to return to reassure the others that she was safe.

Jane took Archie's hand. "I remembered what you said about the *Tannenbaum* and how special it is to you. I wanted . . ."

Her words trailed off, and Archie was overcome, unable to believe that she would go into the cold, dark woods alone to find a tree for him. "Jane, I . . ." He had no words to express how deeply her gesture touched him. The swing from panic to relief to tenderness tumbled his emotions all over one another, and his mind was still attempting to catch up.

Jane watched him, the crease between her brows deepening. "I didn't mean to frighten you. I am so sorry."

"I told you I would always worry about you."

She nodded. "I remember."

"And after last night . . ."

"I know. I realize now how my absence must have appeared to all of you." Her cheeks, already pink from the cold, deepened into a blush. "I don't know what overcame me last night. I am so sorry for ruining the evening."

Archie stopped at the top of the hill. He cupped her chin,

lifting her gaze. "Nothing was ruined. You have no need to apologize." He pushed out a breath, remembering what Jonathan had told him: *talk to her—plainly—and then listen.* "Jane, I am the one who should apologize." Seeing her confused look, he continued, "For my actions two nights ago. I should never have taken such liberties, kissing you without your permission. I know it upset you. And I never intend for you to feel ill at ease in my company."

Jane walked silently, and Archie's heart sank. She was still uncomfortable. Perhaps she didn't intend to forgive him. He'd overstepped, assumed too much, and ruined his chances with the woman he loved. Maybe he'd never had a chance in the first place. His stomach began to feel ill and his rib cage tight.

"I was not upset," Jane said, her voice quiet.

"Don't spare my feelings. I saw your tears. It was very wrong of me."

She shook her head, walking slower and still not looking at him. "I was disappointed." She paused, then stopped altogether.

"Disappointed?"

She let go of his hand, wrapping her cloak tighter around her. "Archie, I was disappointed, not because you kissed me, but because I thought—I hoped—you would *kiss* me."

Color flooded her cheeks, and Archie's mouth gaped open. His power of speech deserted him altogether.

She turned and hurried toward the cabin, waving her hand and calling out to her sister when she got close.

Archie remained where they had stopped. She'd hoped for a kiss? And not just a kiss, but a *kiss*? Had Jane cared for him all along? His mind jerked back into action, and he replayed the events of the last few days, seeing them in a new light. A trickle of hope made its way into his chest. It grew, pressing outward and filling him with warmth and joy. He walked slowly back to the cottage, letting the feeling settle in his bones.

Well, Ren, he thought, a smile pulling at his mouth, *your absurd advice was not so foolish after all.*

Chapter Eight

Christmas day was a flurry of activity. The men made trips back and forth from the cottage to the manor house and the Cringlewoods' home. They returned with tablecloths, dishes, food, and even an extra table. Kathleen directed the furniture arrangement, and Eliza supervised the cooking. Tom helped Simon bring the goose and other food from the Cringlewoods', and the women helped with the final preparations.

Jane could not have imagined working so hard preparing for the Christmas feast or enjoying herself so much as she did it. The ladies sang Christmas hymns as they worked, and Kathleen told stories of holiday celebrations when she was a child. Even Eliza joined in the singing. To Jane, it felt like belonging to a family—something she hadn't experienced in a long time.

She glanced up when the door opened and Archie carried in a pair of chairs from the manor, but when she met his gaze, she quickly looked back down at the wreath of holly she was arranging around the candlesticks. She still could not believe what she'd told him earlier—that she wanted him to kiss her? What kind of young lady confessed something like that to a gentleman? If anyone else were to find out, they'd surely think her a tart.

She should apologize. Find a moment alone with Archie to set the record straight. If it were at all possible, convince him not to reveal what she'd said to anyone else.

Once the table was set to her satisfaction and the food warming, Kathleen declared they should all dress for dinner.

Jane pulled the ball gown from her trunk. She shook it out, admiring the lovely velvet and gold trim. "It seems too ostentatious for this simple cottage," she said, holding the dress in front of her.

"Nonsense." Kathleen motioned for her to turn around and helped her slide the dress over her head. She pulled tight the strings. "A special day calls for a special gown." She played the part of lady's maid, arranging Jane's hair atop her head and allowing strands of curls to hang down around her face and shoulders. As the room contained no mirror, Jane had to trust that Kathleen's elegant taste applied to hair styling, as well. "Now turn around, dear, let me see you."

Jane spun, loving the feel of the heavy fabric of the skirt.

Kathleen's face softened into a warm smile. "Lovely."

"Thank you." Jane smiled and then, on a whim, gave the older woman a kiss on the cheek. "Happy Christmas, Mother Kathleen." She fetched a package from her trunk and stepped out into the main room.

The smell of Christmas supper filled the air. The tables were pushed together to make one long banquet table, set with white cloths and sparkling china. Holly, ivy, and candles decorated the center, the flames sparkling on the goblets and silverware. In the corner, taking up more of the small space than was reasonable were two evergreen trees. Archie had brought small tapers, ribbon, and glass baubles from a box in his luggage, and the ladies had adorned the branches. With the candles lit, the trees were every bit as beautiful as he'd described.

As Jane stepped toward the trees, Archie climbed down the ladder. When their eyes met, he fumbled, losing his footing, but regained it quickly.

He'd shaved and wore a dark coat with tails that touched the backs of his knees. His hair was combed and his cravat carefully tied, although she didn't think he had a mirror either. When he saw Jane, he bowed.

She curtseyed.

Archie walked toward her, meeting her in the space before the trees. He took her hand, studying her. "Jane, you look—" He swallowed. "You look beautiful." His voice was low and serious.

"Thank you." She glanced down, holding the skirt of her dress. "Maryann and Kathleen insisted upon the dress, but I think it is rather formal for—"

"I hadn't even noticed the dress."

She looked up, squinting as she wondered at his meaning.

"*You* look beautiful. Radiant, even. I have not seen you look this happy since . . . well, since I've known you."

"I am happy."

He nodded, turning toward the trees.

"I'd always thought *eine Tannenbaum* to be the most

delightful part of Christmas, but do you know what is even more delightful?"

"No," she said, feeling nervous that he'd bring up her earlier confession.

"*Zwei Tannenbäume.*" He spoke the words carefully, pronouncing the German words with a perfect accent. "Two Christmas trees are much better than one, especially knowing the sentiment behind them."

She wondered for a moment if he were teasing, but saw no sign of it in his expression. "Do you mean because we each crept out before dawn, hoping our tree would be a surprise for the other?"

"Exactly." He moved her in front of him to admire the trees, resting his hands on her shoulders. "I cannot remember any gift ever meaning so much to me, because I know what you sacrificed to bring it about."

"And you did the same," she said. Jane glanced down at the package in her hand. She turned, holding it up between them. "I brought you a Christmas gift."

Archie tore off the paper and opened the box, lifting out the small nativity.

"It's from Bavaria," she said. "The man at the shop told me it's meant to hang from the ribbon."

He held it up, studying the image, then looped the ribbon over a branch to allow the carving to dangle beneath. Stepping back, he studied the effect. "It is perfect."

Jane felt pleased with his reaction. "I am glad. You are not an easy person to shop for."

He shrugged. "I think you did quite well, all things considered—with *both* gifts." He watched her, his eyes growing thoughtful. "And I have something for you as well."

She shook her head. "You already gave me a gift—the book. And I love it. There is no need . . ." Her words trailed off when she saw what he held: a sprig of mistletoe directly over her head.

Heat flooded over her cheeks. He was making a joke; he had to be. Her first instinct was to hurry away, perhaps hide herself in the bedchamber. But she glanced up at Archie's face and froze.

His eyes were earnest and hopeful. He waited, brows raised, looking a little bit frightened and very vulnerable.

Jane stepped forward instead. She touched her fingertips to his coat lapels as his hand cupped her cheek and the other, dropping the sprig of mistletoe, circled around to press on her back. He bent his head, still holding her gaze, until she closed her eyes the instant before his lips touched hers.

She was not prepared for the softness of his lips nor the heat that spread from their contact, making her heart pound and her knees weak. When he drew back, resting his forehead against hers, she let out a sigh. She closed her eyes again, wanting to melt against him. "I like that gift much better," she whispered, not wanting to shatter the moment.

Archie chuckled. "Jane, my darling, I am in love with you."

Her eyes popped open, and she drew her head back, not believing this—any of it—could be real.

He must have seen the question in her face. "Do you think I give Christmas trees, classical books, and kisses to women I don't intend to marry?" He tightened his arm around her, moving the other to rest on her hip.

"Marry?" Jane's mind whirled. "You wish to marry me?"

The side of his lips pulled up in a smile. "More than anything. If you will have me."

She saw the truth in his eyes. Archie did love her. Tears sprang into her vision, blurring the lights on the tree. She thought she might float right up to the ceiling. "I love you, too. Of course I will marry you." A nervous laugh burst out of her mouth.

Archie joined her, chuckling and looking relieved. "I think that calls for another kiss, don't you?"

She nodded, closing her eyes.

His lips barely brushed hers before she heard applause. She jumped back, but Archie kept his arm around her.

Jonathan, Maryann, Kathleen, Eliza, Simon, and Tom came out from the rooms at the back of the cottage.

"Congratulations!" Maryann pulled her sister into an embrace.

"Oh, I am so happy for the two of you." Kathleen smiled, clapping her hands together.

"I thought supper would get cold waiting for you to finally get up the nerve," Jonathan said in a grumbling voice, but his eyes were bright. He slapped Archie on the shoulder. "Couldn't be happier for you, my friend."

Jane's cheeks felt like they were on fire. They all knew. They'd hidden in the back rooms, watching and waiting. She wanted to hide herself. But looking at the gathered crowd, her embarrassment ebbed away, replaced by a swell of affection for each of them: Maryann and Jonathan, her treasured family; Mother Kathleen, who treated her like a beloved daughter; and Tom and the Cringlewoods, who had shared their Christmas, making it magical. She glanced up at

Archie, *her betrothed,* and a thrill moved through her. She could not keep the smile from her face.

Archie had planned the perfect Christmas, and nothing had gone as expected. Somehow, though, the unexpected had made everything exactly right, and now she had a lifetime of perfect Christmases to plan together.

About Jennifer Moore

JENNIFER MOORE is a passionate reader and writer of all things romance due to the need to balance the rest of her world that includes a perpetually traveling husband and four active sons, who create heaps of laundry that is anything but romantic. She suffers from an unhealthy addiction to 18th-

Jennifer Moore

and 19th- century military history and literature. Jennifer has a B.A. in linguistics from the University of Utah and is a Guitar Hero champion. She lives in northern Utah with her family, but most of the time wishes she was on board a frigate during the Age of Sail.

You can learn more about her at:
www.authorjmoore.com

More Timeless Regency Collections:

Don't miss our Timeless Romance Anthologies:

www.ingramcontent.com/pod-product-compliance
Lightning Source LLC
LaVergne TN
LVHW021758060526
838201LV00058B/3150